VOICE

OF

FEAR

HEATHER GRAHAM

VOICE OF FEAR

mira

Recycling programs
for this product may
not exist in your area.

ISBN-13: 978-0-7783-8718-3

Voice of Fear

Mira
22 Adelaide St. West, 41st Floor
Toronto, Ontario M5H 4E3, Canada
BookClubbish.com

Printed in U.S.A.

For Jennifer Price with tons of love
and all the thanks in the world!

VOICE OF FEAR

PROLOGUE

Alfie leaned against one of the historic cemetery's obelisk memorials, one that had been commissioned and crafted to honor law enforcement killed in the line of duty.

Like himself.

Not many remained "in spirit" as he did, though he did have friends among the other dead buried in the cemetery, both officers and agents who had served their time, retired, and died peacefully of old age, and those who'd met a violent end in the pursuit of justice.

Day was just breaking. Dead or alive, he had always loved the beauty of a new dawn. And so, for a minute, he just watched the sun rise. He couldn't feel the warmth anymore—neither could he feel the cold of a snowy night. But he could remember the heat of the sun and smile because simple things in life were so good, and it was important in death to remember them.

Though he remained, he had seen others go on in a spectacular ray of light, wondrous in itself. And when it was gone, so was the soul of the departed.

But he knew why he waited.

It was Susie.

Sweet, innocent, optimistic—no matter what life dealt to her.

He had arrested her once when she had been on the streets, but he'd heard her story, and he'd known why she had run away from her home. On the streets, it was too easy to turn to prostitution, and prostitution too often led to drugs.

She had been so sweet, so naive, so desperate. She had been relieved to be arrested.

At first, he hadn't believed the stories she'd told him. That there was a criminal mastermind out there who controlled a whole network of people, who was at the helm of all kinds of illegal activities—arms deals, prostitution, murder for hire, drugs—and who sanctioned and supported all kinds of crazy killers.

Alfie now knew that the Krewe had a good idea of who the mastermind was.

Rory Ayers.

Finally incarcerated because his ego won out over his insidious plans. But he'd had a long reign as a criminal kingpin, and even in jail, still seemed to hold power over life and death.

At first, Alfie thought Susie had seen one superhero movie too many. He thought she had invented some diabolical comic book villain in her head because she couldn't accept the life she'd come to lead.

But when he'd made a point of going to a friend who was the prosecutor for her case, they'd managed to get her probation and a stay at a halfway house. She wanted to be off drugs; she wanted nothing more than a nice, normal life.

She was just a kid. A sweet kid. The daughter he might have had one day.

But she had disappeared from the halfway house. And when that happened, he went over every statement he'd ever taken from her. He'd found and interrogated a pimp who had pushed her out on the street. And putting it all together, he'd concluded she had known there was a compound of supposed family homes and commercial properties where business was being conducted—the business of illegal arms deals, every illegal drug known to man, and more.

Susie had once told him she was always careful. She was so afraid "they" might get her. At the time, she could never quite identify "they," but she claimed "they" were out there, and the whole hierarchy was so complicated and convoluted, there was no hope if "they" decided you were done.

Alfie's superiors had looked at the evidence. They had gone in with SWAT and FBI assistance. They'd believed they had the element of surprise. They'd been wrong. The shoot-out was one of the largest and most deadly area law enforcement had engaged in.

They took down a massive criminal empire.

But he hadn't found Susie.

And he had died in the effort, looking for her so desperately he hadn't even realized he was dead until he'd found his old partner, quiet tears running down his cheeks as he knelt by Alfie's body.

It was a shock to be dead.

He didn't even remember the pain. But he knew, almost immediately, that he would linger. And he believed it all had to do with the events of the day: the fact that their surprise raid had not been a surprise, and there had been no sign of Susie.

And while they had made a massive dent in the "empire," they hadn't taken down the man they were after—a man referred to as John Smith.

There were clues as to the identity of this man. It had been suggested through various minor criminals they'd picked up and incarcerated that John Smith just might be Rory Ayers.

And it was all happening again.

Alfie straightened. He'd been waiting as morning had broken. He was glad to have friends among the dead—and among the living. He'd stumbled upon Krewe members by happenstance when they'd been at the cemetery. Now, when he knew something was up—when he could help in any way—he hitchhiked a ride from an unsuspecting driver and headed to Krewe headquarters.

They were more than willing to help him, and had tried to do so before. But he believed rookie Krewe member Jordan Wallace was on to something that might have to do with "John Smith," or the man who had been running things when he had died. A man who had cleanly disappeared while his thugs were left to willingly die for him.

Why? Why take bullets for another man?

Alfie thought a series of recent Krewe cases might have been connected. One of the men arrested during an attempted Embracer murder had given them a description of the man who had recruited him.

A man who had called himself John Smith.

Alfie hadn't recognized the man from the drawing. But it could have been a man they had in custody. A man named Rory Ayers. Not as he appeared now. But a man could easily change his appearance.

Alfie knew Jackson Crow, field head for the Krewe of Hunters, believed him—and believed in him. There was someone pulling a lot of strings. A master puppeteer who could make people do things they had an itch to do—and things they didn't want to do.

Alfie wasn't waiting for a Krewe member right now, but rather a man who had his own brand of talents and who was, by chance, related to a Krewe member.

He smiled in relief. He could see Patrick Law was making his way toward him. He'd reached out to Patrick because he'd been concerned about Jordan.

Of course, worried as he was, Alfie could have hitchhiked to the Krewe headquarters. But he wasn't sure why he was so worried. Though young, Jordan Wallace was a competent agent. She was on an assignment with the full backing and support of Jackson Crow and the Krewe of Hunters. And what she was doing wasn't crashing into a den of vipers, per se. Her intent was to watch over possible victims.

From the time Alfie had met Jordan, she had wanted to help him. And he wanted to help her. She was young, bright, a crack shot, and a hell of an actress, which made her excellent for undercover work. Maybe too excellent. Just as Susie reminded him of the daughter he might have had, Jordan reminded him of the sister he might have had because of her energy, her passion, and her love for others.

"Hello!" Patrick called to him.

"You came!" Alfie said. He had never suspected Patrick would blow him off on purpose, but sometimes life had a way of getting in the way of promises—especially when those promises were made to the dead.

"As I said I would, Alfie," Patrick said, frowning slightly at the idea he'd expect anything less.

"Well, thank you, Dr. Law!"

Patrick winced. "I never go by Dr. Law."

"But you are a doctor, right?"

"Of psychiatry. And I have my degree in psychology. But I've never liked people calling me *doctor*—Patrick is good. Anyway, I needed to let you know one of the first things I've been tasked with is interviewing Rory Ayers. Apparently, he's still crying 'lawyer,' denying he was ever involved in anything, and we're all idiots, and the entire facility where he's being held is corrupt. But we are going to work on your case. Megan is getting the records together from various police departments and law enforcement agencies regarding the event that—that took your life. I wanted to hear—"

"It's going to have to wait," Alfie said.

"Pardon?" Patrick said, surprised.

Alfie smiled. Patrick Law was in his late twenties. That meant little; Alfie knew about his credentials and the many cases he had worked alongside police in the state of Pennsylvania and beyond. Alfie knew Patrick from cases his sister Colleen, a Krewe agent, and his other sister, Megan, an editor and accidental consultant, had worked.

Patrick had come to check on his sisters. The siblings were a real trio—triplets—all with strange abilities. While Alfie had many friends at the Krewe, he had most recently worked with Mark Gallagher, Ragnar Johansen, and Colleen Law— and even Megan Law because of her strange abilities—on the Embracer killings. And he'd met Patrick, of course.

Patrick combined the best of qualities when it came to law enforcement. He understood the human mind. He seemed to know when talking might work, and when violence could be avoided.

But he also knew how to move quickly and effectively when talking wasn't an option.

He had empathy for those in trouble through no fault of their own.

And he knew when tears were real.

And when they were not.

Alfie was glad Patrick was in the DC area.

Because he needed help. Real help.

"There's a situation going on I'd like to monitor."

"Alfie, you could have done so—"

"Ah, but you're alive. You have a car; you can drive. You have a phone, and you can make calls. I need help right now from the living—for the living."

Patrick arched a brow. "What's going on, Alfie?"

"I need your help, Patrick. Please. Keep your phone out. I'll explain along the way."

CHAPTER ONE

"No!"

Jordan didn't know the pretty redhead who choked out the muffled word. She was among the many young women, including Jordan, who had been kidnapped that evening.

She did know the young woman was terrified.

Jordan was somewhat terrified, too. But she was also a trained FBI agent. She had excelled at Quantico, and she'd been incredibly gratified to join the legendary Krewe of Hunters, where she'd been accepted and respected and was already known for her undercover work. Jackson Crow had warned her, though—never be caught off guard.

She'd thought she *had* been careful, but now that seemed ludicrous. Her service Glock had been hidden in her clothing in her bag, beneath some towels. She had never thought the danger might come from beneath her in the water as she dressed the part of a woman on vacation in a blue bikini.

Now it was her undercover work—and failing to realize Jackson had meant *never, ever, not for a single second, be caught off guard*—that had brought her here. She didn't know where she was exactly, though she had tried to listen to every sound she'd heard as they had driven here in what seemed like a van despite them referring to it as "the meat train," noting every twist and turn they had taken. She hadn't been knocked out as some of the girls had been. The big man they called Lefty had disliked her from the start and had given her a good knock on the head, hard enough to send her reeling and for him to bind her hands behind her back. Of course, she had fought him. She liked to believe if she hadn't been taken by surprise in the pool, she might have beaten him and escaped to save the others. She had gone through many self-defense classes. She knew how to kick hard enough to send someone off-balance, how to lock her elbows around an attacker's neck, how to duck, twist, dive, and deliver a killer right hook. But she had neglected Jackson's one warning: *she had been caught off guard.*

Who the hell kidnapped someone right out of the water at a hotel pool that was popular with tourists and locals, anyway?

He'd hit her good—but he hadn't tied her quite so well. She'd left her gag in place and used every ounce of her senses and strength to work at the rope around her wrists.

If he'd hit her any harder, she might not have picked up on the men calling the vehicle they were in "the meat train" or realized in terror where they might be going—an old packing plant or slaughterhouse.

She feared that, once inside, there would be a deep cellar or basement. There would be cells of some variety, a place where the men kept their "meat" before it was sold.

But the van door had opened and two men were outside arguing about the product.

Jordan knew they were arguing about her. Lefty thought

he should have a turn with her since she was clearly in her twenties, no pure angel to be sold to the highest bidder.

His partner was yelling they weren't paid to sample the merchandise.

This was her chance.

"No!" the redhead cried out again. She, too, had been bound and gagged.

Jordan freed her wrists and twisted to start working at her ankles. She was up in a flash, tearing at the gag in her mouth.

The redhead was sobbing and rambling beneath her gag.

Jordan knew why. There had been talk on the street. That talk had turned into the reason she was here now.

Months ago, the body of a woman had been found floating in the Potomac River. She had never been identified. She had been shot through the heart after being beaten. Rumors began to swirl. Sister Mary Kathleen had gone to the police, claiming homeless youths who had used her shelter had just disappeared.

Then a high-profile someone had disappeared. The daughter of a congressman.

Jordan had already been working undercover as a sex worker. She had started out walking the streets. But when the high-profile woman had disappeared, she'd changed her identity, pretending to be a college girl on holiday. She became friends with a group staying at the Castleberry Estate— an old mansion that had been turned into a five-star hotel with outbuildings, a spa, four Jacuzzis, and a giant, meandering pool that curled around a bar and offered charming, smaller pools within the larger one, between little concrete "islands" that were flush with foliage.

It was the last place Chelsea Moore, the congressman's daughter, had been seen. She'd met up with high school friends who had come down from college. Rumor and fear suggested whoever was taking women was killing them the moment they caused a problem.

The lounge chairs where she'd sat with the girls she'd befriended had been no more than twenty feet away. Belinda Hoyt and Terry Unger had been lounging on the chairs when Ellie Ferguson had insisted they race across to the bar.

Jordan was a good swimmer, a strong swimmer, but the man had come out of nowhere; and she'd twisted and fought and then gasped for air, kicking and struggling away, but it had been too late. Bursting to the surface for air, she'd been met with the slam of a fist. A glance at the lounge chairs revealed that Belinda and Terry were gone—they had disappeared in seconds. The world had become a fog. And then she'd found out what was happening to the missing women. It was what she and one of the Krewe organizers, Angela Hawkins Crow, had suspected: a sex-trafficking ring.

In her daze, she'd noticed the men who had taken them in the meat train had not been armed. They were arrogant and confident in their ability to manage the six women they had taken—Belinda, Terry, Ellie, herself, plus the redhead and a blonde. They had been taken at closing time, when families were all inside, when the pool bar was winding down, and the night life inside the place had begun. It happened swiftly—so swiftly no alarms had been raised. They would be by now, of course. But the girls were long gone.

Jordan was determined she wouldn't be locked up. She believed the traffickers were getting their "merchandise" out of the country as swiftly as possible. She had to break free and run. She wouldn't be caught off guard this time. And she was certain she could outrun Lefty even if he did have a mean left hook.

That was the only way to bring help to the others.

The men were starting to turn toward the van; the wide hatch door was open. Lefty was about to hop up.

Jordan slammed him hard with a right-foot kick just as he stepped up. As she had hoped, he was in agony—and off-balance. He fell back hard, crashing into his slimmer partner, knocking him off his feet as well. She leapt from the truck, searching the area. They were in an alley behind a large building.

An old meat-packing plant, just as she had suspected.

She had to reach the street.

She ran. She was halfway through the alley when she heard Lefty's partner shouting.

"Get back here—unless you want every single one of your friends shot in the head!" he warned.

She slowed, then turned around. She stared at him, shaking her head. "The FBI is on to you! I'm not alone!"

Of course, she *was* alone.

The partner started off toward her again. "I'm gonna tell the boss! I get to shoot her!" Lefty shouted. He was still gripping his crotch.

"They are on their way; you'll hear the sirens any minute!" Jordan warned.

Night had fallen. The alley was dark. Only moonlight provided a dim glow.

"Bull! You're dead, bitch."

"I don't think so," a voice said.

Jordan spun around. To her astonishment, she knew the man standing behind her, a no-nonsense Glock 22 in his hands, aimed at the kidnappers. He wasn't in a uniform; he didn't have one. He stood at about six-three, and he sure as hell looked the part of a man who wouldn't hesitate to fire if necessary.

And she knew he had dialed a certain number on his phone before he'd accosted the men, and that there would *be sirens soon.*

"Patrick Law?" she whispered, stunned he was there. He wasn't Krewe; he wasn't a cop. The man was a psychiatrist!

Lefty's partner took off running in the other direction. Lefty was screaming, heading into the building to get away, limping as he continued to clutch his groin.

"I've got the runner," Patrick said. "Wait! You're not armed. Help is coming."

He headed after Lefty's partner, who, ahead, in the alley, suddenly tripped on what appeared to be nothing at all. Then Patrick was standing over him, warning him not to move.

Jordan heard sirens.

Within seconds, emergency vehicles, police, and SWAT teams were on the scene, crowding into the alley along with a dark SUV filled with members of the Krewe.

Which was good for Jordan; the police officers were trying to help her, assuming she was a random victim. They brought her a blanket and urged her to the rear of one of the rescue vehicles. Bruce McFadden from the Krewe helped her explain she was FBI. She told them the real victims were in the van and in the warehouse and that they needed to hurry.

The traffickers might decide to murder the girls being held in the old slaughterhouse as they tried to escape.

Chaos exploded. Jackson Crow, supervising field director for the Krewe, helped lead a team as the police busted into the building.

An officer moved forward, taking the prisoner from Patrick Law. Agents and officers were helping the girls in the van. Police and Krewe in vests, weapons ready, were heading into the back of the warehouse, while others had already stormed the front. Bruce McFadden gave her a nod before joining those entering the warehouse.

Patrick Law walked back toward her, frowning and shaking his head.

"What the hell were you thinking?" he asked.

She felt her temper sizzle. Patrick wasn't Krewe and he wasn't a cop. His sister Colleen was Krewe, as was his brother-in-law, but he was a criminal psychologist and psychiatrist in Philadelphia. He had the look of a cop, though, or at least a man accustomed to authority—tall and lean but well muscled, with a rock-hard jaw and eyes that seemed to burn with green fire. Sure, she knew he saw action at times with the Philadelphia police, but his expertise was in the psychology of the criminal mind.

She had met Patrick and his consultant sister, Megan, when she had been undercover on a different assignment, one that had gone well. She'd assumed then he had been an agent, as he and Megan had been with Special Agent Ragnar Johansen.

Before that particular undercover assignment, Angela had ensured Jordan had a tracking device in her phone so that other agents would be following. That day, she'd been taken on purpose. Today, things had not gone as planned, and Patrick was staring at her as if she'd been an errant child.

By then, Jordan was standing by Jackson's SUV with a blanket around her shoulders. She wished she was wearing a vest and breaking into the warehouse with the others. Her fear for those being held inside was not without merit. But she was in her bikini and a blanket, with no weapon and no vest. And unarmed, she was a liability to others. But she was hopeful Jackson might return with a backup gun she could use and instructions for her to move in.

"You could have gotten them—and yourself—killed," Patrick continued. "What were you thinking?"

"What was I thinking?" she demanded. "I was doing my job! I was—"

"Your job? You weren't armed; you had nothing to use against those two thugs. You—"

"Gee, and to think I was going to say thank you," Jordan said sarcastically. "I was going to ask how the hell you managed to find us."

He didn't get a chance to answer because they were suddenly interrupted by another voice, an excited voice.

But one that didn't belong to the living.

"I tripped him! I did it! I managed to trip him!"

It was the ghost of one Sergeant Alfred Parker—"Alfie," as he was known—a man killed in the line of duty, still looking to find the lost victim of the criminal enterprise that had taken his life.

Patrick Law looked at Jordan and answered her question. "Alfie. That's how I managed to be here. You told him about what you were doing. He was afraid you might wind up in a bad position, trying to blend in with Valley girls."

"They aren't Valley girls," she said dryly. "They're from Northeastern Ivy League schools."

"I was watching," Alfie said. "I told you I'd be playing my part. I brought Patrick with me to the hotel. We followed as fast as we dared, and Patrick called in for help."

"Thank you!" Jordan said sincerely to Alfie.

"You've been trying to help me," Alfie said quietly. "So have Patrick and his sisters, Megan and Colleen. And Mark and Ragnar—Red and Hugo, of course. And Jackson."

Colleen, Mark, and Ragnar were part of the Krewe, as were Red and Hugo, though they were K-9 members.

Patrick, Colleen, and Megan were triplets. Megan had gotten involved with the Krewe when she was working for them as a consultant and was now engaged to Ragnar. But she was also an editor; and while she was ready to help if needed, she liked her work and managed to keep the job she loved via telecommuting and the occasional jaunt up to NYC a few times a month.

Jordan had liked both Colleen and Megan. She had even liked Patrick.

But while they had been part of the team following her GPS signal on the previous case, Ragnar had been the one to burst through the back as she had been placed in a coffin. She'd been awake and aware and ready to pull her weapon because of Megan's quick moves at the bar from which she had been taken. Everything about that plan had worked.

And Patrick hadn't been a jerk that day.

Maybe this wouldn't feel so bad if she wasn't still reeling from the breakup she'd gone through soon after. Because, apparently, girls just shouldn't involve themselves in danger.

Alfie was shaking his head.

"All these criminal enterprises… I'm telling you, there *is* a mastermind behind it all. And I can't help but think we're looking to solve an old crime, that when I died and the troops went in, they missed the head of the snake. When you told me you were working undercover, well… I said I intended to help you. And being a ghost—with less than 1 percent of 1 percent of the world population able to see me—I had to follow. And did you see that? The fool couldn't see me, but I could trip him! The power of the mind—or the soul—is amazing!"

"Thank you," Jordan said again. "Thank you so much, Alfie. And bravo on managing to trip the man."

"No. No," he said, shaking his head strenuously. "Thank *you*," he told her. "You guys believe in me. And I believe every case your Krewe solves brings us one step closer to finally ending a reign of terror."

"We haven't really helped you yet," Jordan said. "We haven't...found Susie."

"I want to believe she is out there, somewhere, living happily under another name, maybe in the Southwest," Artie said. "I keep believing." He shook his head suddenly. "But this... this setup is almost the same as it was the night I was killed. There was a man, some kind of leader—called John Smith by everyone—who was never found. I believe he moved on. Maybe somewhere else—maybe right here, with this being part of his new conglomerate. And for what it's worth," Alfie added dryly, "I don't think the guy's real name is John Smith. Whoever he is, he scares the hell out of his people. They would rather be shot down than captured."

"Some people can strike that kind of fear into others," Patrick said. "Then again, there is always someone who will crack. Our survival instinct is strong. But when a man or woman has a family and their children might be threatened, yeah. In most cases, maternal and paternal instincts can put a check on the innate desire to survive."

Jackson Crow came out of the building, heading toward them. "Alfie, thank you, my friend. Patrick, you're deputized. You know the routine. The place is a maze. We have dozens of officers and agents, but it's something of a prison with a lot of winding corridors and plenty of rooms with cages. Most of the captors are scurrying, but we need to avoid them killing their victims as they go. SWAT has the front entrances covered into the surrounding area. There's a big park just down the way, and if we lose people there, well, we need all hands on deck."

"Jackson, I need to get in there," Jordan said, her words passionate and her concern very real.

"Of course. You need to be suited up with a weapon and a vest," he said. "I've got something in the back of the SUV. Follow me."

"I'll consider myself deputized and join the troops," Patrick said. He turned, drew his weapon, and headed for the building.

"Be careful! The last time there was a case like this…" Jackson began. He paused, wincing. Alfie was still with them, and *the last time there was a case like this*, Alfie had been killed. The Krewe hadn't been on the case then—other FBI teams had been involved—but they knew about it. They knew not just because of the extensive records, but because of Alfie.

"I'm going in, too. Not much they can do to me anymore," Alfie said, shrugging. "But I'm still damned good at watching a partner's back. Well, you know. When the partner has a Krewe talent, that is. What the hell—I'm going with Patrick!"

He hurried after Patrick Law.

"Jordan, come on," Jackson said.

She followed him to the back of the SUV.

"You don't happen to have any extra clothing as well, do you?" she asked.

"Oddly enough, I do. Angela always keeps workout clothes in both cars. We both take whatever free half hour we can find here and there to go to the gym," he said.

"I don't know how you two do it," Jordan muttered. "Both in high-powered, twenty-four-seven positions, and parents to two kids."

"A lot of vitamin B—and coffee," Jackson said lightly.

In the back of the car, he quickly found Angela's bag and

handed it to Jordan. She found stretch pants and a T-shirt and even a pair of sneakers. The sneakers were a little big.

But she was grateful for whatever she could get, realizing her feet were burning from the barefoot running she'd been doing.

Jackson lifted the lid of a compartment in the back and then keyed in the code to the iron box there.

He had a Glock 19 and he handed her the gun and extra ammunition, then dug into another compartment for a vest.

Jordan donned everything quickly and met his eyes. "Let's go."

As they headed toward the building, the scene became chaos with women running from the hallways, directed by officers from the SWAT team. They were all clad in white sheath-like garments, like dolls in matching gowns.

Like prison garments. The captives appeared to be clean and healthy—but then again, if you were selling human beings, you'd want them to be in pristine condition.

Some were screaming, some were crying, some were laughing and choking at the same time, running into the arms of whomever they could find.

But amid the throng leaving, Jordan noted a woman who stood out. She was attractive but at least fortysomething—older than the others.

She was not wearing a sheath. She wasn't running toward any of the EMTs or rescue vehicles, but rather looking to the end of the alley. And she was looking furtively over her shoulder, trying to be casual but moving quickly.

Was the woman one of the captors? Not technically a captor, but a warden of sorts perhaps? Maybe the person who dressed the girls up in simple shifts, saw that they were clean and hygienic, ensuring the quality of the product they were reduced to being?

"Jackson!" Jordan called, pointing and turning to take off in pursuit.

The woman stopped, turned back, realized she had been spotted, and started to run. She was fast.

Jordan was faster. She hadn't trained for a marathon for nothing.

Still, the woman made it to the end of the alley and swung around at the edge of the building, heading toward another warehouse.

But by then, Jordan was on her.

She tackled the woman, and they went down hard on the pavement near large dumpsters just around the building's edge.

The woman screamed and thrashed wildly.

"I thought you were helping! I thought you were rescuing me. What is the matter with you? Let me up! I will sue! Police brutality!" the woman screamed.

She had neatly coiffed blond hair, and much of it was now sticking up in the air. Her makeup was perfection. She was furious, spitting as she spoke.

"I'm not a cop, so no police brutality," Jordan said. "And I'm afraid we'll have questions for you all. Grateful to be rescued? Oh, I don't think so; grateful people say thank you. They don't run."

Jackson reached her side. "Well, well," he muttered, hunkering down to leave Jordan free to rise as he took the woman into his custody, rolling her over to cuff her with her wrists behind her back. "Look who we have here."

"You know her?" Jordan asked, surprised.

"Marie Donnell. She did a few years in a federal lockup. Back at it, Marie? Only you're not renting out your wares these days—you're selling them," Jackson said.

"No!" the woman raged. "I was a prisoner this time. How

dare you? You can't use past crimes in court. Besides, I was taken by these awful people. I was a prisoner."

"A prisoner in a thousand-dollar suit while the others are in linen gowns, huh?" Jackson said. "Ah, Marie, come on. Detective Flannery is here—I'm going to give him the pleasure of dealing with you."

Jordan didn't know Detective Flannery. He was apparently with the local police, and she assumed that Marie Donnell knew him from years before.

Whatever. Jackson had the situation covered.

"I'm going in," Jordan said.

Jackson nodded.

"Good eye," he told her, leading Marie Donnell away.

As she headed back toward the building at a sprint, she could hear the woman cursing Jackson with one breath and swearing her innocence with the next.

Jordan headed into the building. One of the SWAT officers was directing law enforcement the best he could amid the fleeing women. He motioned Jordan to the right, reminding her, "We need the captors alive. Do your best."

She nodded. *Do your best.*

That meant she should try to take the captors and caretakers here under arrest; but if they were shooting at her, hell yes, she'd have to shoot back.

She took the direction he had indicated. Officers were breaking in doors along the way.

Many of the rooms were empty.

But ahead of her, a door was ajar; she slid against the wall and looked in.

There was a woman wearing a shift on the bed, but she wasn't alone. Patrick was with her. He had ripped up a sheet and was creating a tourniquet for the woman's leg. It appeared she had been shot.

He must've heard Jordan because he looked up. "We need an EMT in here, pronto!"

She turned and shouted to one of the officers in the hallway. Jackson had supplied her well, but she didn't have a phone or a radio on her.

She hurried back into the room and saw there was a man down on the floor. Patrick had shot him and kicked his gun into the far corners of the room.

"Can I help?" she asked.

"I think I've got it until we can get an EMT. He nicked an artery, I think. We need someone in here fast. This hall should be clear. I'm afraid to carry her out and start the bleeding up again," he said.

His attention was on the victim until he suddenly swung around, warning, "He's conscious!"

Jordan turned quickly. The man on the floor had bled heavily, but his fingers were twitching, and he was reaching down to his ankle.

She saw he carried a second weapon. One he was trying to reach.

He just might have the strength to pull it out.

When his fingers curled around the butt of the small gun and shakily brought it up to aim straight at her, she got off a shot removing a few of his fingers.

He roared in pain and stretched out, convulsed, then lay still.

Jordan hurried to his side.

They were going to need more than one EMT.

The operation stretched into the night. In all, there had been forty-four captives in the warehouse, mostly attractive young women, but a few teenage boys had been held captive as well. A few of the captors had been taken alive, but they'd fought so furiously that most were in the hospital. The captives had all been questioned. Many had been runaways or sex workers, but one young woman was a hairdresser on vacation in the Capitol. And Jordan's so-called "Valley girl" friends had been college students, enjoying a break.

The police and the Krewe would be handling it as a joint investigation. Because of her key role in the operation, Jordan found herself at headquarters as it neared midnight, waiting for Jackson to finish his questioning of Marie Donnell.

Both the young woman and the man who had been in the room where Jordan had come upon Patrick were in the hospital. The woman was doing well. The EMTs had been impressed with Patrick's makeshift tourniquet, telling him that he might have saved her life.

The man with blown-off fingers had suffered a seizure and had been put into a medically induced coma.

A day that had begun with a pleasant poolside breakfast had turned into hell—but a hell that she had to admit had been better because of Alfie. And Patrick. She was alive—and so were so many victims.

That meant it had been one hell of a good day.

Patrick Law had remained at the warehouse while she, Jackson, and a few other Krewe agents had headed to headquarters, along with a select group of captives.

Jackson had been determined to get at Marie Donnell. She was capable of appearing demure and frightened. He knew better, and Detective Flannery agreed that Jackson just might get something out of her, using his "Krewe magic," as Flannery called it.

Donnell hadn't demanded an attorney, but she'd refused

to back down on her claim she'd been held captive as well. She kept crying and asking for food and drink, which was provided to her.

Jordan was in Angela's office, where Jackson's interview could be watched on the computer screen via the conference room's camera as Jackson brought in another cup of coffee for Marie. Angela sometimes questioned people, but she usually kept to her office for observation. Angela was glad to have Jordan with her, as many of the agents involved were still working with other departments. "Two eyes are always better than one—wait, I mean two sets of eyes."

But as they prepared to sit and watch Jackson try again, there was a tap at the door.

It was Patrick Law.

Jordan was surprised when Angela greeted him warmly; she hadn't thought Patrick Law had been that involved with the Krewe other than having been there on the day Jordan had set herself up to be taken by one of the "Embracers." And he had been at the gun range when part of the last case had gone down.

Patrick was a psychiatrist, after all. That meant he typically dealt with criminals after the fact, or possibly in figuring just how far their criminal acts had taken them.

He glanced at her and nodded. She found herself wondering how he'd been so quick to figure out the man in the room with them had a second weapon.

She didn't know why she was feeling so resentful. Patrick Law had saved her life—possibly twice. But he had all but chastised her as if she'd somehow messed up. Yes, she had been in a bad position. And the outcome could have easily been worse. But she'd had no choice, really; once they'd been brought into the warehouse, her chances to escape would have been nil.

"Thanks for joining us," Angela said to Patrick. "You just might see what we don't. Draw up that last chair, if you don't mind."

Patrick grabbed a chair that was uncomfortably close to Jordan's. He didn't seem to notice. His attention was on the screen.

Jackson had taken a seat across from Marie. He waited as she sipped her coffee and then said, "Marie, help us, and we can help you. There's no way that you were one of the captives; you are impeccably dressed, and you were trying to slink away—"

"I knew you would think I was guilty," the woman cried. "Those horrible people! They might have known about my past, too. I was at the library, and when I left, they just swept me up."

"Marie, you're going to go down—just how far is what's up in the air," Jackson said calmly.

She shook her head. "You need evidence in court. You don't have a shred of evidence against me."

"I'm sure we'll find lots of shreds as we finish tearing apart the warehouse," Jackson said. "And talking to some of the captives."

"*I* was a captive!"

"Really? Like I said, it will be curious to know what the young women and men being held there will have to say."

"I— They're all liars! I was treated better than others. They will hate me for that and lie about me!"

Jackson smiled at her. He opened a folder he had in front of him, and produced a sketch done by Maisie Nicholson, one of the Krewe's amazing sketch artists.

"Who is this?"

"I haven't the faintest idea. It's a sketch," Marie said.

"You've never seen this man? I hear his name is John Smith."

Marie looked at Jackson. "I don't know a John Smith. And I don't know this man."

"Well, I guess it's time you got your attorney," he told her. He rose.

She did the same. "No! You've got to let me go!"

Jackson walked out of the room. Marie continued to rant and rave as he did so.

"She's lying," Patrick said, looking at Angela. "Of course, we all know that. But there's something more going on. Her mind is a mess, and I'd guess fear is the reason for it. She's afraid to talk—and she's terrified of being locked up. She's got a special reason for wanting to get out of here and not be incarcerated."

"What is it?" Angela asked.

"Like I said, she's afraid."

"I'd be afraid of prison," Angela said.

Patrick shook his head, his eyes intense as he said grimly, "She's afraid of being killed once she's in prison. I believe there's more than that, though. I think Alfie may be right; there's a major connection here."

"To John Smith, yes. We've been questioning Ayers, looking high and low for more connections between guards and prisoners and attorneys."

"Well, whether it's Ayers or not, there is someone at the top who is protected by use of threats against the family members of those working for him. I think he's been running major criminal rings, including the burial murders that were stopped recently. We keep thinking Rory Ayers is manipulating everything from behind bars, but we don't know how. A lot of the people who died today knew what was coming. Because the big boss is afraid someone will talk, and his minions know if they don't die, someone else will."

Angela nodded gravely. The door opened and Jackson entered. Angela asked Patrick to relay everything to Jackson.

"They'll hold her in a federal facility in isolation," Jackson said.

Patrick nodded. "She's scared to death. Though there is something behind her fear. She just might break. I'd hold on to her tonight, then have someone let it slip she might be going into the general population. Which would be too bad. If others think she did talk, that might frighten her into believing she needs our help. And she was lying; she recognized that drawing."

"The drawing isn't Ayers," Angela said.

"Not as we see him now," Patrick said. "If Ayers is John Smith, he plays it safe. He makes sure he's nothing like his usual self. The drawing could be him—all he had to do was use some putty, stage makeup, change his hair… He could do anything he wanted. Until he got too cocky and was caught."

"But is it possible? That he's pulling strings while incarcerated?" Angela posed.

"If so, we have to find out how," Jackson said. "Damned magician. We'll need to keep close tabs on Marie. She might not know everything, but she could know enough to give us something. Patrick, thank you. You'll stay on this?" Jackson asked.

"I promised Alfie."

"I love consultants," Jackson said, grinning.

"And I hope to hell I prove worthy," Patrick said.

"It was your move that got the troops out," Jackson said.

"So many saved from possible death or lives of servitude. Of course, the congressman—tough as he can be during his campaign speeches—was in tears over getting his daughter back. All in all, it was a good day."

"I just wish—" Jordan started before breaking off.

"You wish we could have found Susie?" Patrick said.

She nodded. "Every life is equally important," she said. "And I still wish we could find her for Alfie. He's done so much for all of us."

"We won't stop looking for her. If we can break any of this wide open, well, we may be on to something and it all relates back," Jackson said.

"Where is Alfie, anyway?" Patrick asked, frowning.

"He's with the police and social services. They're trying to make sure we separate the good guys from the bad, probably also hoping for some intel we can use. The problem is, those held captive don't know much beyond how they were taken— and how they were kept. Marie and the few captors who were shot but didn't die are our best bet for information. Alfie can go where we can't, so he might learn something." He looked at Jordan, nodding a bit grimly. "My office?" he asked.

She nodded. She was afraid Jackson was going to put her on desk duty. He probably felt she'd made the wrong moves that day.

Except he'd allowed her into the building—and she had managed to catch Marie Donnell before the woman could slip away.

Patrick Law headed for the door. She was surprised when he turned back and looked at her.

"It all turned out okay," he said quietly. And she thought he smiled. That his words maybe meant more than he was saying. He gazed at Jackson, adding, "Krewe are special—in so many ways."

"We need you. You could join anytime as more than a consultant, if you're willing to go through the academy," Jackson told him. "You're more than a little special yourself."

Patrick laughed. "That can be taken many ways. Anyway, I'm here. I'll be here; I'm helping Megan compile everything she can dig up on Alfie's case."

"Thank you again," Jackson said.

Then Patrick was gone. Jackson shrugged. "We don't really need to go to my office; I just wanted to tell you—"

"I know. I'm sorry. I did put myself in a position—"

"As it happened, the day went well. And I understand what you were trying to do, and who the hell would expect what did happen?" Jackson said. "But—no more. No undercover without a partner, without backup, someone on observation at the least—"

"Alfie was—"

"Someone living. The dead can't make emergency calls," Jackson said firmly. "But that's my department, and I'll work on it. Anyway, it's been one hell of a long day. Go home. Get some sleep. All in all, a hell of a long day, but a good day. Not an officer or agent was killed and only a few suffered minor injuries. A lot of people were rescued. Get some sleep."

"Thank you," Jordan said, trying not to show just how relieved she felt. "Oh, I don't have my car. It's at the hotel."

"We'll get you to it. I can't leave yet, but we have a few agents still here. We'll get you a ride home."

Jackson opened the door, and as he followed her out, she turned and asked, "Do you believe everything Patrick Law says because he's a psychiatrist?"

He smiled and said, "Because he's a Law. They have special talents—*he* has a way of practically seeing into the human mind. Anyway, looks like he's still here. Talking to Bruce

McFadden. Hey, Patrick, Bruce, can one of you drop Jordan off at her place?" he asked.

"If she can wait a few minutes—" Bruce McFadden began.

"I'm going now," Patrick said. "If you're ready, I'll drop you."

Jordan forced a smile. She wasn't sure she wanted to spend any more time with Patrick Law that day.

That had to be it; he had been caring for the female victim, but somehow, he'd seen the mind of the man who was about to reach for his weapon!

A ride home. She could handle that.

She saw him smile. Surely, he knew she'd prefer a ride from just about anyone else in the world.

"Yes, I'm ready. Thank you," she said flatly.

He nodded to Jackson, and they left the offices and walked into the parking garage.

CHAPTER TWO

"I'll get you home, safe and sound," Patrick said, smiling at Jordan as she slid into the passenger's seat.

She gave him a very pleasant—and very fake—smile.

He realized he'd come down hard on her. And maybe that was good.

But maybe it had been unfair. Because if they had gotten her inside the warehouse, there might not have been a way out. But she had still risked her life—and inadvertently risked the lives of others—through her actions, even if she'd found herself between a rock and a hard place.

Patrick wasn't sure why he was so drawn to the story Sergeant Alfie Parker had given them, but there had been something in the ghost's words that haunted him more than any ghost had ever managed. Alfie deserved justice.

He would have loved to have known the man in life; Alfie Parker was a good guy, the kind of man you'd always want on your team. None of them—at least, none of the small percentage of people who could communicate with the dead—

understood why some souls remained, while some did not. It was assumed that souls lingered because something had been left undone, because justice needed to prevail, or because an event had been so traumatizing that too many remnants of history remained in the air.

Patrick didn't have answers. But he'd been lucky. It was an odd thing, growing up as a triplet. He and his sisters were close. As the only boy, he was a bit of an odd man out, but in other ways, Megan had been. She loved words. She would help in any situation that she could, but she preferred a life in which most days were dedicated to working in a day-to-day rational world rather than dealing with guns and crime and prison. She believed stories influenced lives, whether they entertained, taught, or did both. In her time as an editor, she'd seen how stories could change people's lives.

And that was great.

But for him, it had always been the mind—and law enforcement. He'd known at a very early age he had a skill for "seeing" inside the human mind. And while their strange talents had become evident to each of them when they were young, their parents had merely thought they were playing with imaginary friends. As a threesome, they had realized other people might think they were crazy, but after Colleen had "heard" an unconscious woman calling for help from the trunk of a car, their parents had become involved.

Jordan was watching him, he realized. They'd reached his car and were sitting in it; he needed to start the engine.

"You were deep in thought," she said.

"Yeah, sorry."

"Were you reading someone's mind?" she asked. She sounded a bit dubious—more puzzled than anything else.

He shook his head. "I guess I was just thinking about Alfie and this…strange sixth sense that brings us all together."

She smiled, shaking her head. "Hmm. Deeper than that."

"No, seriously. I mean, my sisters—"

"I know your sisters. I met Megan on the day I was bait, and I've met Colleen in meetings. Both your sisters are great. You're lucky to have each other. The three of you are close, right?"

"We are."

"And your folks?"

"My folks are good people. They always warned us about not sharing certain things with others so they wouldn't think us crazy, but they believed in us themselves."

"Sounds like your folks handled it well. My folks told me I'd be locked up in a loony bin."

He laughed and saw she was smiling. It wasn't a fake smile anymore.

"All the Krewe agents I've gotten to know so far are wonderful," Jordan continued. "Adam and Jackson have a talent for hiring good people. And Colleen, I guess she wanted to get into this kind of thing from the beginning, right?"

"Colleen's call to law enforcement came early—her bizarre 'hearing' saved a life. Of course, she went to my dad for help and—thankfully—he believed her and checked out the trunk, called the cops, and saved the would-be victim."

"And you?" she asked.

He looked at her and shrugged. The question was honest.

"My decision to do what I do came a little bit later. And I was lucky that day. You know what it's like to be young, to believe something, and to know if you try to explain it, most people will just ignore you. But the young woman who had almost become a victim of a serial killer believed me. And in this instance, the intended victim's brother was a cop. I'm not so sure he would have trusted me, but she did, and he wasn't just any cop—he was one of several detectives assigned to the case. He was getting desperate because, for almost a year, we had a serial killer working in Florida. I happened to be in line behind the killer at a coffee shop. I never know how to explain this, but I was really thrown by what he was…emitting? His thoughts seemed to be pounding in my head. He was watching the young woman in front of him in line and he was…in whatever sick kind of obsession a killer feels before he takes a woman. I knew he intended for her to be his next victim. Like many killers who preceded him, this guy was intelligent, articulate, and charming. He teased the woman playfully, joked with her. Just light stuff—polite. Nothing harassing or sexual in any way. But I knew he meant to follow her."

"How old were you?"

"Sixteen—old enough and way too young. I was afraid to tell her the man behind her meant to follow her, see where she went, and find her alone at night. I was also afraid not to. At sixteen, I was already tall, and I looked older than my age. I was afraid she'd think I was hitting on her in a weird way. Obviously, I never did tell her I saw something calculating in the man's eyes, almost heard his excitement at the prospect of having her and thinking about all he might do to her. I never did say I knew what was going on in the man's mind."

"So, how did you convince her and her cop brother?"

"I told her I heard the man whispering strangely. Of course, he didn't know I heard him, but it had sounded real enough. And I had followed the guy as he followed her to her place, saw she lived in a duplex, and scoped it out."

"I can see your dilemma there. Were you afraid you might have looked suspicious yourself?"

"I'm sure I must have been. Like I said, I was a big kid. Until the coffee shop, I'd had nothing on my mind but the football game I'd be playing that night. Anyway, she must have believed something I said because she called her brother, and I told him what I'd 'heard.' The guy had given a few specifics, and, though it was awkward, I told her brother everything. He, of course, checked me out, but I was a high school junior. I had alibis for every night there had been a murder. Anyway, too late to make a long story short, but I went to the football game. The young woman's detective brother and his partner staked out her place; and sure enough, around midnight, the killer picked the lock and headed into the bedroom…and the detectives took the man down."

"Wow. You caught a killer at sixteen. A serial killer at that."

"No, the detectives caught the killer. My parents begged them to keep my name out of the papers. So it was explained they brought him down on an anonymous tip. And that was fine with me—I was grateful. I didn't want to talk to anyone about it. Except for my sisters; it was nice that we were all…weird."

"Weird—and wonderful," Jordan added.

"Yeah. Thanks. Of course, I did spend some time at the police station. And that was when I determined what I should do. When one of the detectives told me they'd been seeking the man for weeks, he added, 'Hey, kid, you must be a mind reader or something.'" He grimaced. "Anyway, psychology and psychiatry it was. Both professions have a great deal to do with learning to read the human mind. But I should be getting you home. I need an address," he said lightly.

"I'm going to pick up my car—at the hotel," she told him.

"Yeah, of course. Sorry."

"You didn't know that by looking at me—staring into my eyes and through to my mind?" she asked, the slightest bit of humor in her voice.

He kept his eyes on the road, a dry smile coming to his lips. "It doesn't work that way. If it did, I could be working on world peace and solving global problems."

"Hmm. So, you're a psychiatrist and a psychologist?" she asked. "Degrees in both?"

He nodded.

"I still don't really understand what you do," she said. "Or how it works. You work for the police—but you don't work for the police?"

"I'm an independent consultant," he said. "Makes it easy to travel to different places. I've worked with different departments in the greater Philadelphia area, but I've also gone to New Jersey, New York, and a few other states for various situations."

"All these departments know you're a mind reader?" she asked.

He shrugged. "No. It's not as simple as being a mind reader. Sometimes, I know from a person's words what they're really thinking—a lot like Megan, in a way. But sometimes it's something else—as it was with the killer in line at the coffee shop that day. People can almost cast off their thoughts. Almost like speaking aloud to yourself when you think no one is listening. And when you read the thoughts behind certain words, it makes it easier to say the right words back or know when words won't work at all. So, with the cops, I do different things. I work negotiating hostage situations when necessary. I'm told I'm good at it."

He kept his eyes on the road but knew she was looking at

him curiously. "But, if you're not in front of someone, how do you read their expressions, or—"

"Their minds?" he asked. "A lot is in the voice at the other end of a phone. Sometimes, you are face-to-face. But you're right. Most of the time, you're on a phone, or speaking through some kind of device. Sometimes," he continued, "it is just the psychology of a human being. You can tell when someone is desperate, and you can tell when they don't want to kill."

"Impressive."

"But what it comes down to is like all police work. A good cop—or a good agent—uses a mixture of hard evidence, forensic science, and gut instinct."

She had given him an honest compliment.

It was time he did the same.

"You've been pretty impressive yourself."

"Um, thanks."

"So. What about you?" he asked. It was always difficult to explain himself. Just as he knew it was sometimes difficult for his sisters. And why they had their strange gifts was something they might never know. It was odd he had explained as much as he had to Jordan Wallace, but he was admittedly curious about her.

"What about me?"

"Yeah. I just gave you my whole sordid story. So? What made a beautiful young woman decide constantly risking her life was a great way to live it?"

He glanced her way. She smiled at that.

"First, thank you. My dad was FBI. He...he had our gift or curse, too, but long before the Krewe came about, and he kept it to himself. Anyway, I loved seeing him and his friends at my house, though he had retired by the time I was about ten. He was almost sixty when I was born—twenty years older than my mom, but they were both thrilled to have me and…they were amazing parents."

"Were?" he asked softly.

She nodded. "Just lost Dad two years ago. He was eighty and told me he'd lived a great life and had me as a bonus—the best thing in life. I loved him so much. And my mom. My mom is doing fine, living with her sister in Hawaii. I get out there when I can, and she comes here frequently." She smiled. "She loves Hawaii—what's not to love—but she loves coming back here, too. She was born in DC, as was my dad." She grimaced. "I have an ancestor who was in Lincoln's cabinet."

"Patriots all," Patrick said.

Jordan shrugged. "Law and order and our inalienable rights," she said. "Absolute equality for all, um, truth, justice, and the American way."

She spoke lightly, but he thought there was something serious in her tone. He glanced over at her. He hadn't been lying or flattering her—she was a beautiful woman. Long, blond hair, enormous blue-green eyes, and a face that might have been sculpted by a master.

Patrick thought she was perfect for many undercover details. Because far too often, the men behind certain criminal enterprises just didn't suspect that a woman as beautiful as Jordan might be blessed with a tremendous—and cunning—mind. The alpha dispositions that had led them into believing they could be crime lords wouldn't allow them to see someone like Jordan as a threat.

She was passionate about her work.

He just feared her passions tended toward the reckless.

"Hey," she said, turning to stare at him, almost as if she had read *his* mind. "I was careful. I just blended in with the girls at that hotel, which, as you saw, worked. Come on—be honest! Would you assume kidnappers were going to snatch you from a popular hotel pool *while you were in the water?*"

"Backup," he said softly.

"Back up to what?" she asked.

He smiled. "Backup. Like making sure there's another officer or agent in the area."

"It's hard to be undercover with backup. Trust me. Our agents have gone undercover alone many times. You blend in, become part of a group. You can't draw suspicion."

Patrick didn't say anything. They had arrived at the hotel parking lot.

"What am I looking for?" he asked her.

"The little red compact over there," she told him. "I can get out anywhere."

"No, I will take you to the car and watch you get in."

"You know, I was head of my class at the academy," she told him. "I am pretty good at self-defense."

"Then you should know it never hurts for someone to have your back," he told her.

She sighed.

"Right, right, right. I get that."

He smiled. "Yeah, well, I just had to make sure. Jackson wants us working together."

She didn't glance his way. He thought her jaw tightened, but then she turned to him and smiled. "We're going to stay on this with Alfie?"

He nodded gravely, watching her.

"You're reading my mind! Stop that!"

He laughed. "No, I swear. Not mind reading. You want to be with me just about as much as you'd want to be with a giant mosquito—but you'll do it. And we'll work great together because we both really want to help Alfie—and ensure justice is served. He might be right about a potential connection. Go back. John Smith could be the crime lord pulling several strings. Maybe the past and present have collided. So if we don't stop things now, there may be a greater hell to stop in the future."

"That wasn't reading my mind?" she asked.

He shook his head. "No. Human nature."

"Pretty good," she told him. "Except for one thing."

"What's that?"

"I was thinking cockroach. Not mosquito. Anyway, thanks for getting me to my car. And good night."

But she didn't get out of the car. She hesitated. "Thank you."

"It was just a quick ride."

"No. Thank you for being my unexpected backup, saving my life, and most of all, telling me about yourself."

"Sure. Hey, text me your home address. I'll get you in the morning."

"Do I need to text it?" she asked lightly. "I mean, I'm thinking it right now."

"Text me your address," he said, sighing dramatically.

She smiled.

"I can get you, you know. I'm actually an excellent driver."

"I don't doubt that. My car is bigger, though. More comfortable. Nothing wrong with yours. But—"

"Hey. It's cool. I'm definitely not going to fight about whose car we take." She was quiet a minute, grinning at him. "As long as I get to drive sometimes."

"I believe you're an excellent driver. No problem."

"You *believe* I'm an excellent driver? Or you're hoping?" she asked lightly.

He sat back in his seat, grinning. "Nope. You excelled at

the academy. You're known for being a crack shot. You've handled several undercover assignments well—from what I understand—even if I did go off the handle about you being reckless getting to know your—"

"Not Valley girls."

"Friends," he acknowledged, seeing she was smiling. "Your new friends. Beyond that, you have a capable and cunning mind, and mostly good survival instincts. That leads me to believe you're a good driver."

"Uh, great. Thanks."

"You are more than welcome to drive as often as I drive— my car is just more comfortable."

She grinned at that and hopped out of the car but paused, looking back in at him.

"Thank you. Sincerely."

"You're welcome. Just remember, we all need backup."

She nodded. "Got it. Honestly!" She turned and hurried toward her car.

He waited until she reached it, revved the engine, and waved to him.

He waved back.

He was tired as hell and it was time to rest.

As he drove, he realized he was glad that he'd turned down invitations from his sisters to stay with them in their respective homes. He truly loved his sisters—and Colleen's husband and Megan's fiancé were great, too. But he hadn't wanted to intrude on relationships that were still so new.

Now he was glad because he needed alone time.

The clean and quiet—physical and mental rest—of a hotel room was going to be just fine that night. He'd wind up going over the case anyway.

But when he reached his hotel room and settled in bed, his

mind was still racing. He'd spent a lot of time with the ghost of Sergeant Alfie Parker. He wasn't the first. Jackson Crow had tried to follow any remote clue that came to light about a man named John Smith. And while the Krewe of Hunters encompassed many agents, there were fifty states in the Union, with a national population of over 330 million. Though the FBI was specifically assigned to work stateside, they were still asked occasionally to consult in other countries. While Patrick wasn't Krewe, he knew just about everything about it. His sister Colleen's dream had been to join the unit, and he had therefore researched it thoroughly. Simply, Jackson never forgot Alfie Parker. But he was also busy finding the right agents for what others considered strange or occult situations, or murders with "paranormal" undertones. The powers that be didn't believe in ghosts or things that went bump in the night, but law enforcement had long accepted the fact there were those out there who thought of themselves as vampires or werewolves or who practiced strange rites that, on occasion, meant the devoted were into sacrificing animals—including human beings.

Those powers that be were relieved to hand such cases to the Krewe. That, of course, was the official line. Krewe members were experts on the strange and unusual.

Which meant that while leads could be followed, the battle that had taken Alfie's life was considered a dead end by the bureau. A "haunting" case, but a cold one.

But it wasn't cold at all. It was burning hot.

Jackson Crow had determined it would be solved, because he was convinced it was related to what was happening now.

Patrick wasn't Krewe himself. But his sister was, as were both sisters' significant others.

Jackson had given him Jordan Wallace.

Again, passionate and capable.

And reckless.

Alfie believed in her wholeheartedly.

And if Jordan hadn't been so unwavering, dozens of human beings would still be prisoners, ready to go to the highest bidder for whatever that bidder had in mind, including snuff films, he imagined.

If nothing else, working with her was going to be interesting.

Alfie Parker's situation had haunted Patrick since he'd met the man, heard about the situation and his long-lost Susie.

Now Jordan Wallace was managing to haunt his mind equally. He tried to dismiss the intruding thoughts.

But they wouldn't go away, instead haunting him into sleep and beyond.

CHAPTER THREE

Jordan was downstairs waiting when Patrick Law drove down her street. After their initial interaction on the case, she didn't intend to give him any reason to find fault with her—though he had been decent during the ride home. She'd stayed up staring at the ceiling, unable to enjoy reruns of *The Golden Girls*—something that often lulled her to sleep after a long day. She was lucky to be alive. She knew it. And since she was alive, she shouldn't still be bristling as she was over Patrick's initial comments. Especially after he had opened up to her; she wondered if he ever did so with someone who wasn't in the Krewe.

"Okay, so we're off to the hospital," he told her as she slid into the passenger's seat.

"Oh?"

"Angus Macon and Raul Kent."

"And they would be…two of the surviving captors working at the warehouse?"

Patrick nodded.

"MEs have been busy determining the identities of those who were killed, and Angela and the team will begin hunting down their known relations and the whereabouts of those relations."

"You sincerely believe whoever is the head of this thing is holding the wives, children, or other family members of those working for him to make sure they never talk?"

Patrick nodded. "Our human instinct to survive is strong—barring mental illness. But we're also capable of loving others more than we love ourselves. If you want to guarantee someone keeps a secret, there's no better way to do it than to hold something over them even greater than the threat of their own life."

"And you got that from listening to Marie Donnell?" she muttered.

He shrugged. "Everyone who was at that warehouse—captive and captor—needs to be questioned. Macon and Kent were unconscious following surgery, but they're awake now. Apparently, Macon hasn't said a word. Doctors didn't know if it was a natural delirium after surgery, but Kent woke trying to rip his IV out of his arm. That may have been intentional, but we haven't given any names to the media. No one knows who died and who survived after the shoot-out. We have to convince him he's safe—that it's been reported that those involved are either dead or critically wounded."

"And you think we can do that?" she asked.

"I do. I have faith," he said.

"Even in me?" she asked lightly.

"I think you'll do very well," he told her.

She frowned suddenly, hating that she felt a sense of resentment again. She was the one who was Krewe in their duo—Patrick was a consultant. But Jackson had given the day's assignment to Patrick Law.

"You okay?" he asked.

"Yep, sure, of course," she said.

"Hey," he said lightly. "We're playing mind games here, which is why Jackson briefed me, the psychiatrist."

"Naturally. And quit reading my mind."

"I wasn't reading your mind. Human nature."

She smiled. "Would you be…?"

"Resentful?" he asked with a shrug. "I'm more on point. Whatever, however, to get to where we need to be."

"Applaudable," Jordan said.

"Not so much. Because I've come to know you. A little bit, anyway. And no matter what your feelings, you'll do what's right. That's applaudable."

Jordan laughed. "Okay, I give it to you. You're trying. You laid into me yesterday when it wasn't your place to do so—whether you were right or wrong. I am a federal agent. Jackson is my immediate supervisor. But you want us to manage to get along amicably and hopefully learn something that will stop a lot of horror."

"Well done," he said. "See? Not mind reading. Human nature."

"Not really," Jordan said.

"Oh?"

"One or both of us could have still been assholes about the whole thing," she said.

She was glad when they both laughed at her comment. More at ease. She'd spent too much time thinking about him and realizing she hadn't just been resentful—she'd been resentful because it was him. He was respected. He presented the perfect competent figure, tall, strong, exceptional in the looks department, and admired by his peers. She didn't want his opinion of her to matter. It did.

At the hospital, they found that both an agent and an officer in uniform had been assigned to look over the rooms where the prisoners were receiving treatment. They greeted them and were able to speak briefly with Dr. Simone, the surgeon who had removed the bullets from both Angus Macon and Raul Kent. The patients had both survived surgery, and while it might be a long road back, both were doing well.

"Macon barely responds to his health team. I don't think you'll get much out of him, nor can I offer you more than five minutes. He's older, in his late sixties, and his blood pressure spikes when he's upset. I know other lives are in the balance. I can give you more leeway with Kent. The man is only thirty years old, and he was in excellent health—other than the damage the bullets did. No vital organs were struck, so I foresee a full recovery," Simone told them. "What happened...hard to say. Some patients go through something we call delirium after hours of surgery, and that may well have been the case. But the nurse with him at the time said he woke in a panic, looked around and saw where he was, and swore something while ripping at his IV needle. He has a sitter with him at all times now, one of our LPNs, experienced with this type of behavior." He grimaced. "His name is Matt Humphrey. He was on the way to a great college hockey career until he wrenched his knee. He's working on his RN degree now. Anyway, he's a large fellow, and he can handle a large patient."

"How long is it safe for us to question Kent—without overtiring him?" Jordan asked.

"You're fine with ten or fifteen minutes with Kent," Simone told them. "As I said—except for the bullets riddling his body, he was in great shape. Lucky the way the bullets hit."

They thanked him. Patrick suggested they start with Macon. A nurse outside the door saw them with Dr. Simone, who nodded her way, and the nurse stepped aside, allowing them to enter Angus Macon's room.

The man looked shriveled and older than his years lying in the hospital bed. Patrick nudged Jordan and she knew he meant for her to start.

"Mr. Macon, I'm Special Agent Jordan Wallace. I need to ask you a few questions."

At first, she thought the man might still be out of it, weighed down by the trauma to his body and the medications he was taking. He stared straight ahead, not even recognizing that she and Patrick were there.

"Mr. Macon, we believe—"

"Feel free to believe what you want," he said. "I cannot answer any questions."

"Cannot?" Patrick asked quietly. "Or will not?"

Angus Macon lifted a thin hand into the air. He let out a short, dry laugh. "Once...once I could rule the world. Might as well say I mowed down a lot of people in my day. I had the power of life or death. Now seems like it's my time. I'm already going to hell. There's nothing I can tell you. I was heat for hire."

"You can tell us who hired you," Jordan said.

He moved his frail hand in the air. "I thought I was okay until those bullets came. Now I know. My time is near. I'm ready for Satan. Bring him on. I like it hot. Burning forever or not. It may all be the real big lie; no Heaven and no Hell. Whatever."

"Who hired you?" Patrick said firmly.

"Some broad."

"Some broad named..." Jordan pushed.

"Called herself the Mother and that was it. Took care of nutrition and hygiene for the product. Hey, some of those girls got better treatment than they were giving themselves. And they were taken off drugs. There you go—the place was a great rehab facility!"

"That's all you know? You were hired by a broad who called herself the Mother," Jordan said. "Was she an attractive woman? Older than the others, dressed neatly, coiffed blond hair?"

"That's the Mother. And you want vicious? She could hurt you to a scream without leaving a mark! But she was just hired help, too, just an echelon up the scale. And that's it. No more talking. I'm going to die here. I've got some mental arguments to make with the devil."

He stared straight ahead again. Jordan and Patrick looked at one another, nodded, thanked him dryly, and left the room.

"On to Mr. Raul Kent," Patrick said.

Jordan nodded. "One minute. I want to report in about Angus Macon's description of the Mother."

He nodded. Jordan made her phone call quickly, and they headed into the hospital room where they'd find Raul Kent.

The man lay in the bed with his eyes closed. He was young, with a full head of thick dark hair, a slim nose, high cheekbones, and a broad mouth. He looked like the kind of guy who might have smiled easily at one point in his life.

The LPN "sitter" keeping watch over him, Matt Humphrey, was in a chair near the bed, reading a textbook. He appeared to be in his very early twenties, built like a linebacker, with hair cut short as if anything else would be a bother. He rose, frowning, as they entered the room.

Jordan quickly produced her credentials and he smiled.

"Sorry. We're told to check everyone out—everyone who

enters, including my coworkers when I don't know them. Of course, the wrong people should be stopped in the hall, but…"

He shrugged.

"Not to worry; we appreciate your care for your patient," Patrick assured him. "But we need for you to step out."

"I'll, uh, grab coffee at the nurses' station and be right outside," he told them.

The patient on the bed, Raul Kent, was awake. He was looking at them with fear in his eyes.

He shook his head. "I have nothing to say."

"There was a complete barrage of gunfire, and you took three bullets. Who did you do that for?" Patrick asked him.

"I should have died; loyalty is everything," Kent said gravely.

"Not so much when it isn't returned," Jordan said softly.

"What does he have on you?" Patrick asked. "Or rather, who does he have on you?" he added softly.

Jordan saw something that let her understand a little of what Patrick had been telling her. There was the slightest change in his face. But Patrick had been right; the emperor of this crime ring demanded loyalty and got it because he held something—*someone*—his subordinates held dearer than their own lives.

"No one knows you are alive," Patrick assured him. "Your person is safe."

Raul Kent looked away.

"They will only stay safe if we're able to get them to real safety," Jordan told him earnestly.

Kent's eyes went glassy. A single tear appeared beneath his left eye. He shook his head.

"I can't tell you what I don't know."

"You are ready to die for someone you don't know?" Patrick asked.

"I knew Ralph Chino; Chino brought me into the business selling drugs. Small time. Then I found out we were lacing crystal meth. But when I wanted out, I went home to find that my wife and two-year-old son were missing. And I was told via phone call they were fine and would stay that way—as long as I never opened my mouth. Live by the sword, die by the sword," he added dryly. "It was my fault; I was willing to sell drugs to get ahead. Not tainted drugs, but hell, drugs that create addicts and... My fault. But not theirs! Natalie never knew what I was doing, and my precious boy, he turned three while I was guarding prisoners who were going to go up for sale to the highest bidder."

The single tear was joined by a torrent.

"Easy, easy!" Jordan said, catching his hand.

He held hers tightly in return, almost unaware of what he was doing.

"Where are they keeping your wife and child?" Patrick asked.

Kent shook his head. "We could only speak by video calls—once a week. Natalie... My wife is beautiful. They warned she could be...that she could be used or sold. And there's a market for children, too—and not one where a loving couple pays a fortune to adopt."

Jordan winced inwardly, not wanting to think anyone could be cold enough to allow the torture and murder of children.

They were here to stop this.

"Ralph Chino—he's the head of the operation?"

"Not the head. But he was one of the key people who saw the head," Kent told them.

"We need to get to Chino," Jordan said, looking at Patrick.

But Kent shook his head. "Chino is dead—I saw one of the SWAT guys take him down right before I passed out."

"Maybe he's here, too?" Jordan said hopefully.

"No," Kent said.

"Three more of the captors are here—"

"No. I saw his head explode," Kent said with quiet certainty.

"Do you realize what may happen to your family if they believe you're dead anyway? Why let someone valuable go when they have them?" Patrick asked.

Kent stared at him hard with growing fear in his eyes.

"No, no, the promise was always that, if we died in defense of the emperor, our families would be rewarded."

"And what guarantee were you given?" Patrick asked.

"I couldn't ask for a guarantee. It was too late. I was a fool; they were gone."

"So, help us get them back."

"How? I told you what I know. Chino was the man who was my contact. And in my line of work, I came to learn when dead was dead."

"All right. Twenty-three men were killed at the warehouse. Four of you are still alive. How many escaped?" Patrick asked.

"There were thirty-five or thirty-six attached to the warehouse at all times, and it was filled with arms. We were supposed to be able to hold off a small army, allowing the captives to be filtered through the immediate buildings, through the park, and into the woods." He shook his head. "But those who ran—ran. The building was filled with cops, and when it came time to run, well, running was allowed, escaping was allowed—being taken alive was not."

Patrick shook his head. "When you did your video calls—what device were you using?"

"Chino's phone," Kent told them.

He was holding Jordan's hand so tightly she almost cried out. With a pained smile, she got him to ease his hold.

"We're going to find them," Jordan told him softly, trying to extricate her hand.

Patrick was staring at him, as if he saw more. But he repeated her words firmly.

"We will find them. When you saw Chino die, it was when the others had already fled?"

"We were bringing up the rear," he said. "SWAT was all over the warehouse building by then." He shook his head. "I wasn't the only one. Some of the lieutenants, or whatever you want to call them—those who answered to the emperor—were required to bring in others. Fools like me."

"How many lieutenants?" Patrick asked.

"Five or six—I wasn't always sure. And there were a few..."

"A few?"

"Just as sick as the emperor," Kent said. His cheeks remained wet.

Jordan wasn't sure how she could feel empathy for a man who had collected people for sale and possible torture and death, but she felt Raul Kent's sorrow was as real as his fear and pain.

"They're out there," Patrick muttered.

"Men so into the money they would die to be part of the business," Kent said.

"What about women?" Jordan asked him.

"There was only one. The Mother."

"Yes, we heard about her," Jordan said.

"The Mother—she was to take care of 'our product.' Though we had lots of products. All kinds of arms. I can't tell you how much money you can make selling arms to certain South American and Asian countries. Sex and guns. All we were missing was the rock and roll," Kent said dryly. He looked at Jordan, possibly believing they'd made a connection. "And death. We sold death. Some of those guys were hit men. So far, I hadn't been asked. I just… I shouldn't have sold drugs. I know it was wrong. But I argued with myself that people who wanted illegal drugs were going to get them one way or another. Addicts will get their fix. I didn't know about the lacing. I didn't know what I was getting into—I swear it. And then my wife and my kid paid the price."

"Thank you," Jordan said.

"We will get to them," Patrick assured Kent.

Kent winced. "I think…"

"Please, you think what?" Jordan asked.

"There may be a few places. I heard Mother talking one day to someone on a phone. I don't remember her words and I don't know if I'm paraphrasing, but something about not putting all our eggs in one basket. I'm just afraid…" He paused again, staring from one of them to the other. "I'm afraid if you find one place, they'll kill everyone at the others."

"A sound fear. We'll get all our eggs together first," Patrick promised.

It was definitely a sound fear. But just how many places were there out there? And how the hell would they ever know if they had found them all?

The Mother. Marie Donnell. She was the one who wanted people spread out, adding that factor of fear to guarantee loyalty.

They needed to leave. And they needed to get on it.

Patrick was thinking the same thing. He was looking at her.

Jordan squeezed Kent's hand one more time. "We will do absolutely everything in our power to find your wife and child," she promised him. "We will find them. And no one will ever know that you told us anything. We promise."

Tears stung his eyes again.

As they left the hospital room, Patrick said, "I told you neither of them would talk."

She realized his words were for the benefit of the sitter, waiting just outside the door.

They could never let anyone know someone had said anything.

They didn't talk again until they were back in the car.

"We're going to need teams on this. We have to cover so much area. And we have to get to the morgue and get our hands on the phone Chino was carrying."

"Right. Let me call Jackson."

"The phone will probably give us clues, if nothing else, to one location. But besides his, we'll need to get our hands on every cell phone belonging to every dead man at the complex."

"And the one belonging to Marie Donnell."

"Absolutely."

Jordan pulled out her phone, calling Jackson on speaker. He was in Angela's office, where they were on speaker, too. Jordan and Patrick told them everything they had learned from Raul Kent—and all they hadn't learned from Angus Macon.

"We have Marie's phone right here and I'll start on it immediately," Angela said.

"I'll get an agent over to the morgue to pick up the personal possessions of the bodies that were brought in," Jackson said. "You have any other names besides Chino for the lieutenants?"

"Just Chino," Jordan told him.

"We're on it," Jackson assured her. "We might be able to pull something off Marie's phone, and you two can get out there—"

"We can't go blazing in. They might strike at others," Jordan said.

"No, but you can find that particular holding house, and keep an eye on it."

"Right, of course. We're going to need warrants, I imagine," Patrick added.

"I can get warrants," Jackson said. "We are going to need to act in tandem if people are being held in various places."

"We'll only act if we witness anything that might indicate immediate danger," Patrick said. "As to the others, and to looking for something in the woods—"

"We'll have you out there as three teams," Jackson said. "I'm not a mind reader, but I believe you were about to suggest the dogs."

"I was. And I was also going to suggest I bring my dog down here. He's been certified in a few areas, searching for missing children and adults—and the dead."

"Bring him down," Jackson said. "For now, head in. Maybe you can pick up something on the phone that we can't. If we come up with anything while you're driving, I'll let you know."

They ended the call.

Jordan looked at Patrick with a dry smile.

"You can see things on phones?" she asked.

"No. And a good tech person with a warrant and assistance from the carrier can do way more with a phone than I can. The thing is, if they were using a company to hold visual calls, those calls may still be found. Remember, nothing ever really disappears from the internet."

"True. So, another dog?" she asked with amusement.

"Another dog," Patrick confirmed. "Brian Boru, or Brybo, most of the time. He's an Irish wolfhound, named after an ancient Irish king." He looked over at her, frowning at first. Then he laughed. "I was about to ask if you have a problem with dogs. But I don't think you do."

"Well, I have met Hugo and Red. We will have to see about your pup," she told him. "Okay, in general, I love dogs. But you came down here without yours. Why?"

Patrick took a breath and grimaced as he drove. "I wasn't sure how long I would be staying. I needed to see Alfie again—and have a talk with him and Megan. A friend is watching him for me. Anyway—I'll have him driven down."

"That simple?"

He glanced her way and shrugged. "I have good friends."

She found herself looking out the window—and wondering if his good friends included a girlfriend. Who else did you leave a beloved pet with?

"Not a problem," she said. "I do really like dogs. I had a mutt named Cairn—because he was mainly Cairn terrier—when I was a kid. The little goofball lived to be sixteen, but then we lost him while I was in college. Now I've been afraid I'm out way too much of the time and sometimes—" She shrugged. "Sometimes I'm undercover, and I may be gone for days at a time. That doesn't seem fair to a pet, so—"

Jordan broke off; her phone was ringing. It was Jackson.

"Jordan and Patrick on speaker," she answered.

"We got a strike off a cell tower."

"You got Chino's phone that fast?" Jordan asked.

"No. We had Marie's already. Head south and west. There's a massive state park surrounded by privately owned land that's mostly undeveloped. I don't have an exact GPS location, but you can bring up a map of the park and the surrounding roads. Somewhere in there, you'll find a place Marie has been calling. I'll get satellite images to you ASAP. See what you can see."

"You still have Marie, right?" Jordan asked.

"We do."

"Did you ask her about any locations?" Patrick asked him.

"How many there might really be?" Jordan added.

"No. I don't want her to know that we're aware there are others being held in order to keep their killer elite in order. Not until I'm sure she's telling us the truth. She could say almost any number and be lying and pretend she told us all she knew."

"Okay. Thanks. We're on it," Jordan said.

"The other phones just arrived from the morgue," Jackson told them. "We'll keep in touch. I'm sending Ragnar, Mark, and Colleen out with Red. If I get more locations, I'll split you up. We need to find all the places where captives are being held and go in at the same time, or we might have a bloodbath. Patrick, once we've got eyes on this one, I'll have you talk to Marie."

"Will do," Patrick said.

"Thanks, Jackson," Jordan added.

They ended the call and she looked at Patrick. "We could use a dog now."

"Mark, Ragnar, and my sister will be searching soon. With Red," Patrick said. "And maybe Hugo."

He hit a button on the dash. His car's screen lit up with a message from Jackson. It was an aerial view of the buildings just to the north of the state park.

"How about that? All these places are on a few acres. I doubt anyone runs into their neighbors frequently, and that looks to be a good size where you might keep captives."

Patrick was driving. He glanced quickly at the map.

"Okay, navigator. Tell me the way," he said.

"The yard backs up straight into the state park. And there are trees to both sides...and a wall, I think," Jordan said.

He glanced her way. "Trees behind the wall?" he asked. "Are you good at scaling walls?"

"I'm the best," she said confidently.

He smiled. "Of course you are."

"Wise guy. No. I can really scale a wall."

"You're going to get to prove it."

"I'm going to assume they have cameras everywhere. And that they know what happened at the warehouse. The media did report the shoot-out. Those goons who escaped probably scrambled out to these places, waiting for their next command."

Patrick shook his head. "I don't think many people knew the whereabouts of the holding sites for the families. There were lieutenants, remember? They knew. So, there may have been a few who survived, as Raul Kent indicated, but not an army. There will definitely be cameras. We'll have to observe from a distance for a while."

His phone started ringing. He glanced at it where it lay on the compartment dividing the bucket seats. Jordan could see it was his sister calling.

"Answer for me, and put her on speaker."

Jordan picked up the phone and greeted her on speaker. "Colleen, it's Jordan and Patrick. We're headed out to a site—"

"We've got it up on the screen, too. We wanted you to know we're on our way," Colleen said. "Meet on the service road that skirts the edge of the park?"

"Sounds like a plan," Patrick said. "You got the dogs?"

"We got the dogs," Colleen said. "See you there."

After a few minutes, they moved down the service road. Patrick found an area to pull off where there was a split in the trees.

Jordan quickly hopped out of the car, trying to see through

the trees and the foliage. It was too dense; they would have to move in and through some of the growth to see anything. She looked back at Patrick; he was out of the car as well, surveying the trees as she was doing.

She spun around, hearing another vehicle, quickly seeing it was fellow agents. Mark was driving. He slid his vehicle into the semicircle of clear space, just behind Patrick's.

Mark, Ragnar, and Colleen emerged from the car, followed by Hugo and Red.

The dogs knew they were on; they stood quietly waiting for commands.

"At ease, guys," Ragnar said, and the two dogs wagged their tails and rushed forward to greet Patrick and Jordan.

She sensed Patrick was watching her. He was making sure she really liked dogs, she thought. And that was fine. She understood. She had learned early on that people who were kind to animals tended to be good people.

"Well, the important guys love you," Patrick called to Jordan.

"Yeah," Ragnar said, walking over to them with Colleen and Mark. "Though we did take down a serial killer once who sliced open a man without a thought, yet couldn't let a stray pup go without a meal."

Patrick laughed, shaking hands with Mark and Ragnar and giving Colleen a hug. Jordan realized she was a little envious. It would have been nice to have a sibling. But they all greeted her, too, with quick hugs rather than handshakes.

Then they went right to the matter at hand.

"Colleen and I will circle around to the far right," Mark said, handing them easily concealed headsets so they could communicate from their positions. "With Red."

"Front left with Hugo," Ragnar told them.

"And we'll take the back. I'm hoping for climbable trees," Patrick told them.

"Take care; we don't want to lose anyone," Jordan reminded them. "We're to observe and make no movements unless—"

"Imminent danger," Mark said, nodding. "But I understand Jackson also wants Patrick to have a chat with Marie Donnell. We'll hold here when you go in."

Patrick nodded, looking at Jordan. "We're on it."

They headed into the trees together, splitting when they neared a barely discernible patch of dirt and gravel in a line that was the divider between state and private property, one that wasn't acknowledged by all the bushes and tree roots.

There they split up, the dogs padding silently beside their masters as Jordan and Patrick moved farther along the scant path to reach the rear of the property. A high wooden fence surrounded it, but Jordan and Patrick both saw a large oak with spanning, low branches. He came behind her as she reached up, and he put both hands on her waist to give her a boost. His touch startled her; luckily, she said nothing. He was giving her the help she needed.

She caught hold of the branch and pulled herself up. He had a hold on it. She caught both his arms, adding to his ability to pull the length of his body up. Carefully, Jordan balanced to her knees, then caught another sturdy branch to stand and get a clear view of the back of the house. In a second, Patrick was up beside her.

They had a solid view. There was an expanse of lawn, and though there were trees within the wooden fencing that surrounded the house, they could easily see past them. There was a large area of nothing but grass, well mowed, and a playground set off to the far right. There was also a small aboveground pool, one that might be enjoyed by a mother sitting with an infant or toddlers playing with pool toys.

The place was set up for children to enjoy, but the windows in the rear sported bars.

And as Jordan surveyed the place, the back door opened. A young woman with soft brown hair falling about her shoulders was being shoved outside by a man with a gun.

She was crying; they could hear her sobs.

She was begging the man with the gun.

As they watched, she was forced to her knees, and the nose of the gun was set to the back of her head.

CHAPTER FOUR

There could be no discussion, no discourse on mind reading, or the true concept of imminent danger—but Patrick's mind still raced. He could almost feel the crackle and pop of neurons in his head like the electric sizzle of a lightning storm.

All in a split second.

The woman was about to be shot. She had managed a terrible transgression of some sort, or maybe she was to die as an example to others.

And they couldn't let that happen.

No choice.

He fired his weapon, hearing a second gunshot at the same time. The would-be executioner was down. The second shot had come from Jordan. They had shared split-second timing, but then, there had been no more than a split second to save a woman's life.

The woman remained on her knees, sobbing, afraid to look up after the gunfire.

Patrick and Jordan looked at one another.

"We've got to get in there," Jordan said.

"Stop them from spreading the word. Get in before someone comes out."

He caught hold of her hands, easing her down to the ground. She was already headed for the wooden fencing that created the wall around the site. When he hit the ground, she was halfway over. With a running leap, he catapulted himself up a few feet, caught hold of the jagged wood at the top, and hefted himself over.

Jordan was already crouched in the yard. He saw Ragnar Johansen was already there as well, hurrying over to the downed man and the sobbing woman. They might simply be out of luck. If there were cameras, they would catch what was happening.

"Colleen, Mark, and the dogs are around the front," Ragnar told them. "We've got to blitz from the rear. Stop what we can."

They didn't need to answer. Ragnar turned to check on the dead man and Patrick caught the arm of the sobbing young woman, drawing her to her feet.

"I'm Patrick Law. I'm with agents here to help. What is your name?"

"Judy. Um, Judy Greeley," she said, blinking, shaking her head, her voice a choked-out sob.

"Okay, Judy, thank you. How many are in there? How heavily armed?"

The woman was still shaking, and terrified.

"Thank you, thank you," she gasped out. "They warned us all the time. We knew to behave, but I didn't do anything! He was going to shoot me in the head. I didn't do anything. I followed the rules. I was terrified—"

"It's all right," Patrick told her, using his most soothing

voice. "Help us save others. How many are in there? They'll be out any second to see if you're dead or not."

"I… Oh!" she cried, looking at the dead man on the ground.

"Please!" he said softly. "The lives of others are at stake."

She winced hard and blinked and seemed to come back to her senses.

"That's Martin…on the ground. Oh, my God, he was going to shoot me in the back of the head. They said I was going to be a warning to the others!"

"Judy. Please. I know this is hard for you right now. We need your help."

"Um…um…inside, Lawrence, Carlo, and Alba."

"How many captives?"

"Vera, Connie, and Tonya, and the kids," she said, seeming to draw sudden strength and adding, "The kids: baby Franklin, toddlers Benjamin, Kayleigh, and Harry."

Three women, four kids. And three armed defenders still inside. He looked at Jordan, who was nodding and heading toward the back door.

Ragnar followed behind her, and Patrick carefully set Judy down on the ground, bringing a finger to his lips. He quickly joined Ragnar and Jordan. Ragnar made a hand motion, indicating someone was coming toward the back door. They flattened against the wall as the door was thrown open.

It was a tall woman—an armed woman—and she had her gun aimed straight ahead as she walked out of the house, wary and ready for any danger.

But they were also ready.

Patrick grabbed her arm, and Jordan slammed a hand down on her wrist, causing her to gasp and drop the weapon. Ragnar spun her around from Patrick and delivered a knockout blow to the top of her head and stooped to cuff her as Patrick and Jordan carefully entered the house.

According to Judy, there were now two captors or caretakers left inside. Lawrence and Carlo.

Jordan moved ahead of Patrick through the kitchen; Ragnar was at his rear. They could hear more sobbing coming from the main part of the house, and glancing at one another, they nodded and hurried on through silently to the archway that led from the dining room to the large living room or parlor.

Colleen and Mark were already inside, negotiating with the captors.

On one sofa, a woman held an infant of six or seven months in her arms, cradling the baby, rocking with the child, and half crooning, half sobbing as she looked at the man in the center of the room, who was holding another woman with a gun to her temple. Toddlers were clinging to the legs of a third young woman, who stood near the woman with the infant, a gun pointed to her head as well.

The man holding the woman with the terrified toddlers at her feet was speaking, shaking his head at Colleen.

"We have all the cards! You can shoot us, but these two will be dead before your bullets ever fly," he said.

The captor was a young man. Patrick noted he was shaking as he held the woman. Not a good thing; the no-nonsense nose of his gun was rubbing against her temple.

"We are to fall on our swords," the other man said. "We'll just take these ladies with us!"

"Don't be stupid," Colleen said quietly. "There's no reason to die. We can help you."

Patrick quickly weighed the situation the best he could. They wanted to take the captors alive in the hopes of getting more information to help them cut off the head of the operation, but they didn't want the hostages dead. And yet, the way they held the women, it would be almost impossible to break them free.

He looked at Jordan and Ragnar, hoping they understood what he planned. They had not been seen by either of the gunmen.

Nor were the dogs visible.

They still held all the cards. He needed to make a move.

He stepped out into the room, holstered his weapon, and lifted his hands.

"Think about this. We can report you all as dead. From what I've seen, dead is the only way to be safe. And we know just about everyone involved is being blackmailed in one way or another. Do you really want to kill anyone? Besides, maybe one of you has someone somewhere who might just be in danger as well. That makes us the best chance you've got. We can keep you alive and get you far, far away. Life is worth fighting for. Come with us; you'll have a chance."

The two men listened. There was a riot of confusion going on in their heads. *They didn't want to shoot. They had probably imagined their part in this was simple guard duty, or maybe one of them had a loved one held at one of the other facilities.*

They could be stalled. One might break out of fear and be ready to die, but if Patrick could just get an advantage of a few seconds.

Only the most demented psychopath could kill a kid in cold blood as collateral damage.

He glanced across the room at the archway where Jordan and Ragnar remained out of sight.

He gave Jordan a slight nod. He had caused the captors to give pause and think.

And so, they were off-balance. Mentally. And whether it was something strange in his personal psyche or the years he had spent at universities, he could read the expressions on their faces and the slightest movement in their body language.

Yep, they were off-balance.

Perhaps only for a second or so, but that would be enough. If Jordan had understood the almost imperceptible nod that he had given her.

And she had.

In turn she nodded across the distance at Ragnar.

Jordan threw herself down and slid across the floor, catching the one man's feet and sending him flying before he could get off a shot. The second man eased his hold on his captive as he twisted around to discover the source of the danger; and as he did so, Ragnar caught him with a precision shot that shattered his arm and sent his gun flying.

There was nothing else to worry about because Red and Hugo—who had apparently been obedient and silent while waiting—crashed through the front and stood ferocious guard over the downed men.

The man Ragnar had caught in the arm howled in pain. The other just stayed down, staring at Hugo, who stood over him like Cerberus from Hades.

"We can't have emergency vehicles pouring in here," Jordan said, rolling and leaping to her feet. "We have to keep this low-key."

"Colleen," Mark said. "You and I will get this man—" He paused, nudging the shot man with his foot. "Hey, who are you? Lawrence or Carlo?"

"Go to hell," the man sputtered.

"Anyway," Mark said dryly, "we'll slide out back with Mr. Go To Hell and get to a hospital as quickly as possible. I'll get Jackson slipping more vehicles down the service road so we can get the hostages to safety and move Mr. Go To Hell's companion down to headquarters. And their friend outside. I don't think there is much help for the other man in the yard, but we'll have to get him out of there, too."

"Go," Ragnar said.

"We'll take Red and leave Hugo," Colleen said. She smiled at Patrick and nodded toward Jordan. "As you might have noticed, he does a great job of watching over a prisoner."

"That he does," Jordan agreed, glancing over at Patrick and studying him. She was surprised and relieved. Between them all, they had made it work. They had one man with a broken, bloody arm, but at least he, like the others in the room, was alive.

The only dead man lay outside. No choice.

"We need to move," Patrick said, stooping down to search the injured man for his phone and kicking away his weapon, then moving on to his companion to find a phone as well. Jordan stepped forward; he started to protest as Jordan went to cuff him.

The dogs growled and made snapping noises.

He turned to have his hands cuffed behind his back. Mark bent down by the groaning, injured man, drawing him to his feet. "We're not cuffing you because of your arm. And since Ragnar is a phenomenal shot, I'd be careful, assuming you'd like to keep the arm. You'll be sitting between me and the dog, who happens to be mine, and completely loyal."

"You don't know what you've done!" the man said.

"Your friend out back was about to execute a woman. We had no choice but to move," Colleen told him. "And I doubt you had time to tell anyone this location has been breached."

"They'll know tonight when the call comes in, asking if all is well."

"Ah," Jordan said quietly. "That shouldn't be a problem. All will be well, because that's what you're going to tell them."

"Then, of course, you could give us the identity of the 'emperor' or whomever the hell you report to. We could get him, and you'd have nothing to fear," Patrick said.

The injured man stared at him and started to laugh, winced instead, and almost sobbed. "They've said he was down, that the cops had him, but that couldn't be, 'cause he's still out there, calling all the shots. And you've saved these folks? What about the others you might have killed with this action? If they find out—"

"If you want to see daylight—and get any threat of a federal death penalty off the table—they won't find out that this facility was breached," Patrick said. He saw Jordan was on the phone, connecting with Jackson. She spoke briefly and ended the call.

"Help is on the way. We need to move," she said, glancing at him and then the others. And he knew Jackson had gotten his hands on Chino's phone, and one of their tech people had figured out the location where Raul Kent's family was being kept.

"We've got Mr. Go To Hell," Colleen said, "and Ragnar can hold here. Go."

She was looking at Patrick, but she quickly turned to Jordan—the Krewe agent in the duo.

Jordan nodded. "If you're all good—"

"We've got it," Colleen assured her.

Jordan stepped around the downed man, gave Red a pat on his head, and looked at Patrick. He turned and started out the back, stopping only to assure Judy Greeley—standing just outside the back door as if she was afraid to move inward—that the others were well.

No one at that location would be executed that day. They would soon find agents and social workers there ready to help.

Then he hurried after Jordan and was impressed by her ability to scale the fence once again.

He followed suit, then checked his buzzing phone for their next location as they headed to the car.

He looked at her briefly after getting into the driver's seat.

"This is just about a mile away," he said, hitting the brake and the button to start the car.

"On the outskirts of the same state park, just farther to the north," she said. "Jackson said he's on the way to that location with Angela—and Alfie. Alfie was at the offices this morning, going over all the notes we've gotten from the victims so far." She glanced at him with a grimace. "Alfie is a powerful force of energy, or whatever it is that we become. He tripped one of the kidnappers yesterday."

"So he did," Patrick agreed.

She had pulled up a satellite map.

"Follow this trail and we'll head in the back. I believe it's a slightly larger facility. From what they could tell from Marie's phone, there are five men working. Eight women and seven children are being kept there. Raul Kent's wife, Natalie, is among them, along with his little boy, Steven."

"Two stories, probably a basement, attic—that's a lot to cover to make sure someone doesn't start shooting if they suspect we're coming in."

Jordan nodded. "We're all on a communication wave through the earbuds. We'll let Jackson know as soon as we're set to go in. He's on his way to the site; he couldn't send out the local police because we're too afraid of the fallout. I..."

Her voice trailed and he glanced her way.

"I wonder what she did," Jordan continued. "The woman who was about to be executed."

"Nothing. She said she was going to be an example," Patrick reminded her.

"But why?"

"I don't know. It did get me to thinking. When Mark and Ragnar started on the Embracer case, they found a woman in the basement of a man named Carver. Then Mark and Colleen found Deirdre Ayers, the daughter of Rory Ayers, buried. Ayers was seriously confident since he was the one who called in the favor, but it turned out Deirdre wasn't his biological daughter, and he knew it. A psychopath such as himself would have no sympathy for her or her mother. But when my sister Megan became involved in it all, agents discovered guards at the correctional facility were making big money getting orders out to other killers—and one of those guards killed Ralph Carver."

"I know," Jordan reminded him. "I was undercover on that case—and it worked," she said.

"Yes, I know," he agreed. "What I can't figure is this—in a moment of supreme arrogance, one of the guards admitted to killing Ralph Carver. But we never did find out who ordered him to do so."

"So, you think that the case we're working now somehow links back to the Embracer case?" Jordan asked.

"I think that the Embracer case was just a piece of a far bigger puzzle," Patrick told her.

Jordan stared at him, frowning, shaking her head. "Okay... if I get what you're saying, this is all happening under the control of one great and powerful criminal who has set himself up, not just as a crime lord, but as a crime *god*, not just using others for their share in criminal revenues, but as a buttress to protect him against ever being discovered?"

Patrick nodded.

"Rory Ayers is still being held behind bars," he said. "Our injured Mr. Go To Hell was saying they'd heard before that their big boss had been picked up, but things just kept on happening. Whomever this person is—Mr. John Smith or someone else—he enjoys supporting sick murder of any kind, which fits with Ayers. It might be part of the feeling of power. Or part of what keeps others in line. This whole thing, Jordan, keeping prisoners to control your little army of bad guys is sick, and brilliant. The more fear this person wields, the stronger he grows. And we don't get him. Except—I think that we have him."

"Rory Ayers?"

Patrick nodded, but then said quickly, "Ahead. That's the house. You can see it through the trees. And look at the fence. Barbed wire at the top."

"We're first to arrive," Jordan said, touching her earbuds. "Jackson, we're here."

Patrick heard a short whistle of air before he heard Jackson's voice in his own ears.

"We've heat sensors on the place. Appears to be fifteen captives, eight women and seven children. Five guards. Looks like there's a playroom upstairs—ten people there, we think children and two moms. Two bedrooms have people in them, and we believe they are the other moms—one person in the hall. A guard probably. Two men in the back; two in the front. We've got to get past them. The house is so out of the way, you aren't going to have anyone selling Girl Scout cookies. But I'm going in at the front as a park ranger; I'll need you two ready to hit the back when the guards there circle around to see what is going on. Angela will be covering me from the front. You're in position?"

"Barbed wire on the fence in back," Jordan said.

"I've got wire cutters in the trunk," Patrick said.

Jordan glanced at him, a slight smile on her lips and a hike to her brow.

He shrugged. "I like to be prepared."

"Let's get in position. The guards at the rear of the house aren't outside. Tech has been searching all our footage for cameras, but we haven't found any," Jackson said. "You will, of course, need to take extreme care."

"Noted," Patrick told him. He parked, slid out of the car, and met Jordan at the rear, where he dug out the wire cutters. He nodded silently to her, and they started through the trees. When they reached the fence, they looked around, then built a makeshift stepladder with fallen branches and bracken. Patrick carefully balanced—with Jordan's help steadying his legs—to snip wire as silently as he could.

There seemed to be nothing coming from inside; so far, they were in the clear.

He dropped the wire cutters, hopped down, and helped Jordan up the bracken. She skillfully used the wooden part of the fence to crawl up and quickly over.

Patrick did the same in time to hear Jackson speak quietly again.

"We're in position, too, behind a pine, watching the rear," Jordan replied.

"They'll burst out or through. No telling which. Be ready," Jackson said.

From the protection of the pine, they could see Jackson approach the house. He looked the part in a khaki park ranger uniform.

He wasn't alone.

But the occupants of the house wouldn't know that.

Sergeant Alfie Parker slid past Jackson. Patrick knew he'd slip in as soon as the door opened and do anything he possibly could to protect the innocent. He had, after all, with the power of his energy, tripped one of the men who had kidnapped Jordan.

They could hear Jackson as he rang the bell at the house, and they heard the front door open.

"Sorry to bother you," Jackson said. "As you can see, I'm from the Parks Department. I'm sorry to inform you, but a recent land survey has shown you've fenced in a few feet of parkland back there. This is a courtesy call, of course, but I'd love just a few minutes of your time. May I come in?"

They could hear the answer, too.

"No, hey, buddy, I'm sorry. This is a really bad time. My wife has her sisters, and my kids have their cousins here; and it's a real family day. But I can come into your office or wherever you want and find out what we've done wrong. Of course, we're going to want to fix whatever the problem may be."

Patrick and Jordan could cleanly see the back door open; they could see the two armed men who stepped out, heading across the back, ready to take shots at Jackson should he refuse to disappear immediately. And they heard another voice from the front.

"Hey, Mark—the kids are getting rowdy. Uh, Mr. Ranger, sir, could you come back at a better time?"

"I just need a few minutes," Jackson said.

Patrick nodded at Jordan; the two men had started to run around. They started a streak across the rear lawn.

"The house," he said. She nodded, heading for the house.

The men turned, seeking the new danger, taking aim at Jordan. Patrick fired in rapid succession. Both men went down as Jordan tore into the house. Patrick sprinted across the lawn, kicking a weapon away from one groaning man, slipping another up into his arms as he rounded the house.

Angela had taken down the one man, and the other lay on the ground with Jackson over him, handcuffing him.

"Jordan?" Jackson asked.

"In the house; I'm going," Patrick said.

He raced past the two men on the ground and through the front, prepared for anything.

But Jordan was seemingly fine; there was a man already handcuffed at the bottom of the stairs. Though there was no sign of Jordan, the ghost of Alfie Parker was seated on the bottom step.

He grinned at Patrick.

"I'm getting really good at this tripping thing! Jordan didn't even have to shoot the bastard. He came rushing down the stairs, and I tripped him. She moved in and cuffed him. I think he cracked his head pretty good on the fall. He's out, but not dead. The more we keep alive, the more people we can question."

"Thanks, Alfie," Patrick said. "Jordan?"

"Upstairs, checking on the hostages."

"Thanks."

Patrick leapt over the man on the floor and skirted by the ghost of Alfie Parker as he hurried up the stairs.

He entered what had been planned as a playroom. There were several women there, most of them young, one of them in her sixties or seventies—probably the mother of one of the players in John Smith's army, he thought.

And Jordan was there, seated with several of the children on the floor, speaking with them. She was explaining what they were going to do with the women. Law enforcement would need to speak with each of them, and social services would be helping them. They would be relocated and remain hidden and protected until they could bring the matter to a close.

Patrick holstered his weapon. She smiled at him.

It had been a successful raid.

But her smile slowly faded. They believed there was a third location.

And there was still the matter of Rory Ayers. Patrick had to have a talk with the man. Find out whatever he could. Because Patrick was convinced Rory Ayers might well be John Smith.

Jordan came to her feet and walked over to him. "This is Patrick Law, and he's here to help. Oh, and, Patrick, the brunette woman over here is Natalie Kent, Raul's wife. And there is his little boy, Steven, playing with the blocks."

Raul Kent hadn't lied. Natalie was beautiful. Tall, lithe, with huge dark eyes and a rich head of sweeping dark hair. He was startled when she walked over to him and threw her arms around him, sobbing.

"She said…she said Raul is alive, and that Steven and I will be okay!" the woman sobbed softly.

The others were looking at him. Hope was in their eyes.

"We have to get everyone to safety," he said clearly. "And then we can begin to sort everything out."

He had spent years of his life studying. Years of school, years of residency. He still had a hell of a time telling anyone they might not see a loved one again. And with the group of people they had discovered today, he didn't know which of their loved ones might have survived and which were in the morgue.

"We'll get this all sorted out," he repeated. "But we need to be very careful now. Others may still be in danger."

"What will happen to us?" one woman whispered.

"Possibly, you'll wind up with the US Marshals Service. We'll need to wait and see about the future. For right now, we will make sure you're safe, and your children are with you and cared for, and then we will work it all out."

"There's someone out there who would still like to use us to control others," a worn-looking brunette said, but she smiled at Patrick. "Please don't get me wrong in any way— we are so grateful to be rescued. But…"

"You're worried about the future, of course," Patrick said. He offered them a smile. "We're all human. Please believe we will do our best. We don't want to see this happen to anyone ever again."

A tiny blonde in her early twenties stepped forward. She was nervous; she wanted to speak, but she was afraid.

"There's another house," she said.

He looked at her curiously. Jordan came around to join him, frowning as they both studied the woman.

"I was there briefly. It's in Central Virginia. There's an old church that was deconsecrated in an old cemetery right by a federal reserve, and there's a wedge of what I'd guess might be private property there. There's an old mansion there that probably dates back to the Civil War, and it looks like it was abandoned. They had a few people there, and—" She broke off, closing her eyes, straining for breath. "They closed the trunk on me, but I could still hear the guards talking. I don't know who he was, but they killed a man there and stuck him in the old cemetery, saying no one would ever know, how it was almost a year ago, and yet they still talked about it and laughed about it and… I know there are others there because there was a woman with me who was dropped off there. They had me in one car, and I saw them take her from the trunk of another car before the door was slammed shut on me."

"Thank you, thank you, sincerely, thank you," Patrick said. He nodded to Jordan. They'd get the message to Jackson if he hadn't heard it through the mics, but when he rushed back down the stairs, he found Jackson was already on his cell phone, describing the location so Angela could work her internet magic and find out where it was.

Patrick waited until Jackson ended the call.

"Should we move?"

"As soon as Angela finds exactly where we need to be. She believes she knows the place, and it's truly desolate, but thankfully, not far. I'll get you GPS coordinates. Angela believes it's the old Mayfield estate. The family died out at the turn of the century and the property remains private, but it's owned by a corporation and usually leased out to movie companies. I'm guessing someone pulling strings rented it for a few years. Hang on, Angela is calling back." He nodded at Patrick and set his phone on speaker.

"All right, I believe I am right about the location. Hanson and Associates owns the property. They're located in LA, and this is the company's only holding in the area. They hired a local caretaker, and I'm going to guess he might be one of the thugs keeping the others prisoner. As far as they know, everything is fine with their rental—paid on time, no damage reports—anyway, sending the info. The house is set back and never had a paved road. There is a path through the cemetery. The church is more of a little chapel with catacombs and a surrounding graveyard. We need to be careful moving in."

"We'll park in the cemetery, out of view," Patrick promised. "I'll grab Jordan and we'll go."

"Take care," Angela warned him. "So far, they don't seem to have any far-reaching camera views. You shouldn't be going without backup, though."

"That's fine. Send backup. But make sure they know they need to stay *back* until they hear from one of us," Patrick said.

"Our people know the dangers," Jackson assured him. "You and Jordan can get going. I'll get this group to headquarters for interrogation—and get the women and children to safety."

"Thank you," Patrick said.

"You've been in this from the beginning; we wouldn't be where we are now without you. Let's hope the third site is the last."

"Yes, let's hope so. And soon, today if possible, I want to interview Rory Ayers. One of the guards at the first location mentioned the fact people had thought they were safe before. They heard whispers saying 'he' was locked up, but more people died. I think Ayers has somehow still been running things from his cell."

"We have gone after Ayers again and again. We thought he was getting messages out about who he wanted kidnapped and killed. But if so, it's going to be hard to find the truth. We've got a problem there," Jackson added grimly.

"What?"

"Ayers was found hanging in his cell, suicide attempt or maybe a murder attempt by a damned magician. He's in the hospital ward, in a coma."

CHAPTER FIVE

Dusk was coming when they reached the site of the old Victorian mansion that was hopefully the last holding site for the loved ones of the crime lord's minions.

Strange light fell over the landscape. Mauves, grays, and streaks of yellow, gold, and pink were floating across the sky, casting an eerie illumination over the old chapel and graveyard. Jordan had always thought she knew the area well—DC, Northern Virginia, Maryland, and West Virginia. And she did. She'd been to colonial parks and dozens of historic places.

But this was different. Abandoned and neglected. A soft lichen or moss seemed to have crept around gravestones, tombs, and monuments. There was a sense of loss and decay about the place, as if it had been lost in time, left to another world.

They didn't venture into the graveyard once Patrick had parked the car. Instead, they crept along the tree line until they saw the old house in front of them.

Once she had been a grand dame, standing tall and narrow

with impressive turrets and two towers, bay windows, and a semicircular porch with handsome columns.

But the paint was peeling, a few of the decorative ginger-bread boards were dangling from the porch's overhang. Old cars sat out front, and there was a playset on a patch of grass that had been poorly mowed.

Jordan didn't realize she had stopped just behind an old oak until Patrick looked at her with a frown.

"Jordan?"

She shook her head and sighed. "That playground is right across the road from a small mausoleum with a broken door, and all those headstones with weeds growing all over them, an angel with broken wings, and aboveground single tombs that look like—"

"They're right out of a horror movie?" Patrick said. "Yep. Thankfully, children are resilient."

"You read the minds of little ones, too?" she asked.

"Sometimes. But also my dad had a friend who lived to be one hundred and two—after having spent several of his childhood years in a concentration camp during World War II. He and the other children knew people were killed daily and that it could be them at any time. But they learned how to find hope and live every moment, continuing to play. I grant you, they may need help. Some people survive bad situations better than others. But, Jordan, we're going to get in there and see to it they have a chance."

"Okay, what's the plan?" she asked. He had discussed the situation with Jackson at the last site. She had stayed with the women and children until he and Jackson had joined, with Jackson detailing how they needed to get them all out without being seen. She had then followed Patrick out and back to the service road and the car.

"We let him know we're here and see if he's gotten anything off satellite data," Patrick said.

She nodded.

She wanted to get in and get the last of the hostages saved, and she wanted for this very long day to be over.

Her mic made a soft whistling sound in her ear and then she heard Jackson speaking softly.

"Okay, so, they're really not expecting anyone here. No one outside; we've picked up just seven heat sensors. It's hard to tell which ones are guards and which are hostages. Two are in each tower. One in what we believe to be the dining room; two in the kitchen. There appears to be no one outside in the rear. There is a parlor, and the dining room is next to it on the left side of the entry with the kitchen in back. There are three rooms to the right of the entry, all empty."

"Windows?" Jordan said.

"My thoughts, too," Jackson said.

She looked at Patrick.

"Windows," he agreed. He smiled grimly at Jordan. "Let's move in."

She nodded.

They both drew their weapons and moved swiftly through the trees and the narrow strip of grass that bordered the house. Nodding to one another, they took side-by-side windows. She looked at him and knew he would hold steady as she went first.

There was no challenge to getting in. The window was open. She hopped onto the sill and quickly crawled in. The room was someone's office. It was empty.

She looked out the window and nodded to Patrick. Pausing, she listened. No sound. She carefully headed to the door to the hall and looked out. Seconds later, Patrick appeared. He shook his head.

No one, so far.

"Damn, make it decent! You're supposed to be a cook, right?"

They could hear the irritated male voice from the other side of the house. Jordan knew she and Patrick were making the same calculations. In the kitchen, one captor, one prisoner.

Who was in the dining room? They had to see before they could save the "cook."

Patrick signaled to her that he would start across the parlor. She would cover him. He was halfway across when she heard someone coming down the wooden steps of the handsomely carved staircase in the parlor before them. She saw Patrick carefully ease behind a faded antique love seat.

The person came down. It was a man of about forty, a pistol tucked into his waistband. He strode toward the dining room and kitchen area, calling out, "Hey! What's the story? Food anytime soon? Hell, it's almost dark outside and I'm starving!"

Jordan hadn't realized just how good Patrick was at what he did until that moment. He rose from his position with absolute silence, caught the man in a headlock that instantly cut off his windpipe and any possibility of him screaming. Within seconds, he lowered the man to the ground.

Jordan hurried over to Patrick.

"Is he—dead?"

"Just out. I've got to get cuffs on him. We need to get to the dining room and kitchen. The guy won't be out long."

"Let's do it," she said, rising as Patrick rolled the man to get cuffs on him. She went to the arch that led into the dining room, pausing to peek in.

Another man of about the same age sat at the dining room

table, frowning as he looked up from the paper he'd been reading. "Saul? What the hell?" he called out.

Saul, of course, couldn't answer. Jordan looked at Patrick. She gave him a weak smile and made a knocking sound on the wall. The man at the table quicky stood, more perplexed than before, but apparently not worried enough to draw the gun stuck into a holster at his waistband.

Patrick grabbed a heavy vase, wrapping it in a throw blanket from the love seat, and found a position at the archway across from Jordan.

She made the noise again but muffled it a little.

The man walked through. Patrick caught him at the back of the head with the wrapped-up vase.

He went down with a grunt. The throw blanket kept the vase from shattering—or making much noise at all.

"Hey!" came a call from the kitchen.

They were both silent. Patrick dragged the man they had just downed to the side and cuffed him as well.

"He's coming," Jordan whispered.

Patrick was back with the vase and Jordan held her position.

"Move, move, get ahead of me!" They heard the man from the kitchen, presumably ordering his "cook."

She let out a muffled sob.

"There had better not be anything wrong. I've got a gun to the back of your head!"

"Please!" came a whimper.

Patrick lifted a hand to Jordan. She flattened herself against the wall as Patrick backed away but stood in the middle of the parlor, where he could easily be seen.

A woman was pushed through the archway into the parlor. She was young, as most of the others had been. Pretty once, worn and too slim now, her features showing her misery, her soft brown hair long and tangled.

"What the hell?" the man who had pushed her through the doorway demanded as he stared at Patrick.

Patrick's hands were on his hips; his weapon was holstered.

"Hey, time to let her go," Patrick said with a shrug.

"Who the hell are you? And what the hell—"

His eyes fell on his co-jailers, both lying facedown and handcuffed.

"What the hell—"

He moved his gun, aiming it at Patrick rather than his now-sobbing captive.

Jordan moved.

There were things she had learned at the academy. Things about speed and precision with her Glock. She'd had a fine instructor, teaching them they wanted the cops and agents to come home, they were the good guys, so while they didn't like killing criminals, when it was life-or-death for themselves, they needed to pull the trigger with speed and accuracy.

But she didn't need to pull the trigger. She had speed and the element of absolute surprise because the man had seen Patrick—he hadn't seen her.

And they needed everyone alive if they were ever going to find the truth behind the deepest bowels of the operation.

She moved like a bat out of hell, grabbing Patrick's vase-weapon from the floor. She hurled the vase and struck the man on the head so hard he went down in a split second with only the tiniest whimper escaping him as he fell.

Patrick looked at her in surprise.

"Nice! You should have played for the majors."

The young female hostage let out a sob that was almost a

shriek. She turned in terror—first, to see Jordan, and then she backed away from them both in confusion.

"It's all right. My name is Jordan. This is Patrick," Jordan said quickly. "We're with the government. We're going to get you out of here."

The young woman shook her head. "They've mixed us all up… There are other places. If anything happens at one—"

"We've been to the other two," Patrick assured her gently. "Upstairs—who is still upstairs?"

"Just Molly and the children. But they're locked in. They never let Molly out of her room; she hit one of them once. She has her son and my daughter. They let me out to cook."

"That's it? Just you—and Molly and two kids?" Patrick asked.

The young woman nodded.

"There used to be another girl. Another young woman, I guess. Very sweet, and so kind, but they came and took her away. They didn't trust her. She was so smart, too. She was etching messages into tombstones, and they finally caught her. They said that she was going somewhere 'special.' She told me once the guys watching us weren't even all that bad—they were scared, too. But…"

Jordan walked over and placed a gentle hand on her arm. "Do you know what her name was?" she asked quietly.

"Of course. Susie. Her name was Susie."

CHAPTER SIX

"Thank you for this," Patrick said.

Jordan was tired. Exhausted, really. But she smiled, her head tilted back, her eyes closed, as he drove.

"You mean that I'm okay to prowl around an old cemetery late at night after the longest workday known to man?"

She cracked her eyes open. He was smiling. "Yeah," he said simply.

"You forget, I care about Alfie and finding the truth as much as you do. It seems more and more likely the cases are related. The man called John Smith seems to be the same person orchestrating everything now."

"And I'd been convinced it was Rory Ayers."

She grimaced. "Maybe it was. We found the places where he was holding all the loved ones hostage. Maybe that's it."

"Maybe, but I was anxious to speak with him, to—"

"Read his mind?"

"I told you, it's not automatic. Sometimes I know something in someone else's head in a way that's as clear as day, and sometimes not. Anyway, I do want to let Alfie know Susie had been a prisoner, and that they took her somewhere."

"You think that's going to make him happy?" she asked, wincing.

"When we tell him we won't stop until we do find her."

"Now I can read your mind. You were about to say 'until we do find her—dead or alive.'"

"I think she's alive."

"But it sounded as if they moved her because she caused trouble. And we know they killed and buried a man in the old cemetery across the path. And while Alfie makes Susie sound sweet—a lost girl, running, just searching for a life and a direction—she might be pretty hardened by now. I don't know. I hope we can find her. But where?" Jordan said.

"She's out there. I know it. I believe it. And we will find her."

They had reached the cemetery where Alfie lay with others who had served as officers.

"Hey, no admittance at night," Jordan commented.

"But we're agents on a case."

Jordan laughed. "And how are we investigating the case right now in this cemetery?"

"Doesn't matter. Just flash your badge and say that, for the moment, your movements are confidential," he said. Then he shrugged. "I'm not really expecting anyone to stop us."

"We're hopping over a wall."

"A little stone wall that's about two feet high?"

"I told you. I care about Alfie and helping him, too. It's just been a really long day, and I don't particularly want to be arrested by the local police." She winced and let out a sigh.

Patrick nodded. He'd been amused, but then his brow furrowed.

"What?" she asked.

"Nothing. I just…"

"What? Patrick, please. Tell me."

"If they killed one man, they might have killed others."

She shook her head. "Susie isn't dead," she said firmly.

"I don't—I don't think she is either. But where might they have taken her?"

When they reached the cemetery, Patrick parked on the road near one of the lowest spots on the wall. He was right; anyone could take a big step over the wall, but there had never been vandalism at the cemetery. It was active and well maintained. Jordan was sure, however, that local police did patrol the area.

Patrick glanced at her. "There are some family mausoleums and several aboveground tomb-style graves. Plenty of places to hide."

She cast him a warning glare; he smiled.

He stepped over the stone wall and offered her a hand. Shaking her head with a sigh, she took it.

There was such a difference, she thought, between this cemetery and the graveyard by the Victorian mansion.

The living visited here often.

They brought fresh flowers.

Headstones and tombs were cleaned. She wasn't sure if it mattered to anyone, once they were dead, if their burial place was maintained. But there was a different atmosphere here, one of love and respect. While at the old graveyard, death seemed to be seeped into the weeds and tree roots that cut through gravestones. The gray seemed to have settled over everything, including the trees and foliage, the old monuments, and cherubs and angels with their cracked and broken wings.

"Alfie?"

Patrick called his name as they made their way to the section that honored police officers.

They didn't see any spirits, but then, the dead didn't necessarily hang around the cemetery. Alfie seldom did. But in this case, Patrick was right.

Alfie was leaning against an old family mausoleum just to the side of the police section.

Seeing them, he pushed away and walked hurriedly in their direction.

"So, anything new?" he asked anxiously.

Patrick went on to explain how their day ended, adding that he hoped they had taken the last of the sites where the criminals were holding the innocent, but he wasn't sure.

"Susie?"

"We believe she's alive. We don't know where yet. But based on what you've told us, I believe that young lady is a survivor. Wherever she is, we'll find her."

"But it sounds as if there were only three locations," Alfie said worriedly.

"Patrick believes it was important that Susie be held," Jordan said. "She's okay. We sincerely believe that. One of the women at the last site—the old Victorian mansion—told us she saw her, and that she was fine. Strong. She's strong and clever, so they needed to be careful."

"And she didn't have a child. They've kept people in control because they had children," Patrick said. "A mother with a child in danger is going to be very careful to follow rules." He hesitated. "Susie was writing notes on gravestones, etching them into the stone, I imagine. The place is remote. There's nothing around but an old graveyard, a deconsecrated chapel, and miles of brush and trees. We'll know more tomorrow. It was decided to let the captors stew overnight and face interrogation tomorrow. If I know Jackson Crow, he had a few conversations this evening."

Alfie smiled. "Long day," he said quietly. "And here you are, crawling around a spooky old cemetery at night."

"We wanted to let you know what we found today," Patrick said.

Alfie nodded. He grinned over at Jordan, who laughed softly.

"Alfie! I've met some of my favorite people crawling around old cemeteries at night. Doesn't matter that they're dead! Not to me, anyway."

"And we, the dead, are lucky friends like you exist," Alfie said softly. "But it is getting very late in the world of the living. Thank you for coming. Thank you for caring enough to bring me all the information that you have. What is the plan for tomorrow?"

"We'll be haunting another graveyard," Patrick said dryly. "We were told a man was killed and buried there. Guards found it funny they were able to discard the body in such a fashion with no one being the wiser. Anyway, we're bringing out a few very special dogs—"

"Cadaver dogs in a graveyard. Interesting," Alfie said, offering them a half smile.

"I said special dogs—as in Red and Hugo. And a few forensics teams to search the area. We're hoping there are not more bodies there—" Jordan began.

"More bodies in a graveyard?" Alfie queried, arching a brow.

"Right," Patrick said. He chuckled and Jordan smiled. He was fully aware Alfie knew exactly what he was saying. "Relatively new bodies," Patrick added.

Alfie's demeanor changed. "You don't think that—"

"No. I don't think Susie is buried there. We were told she'd been moved from that site. I honestly believe she's alive and well. We just have to find where they have her," Patrick said.

"Alfie, we will find her," Jordan told him, her words quiet but filled with assurance.

"I believe you will," Alfie said. "But you two probably shouldn't stay here any longer. Go home. Get some sleep. Just think, tomorrow you get to question all kinds of people, and search through another graveyard."

"We're going," Jordan said.

"Thank you again for coming," Alfie said. He shook his head, smiling. "Crazy people."

Jordan glanced at Patrick, and they both smiled and nodded, giving him a wave on their way back to the car.

"Hey," Patrick said, sliding into the driver's seat. "Kind of a bummer—you didn't have to flash your badge for anyone."

"Ha ha. Seriously. I'm glad you thought to go and see him."

"Yeah, I think it was good. Anyway, it's late, but—"

"You'll be at my place to get me at the crack of dawn, right?"

"Yeah, something like that."

She leaned back. Traffic was light at that time of the night, and they were soon at her place. She was surprised to find it felt weird—he was dropping her off. She'd resented him so much when they had started, and now...

Well, the day they had just shared had seemed like a week or even a lifetime. And they seemed to have a level of communication that allowed them to work exceptionally well together. Of course, she wasn't immune to biology or humanity. Patrick was a striking man, impressive in stance and manner as well as his looks. She was accustomed to men who were fit—a necessity for their work. But he was especially attractive.

He walked and moved and spoke with confidence. He was compelling. In more ways than she wanted to acknowledge.

She really needed to get out of the car!

"See you in the morning," he told her, parking against the curb.

"See you in the morning," she agreed.

She knew he waited and watched until she had gone through her door, closed and locked it. And she was learning the hard way that it never hurt to have someone watching your back. She'd known that before, of course. And there had been times when she had depended on other members of the team. But in truth, maybe she had been too reckless or too certain of her own abilities in the past.

She liked working with others; it was incredible to get to work with the Krewe. She had read somewhere once that INFPs, or "mediator" personality types, able to emphasize and comprehend others to the nth degree, made up 4 or 5 percent of the world population. She knew Adam and Angela had once gotten together to research the past and present. And while they were not alone, only one-fourth of 1 percent of the population had the strange sixth sense that allowed them to see the dead—not by sitting around a crystal ball and waiting for knocks on the table, but by casually having conversations wherever they might be found. Being with the Krewe was special.

And the comradery sure made up for all the awkward friendships and relationships through the years.

Others just didn't understand.

Heading to her room, she found herself wishing she had a cat or a dog.

But she didn't even have a goldfish. Most of the time, she preferred living alone. No roommate to explain her whereabouts to. No worry about hours—or bolting out with the place a mess when she received an unexpected call from work…

Patrick had a dog. One she had yet to meet. She'd gotten to know both Red and Hugo, who were now the beloved canine children of Mark and Colleen and Megan and Ragnar. And they were brilliant working dogs. Hugo had come into it a bit late but had an absolute talent. Red had been certified for many positions for years; he could find the lost, seek out drugs—or find a cadaver.

A dog would have been nice that night.

Or a goldfish.

Crawling into bed, Jordan was afraid she wouldn't sleep. It seemed her mind was on fire, and she was unusually lonely. She never felt that way. She had chosen a path in life, set out on that path, and made it her passion. Tonight, she was lonely. Or at least, she felt alone. Crazy. She had wonderful friends. She was blessed. Nothing had changed.

But it had.

The intensity of the day had gotten to her. It had been a good day, a rewarding day. Many might have died; they had saved lives. They had gotten to three different locations where people had been prisoners. They'd only had to kill one of the captors.

And in time, those they had taken in might have something that would help them reach the very core of the far-reaching empire they'd only begun to uncover.

She stared at the ceiling in the dark and smiled to herself.

Patrick Law had gotten to her.

Whether she liked it or not, they made a good team. Maybe he was reading her mind, but she seemed to understand what he was doing or wanted her to do, down to minute details. They worked well together. Exceptionally well.

And that work closeness…

"Yep!" she said aloud to herself. "Tomorrow is another day. Another long day. And I'm talking to myself!"

She would never sleep.

But eventually, she did.

Sheer physical exhaustion could be a beautiful thing.

Patrick woke before six, dressed, and was ready to head down for coffee when he heard a tapping at his door.

He glanced through the peephole, thinking it was damned early for housekeeping to be coming around.

At first, he didn't see anything. Then he realized the ghost of Alfie Parker was at his door.

He opened it, arching his brows.

"Couldn't you have just come in?" he asked.

Alfie smiled. "Hell, yes. A perk of being dead. But dead or alive, I'd find such behavior rude, so I knocked."

"Very polite of you. Come in, please."

"Hey, I never want to interrupt anything."

"I'm in a hotel."

"Exactly."

"Alfie, I'm here to work—"

"With an exceptional partner. I see a few sparks there."

"We barely get along."

"Sparks," Alfie said safely.

Patrick waved a hand in the air, glad Alfie wasn't a mind reader. His thoughts through the night and the morning had switched back and forth between the case and Jordan.

Hey, he was human, he reminded himself, but he'd discovered his relationships were best kept casual.

"Alfie, we're working," he said dismissively. "Killer hours, which are about to start again. I'm heading down for coffee now. How did you get here, anyway?"

"The usual. You know. Beware of hitchhiking ghosts! I have it down to an art."

"I guess you do."

"So, I pushed you guys out last night without getting the full agenda—other than knowing you're going to an old graveyard to find fresh bodies."

"Headquarters first; between the captors and those we rescued, there are a lot of people to be interviewed. Jackson intends to handle a lot of the interviews himself, but as I said, it's a lot of people. If anyone has said anything that might be of value, Jordan and I will see if we can draw out anything further."

"Okay. I'm ready."

Patrick grinned at him. "May I have coffee first?"

"Sure. I'll pretend I'm drinking it." Alfie grew serious. "I think we may be close, Patrick. So close. Jackson—and the other Krewe members—have always tried for me. But it's time to follow through on what's happening now—and find possible connections to what happened in the past."

Patrick nodded. "You may well be right."

"Aren't you a mind reader?"

"I really wish it was that simple. Sometimes, I know what people are thinking. Sometimes, they may have a barrier of sorts."

"Kind of the same as Megan?"

"Megan's talents lie with words. She can decipher what someone is really saying, like reading between the lines. Sometimes—and I don't know if it's even a talent or a hell of a lot of college courses—but I can hear someone or look at them and know what they're thinking. Jackson is bringing

Megan in to listen to his interviews. Anything suspicious,
I'll take a crack at it. But we're going to talk to the people
who saw Susie."

"Prisoners, right? They won't know where she was taken."

"They might point us to the people who took her."

"Good cop thinking," Alfie said. "Get your coffee. Let's go."

Patrick downed one cup quickly at the hotel's coffee bar
and poured himself a second cup for the ride. Alfie remained
close, silent, just waiting.

A woman behind Patrick in the coffee line shivered slightly
and looked around. Patrick lowered his head and smiled. She
was a person who could sense something—but not enough
to see the dead.

They headed to his car.

"Patrick!"

Walking out, he heard his name called. And looking across
the parking lot, he saw that Karen Crawford had arrived—
with Bry-bo.

"Karen!" he called. He had talked to her right before falling asleep last night about figuring out a way to bring his dog
down as quickly as possible.

He hadn't expected her to drive down before the crack of
dawn.

"Oh," Alfie muttered, seeing Karen. "That's why...you're
nothing but business with Jordan."

Patrick shook his head. "Karen is married. Her wife is as
sweet and as good a friend as she is. They live in my building and have been taking care of my dog. And now here she
is after I told her I needed him."

"That is a good friend," Alfie said. She really was, as was
her wife, Sophie. They were two of the best and kindest people he'd ever been privileged to meet. While Sophie was a

member of a local equity theater in Philadelphia, Karen was a freelance artist. Their chosen fields worked well for them, as Karen could travel with Sophie when she did have a role in another city or state.

"Hey!" Patrick said, hurrying over to meet her and Bry-bo.

The dog, of course, was excited to see him and forgot all his training. He jumped up to greet Patrick and stood even above Patrick's six-three.

"Down, boy, down. Good to see you, too!"

Bry-bo obediently hopped down to stand on all four paws, and Patrick smiled at Karen and gave her a warm hug as well.

"I told you I'd figure out a way to get him," Patrick told Karen. "I feel terrible. You came all this way. What did you do? Start out driving soon after we talked?"

"Nope—it all just worked out beautifully," Karen told him. "Sophie has a bit part in a movie, and she needed to be in DC by ten this morning. So it made sense for us to come after I talked to you. The producers have a hotel in the downtown area, so I dropped her off first and came over here. You're up bright and early. I guess it's a tough case."

He nodded. "I'm off to pick up my assigned partner, but if you two are going to be in the area, maybe we can meet up. Hours will be strange, I guess. No telling when Sophie will be filming. But first, thanks for taking care of Bry-bo, and secondly, you couldn't have brought him at a more convenient time."

"Great!" she said brightly. "I'm going to leave him with you and get back to the hotel to say goodbye to Sophie before she goes in to work."

"Thank you," Patrick said. He gave her a hug goodbye. Bry-bo wagged his tail.

She smiled and headed for her car. Followed by Alfie and

Bry-bo, Patrick walked to his. He opened the back for Bry-bo to hop in. Once he'd gotten into the driver's seat, he called Jordan to tell her he was on his way.

"I'll be outside," she promised.

Alfie was in the back seat next to Bry-bo. The dog seemed to know he was there. He appeared to be happily curled up next to the spirit.

Patrick often thought dogs were smarter than people, including himself.

"Comfy?" Patrick asked, looking at the back seat through the rearview mirror.

"Me or the dog?"

"Both."

Alfie shrugged. "You'll have Jordan up there for company soon enough."

"Hopefully we can find the smoking gun," Patrick said with a shrug.

When they reached Jordan's place, she was already out on the sidewalk, ready to go. Patrick smiled as she slid into the car. Somehow, she still looked nice and professional, even dressed in jeans and a soft blue knit shirt with a light casual knit jacket and sneakers.

"My crawling-around-in-a-graveyard attire," she told him as she met his eyes. "Oh!" she said then, noticing Bry-bo and Alfie in the back.

"Lovely as always," Alfie said. "My dear Jordan, you could wear a canvas bag and still be stunning. I know you agree, Patrick."

"Yep, I agree." Patrick knew Alfie was baiting him. Not going to happen, he determined.

Bry-bo sat up, anxious to meet the newcomer.

"Wow," Jordan muttered. "Is he friendly?"

"Unless he's told not to be," Patrick assured her.

"Hey, there, boy," she said, reaching around to scratch Bry-bo's head. "You are...big!"

"He's an Irish wolfhound."

"Yes, I remember you saying that. How did you get him? Did you drive to Philadelphia and back during the night?"

"My friend brought him down."

"His friend Karen," Alfie said. "A very sweet and lovely woman. I wish I could have met her! Well, you know, I was there, but..."

"Oh, well, it was nice of her to bring Bry-bo so quickly," Jordan said. "That's a good friend."

Patrick glared at Alfie through the rearview mirror. "She's down here with her wife, Sophie, who is an actress. They're filming in DC. I don't know what the project is, but Sophie is a fine actor. They'll be here for a few days, at least. I hope you can meet them. They're great people."

"Nice. Oh! They should see a performance at Adam's theater. Did you know he owns a historic theater in DC? We have actors among the spouses of several Krewe members. In fact, three Krewe members are the sons of famous actors, the McFadden brothers."

"And their delightfully diva-ish mother and their dad are still hanging around. They had a dramatic ending!" Alfie said.

"Yes, I have met all three McFadden brothers and their parents," Patrick said. "And they know this area. As do we." He frowned suddenly. "No one knows every nook and cranny of the many forests, but...maybe we didn't find Susie because there's another holding site that isn't in this area."

"But whoever is behind all this, he seems to be running things from here," Jordan said. Her phone was ringing, and she answered it quickly, noting it was Jackson calling.

"Hey, boss, I'll put you on speaker," she said.

"Thanks," Jackson said. "All right. One of the captors is a man named Brandon Johnstone. He was taken at the first site, and he's willing to talk because his wife and child were found at the third site. I have him waiting for you in a conference room. He's talking because he believes his family is safe now and because he believes we'll put him and his family with the Marshals Service in exchange for him telling us anything he can. I talked to the captives where he was acting as a jailer. He never hurt or threatened any of them, though he made sure they didn't leave. He knows we killed a man, and he's grateful to be alive himself; he's hoping we'll deal so he doesn't do any time at all. If what he tells us about the way he got into it and how involved he was pans out, I'm willing to go to the DA for him. But I'm hoping you'll know for sure if he's telling the truth, Patrick."

"I'm ready to do my best," Patrick promised.

"After, I'll send you out to the graveyard. If Brandon Johnstone is telling the truth, there might be more than one body that wasn't legally interred there. We've been in touch with the holding company for the property and informed the town and county as well. The place was practically abandoned, but it does have a historic designation."

"Which means—"

"If we need to, we rip the place to shreds."

"We'll be there in ten," Jordan promised, ending the call.

"Should be interesting," Alfie muttered. "Cadaver dogs looking for cadavers. In a graveyard."

"None of our dogs are strictly cadaver dogs. Megan's guy is really an emotional support dog. And if I understand it correctly, Red has as many certifications as does Bry-bo here, who has done just about everything a certified dog can do,"

Patrick said, glancing back at the spirit. Alfie was looking out the window, as if he still watched the world. Perhaps he did.

"Okay, let's hear what this fellow has to say," Alfie said. "And then, hell yeah. Let's go rip up a graveyard."

Jordan grinned at Patrick, shaking her head with amusement at Alfie's words.

He smiled in return. He knew they would have both loved to have known Alfie during his life, and they wished they could have done something to have kept him from losing it.

But since death could not be undone, they needed to find a way to give him peace.

They arrived at headquarters and greeted the agents they passed on their way in. All greeted them and Alfie in return. Everyone was interested to meet Bry-bo, and the wolfhound seemed in his element. Bry-bo believed all kinds of admiration and love were his due.

Patrick learned a few agents, Colleen, Mark, and Ragnar among them, were already arriving at the Victorian mansion and the graveyard.

Jackson was waiting for them.

"The cameras are sending out the feed. I'll be with Angela, watching from her computer. To recap, the man's name is Brandon Johnstone. His wife was rescued from the last site, along with their child. We have his wife and child with social services, and we have a dozen agents watching over the home where they're being helped." He hesitated. "We've had another interesting development," he said.

"Oh?" Patrick and Jordan said in unison, glancing at each other as they did so.

"Marie Donnell. I spoke with her again, telling her the more she told me about her part in all this, including whom she was really working for, the easier it would go for her.

She has changed. She doesn't think I can do much to her in court. With a good lawyer, she'll prove she had no choice, and she was just trying to make things better for the women. I'm welcome to put her in general population."

"She's not scared anymore," Patrick said. "We could theorize that's because Rory Ayers is in a coma."

"Exactly," Jackson said.

"We need proof," Jordan muttered. "If not…this could start all over again with the same master puppeteer."

"We do need proof," Jackson agreed. "Anyway, Johnstone is in there. See what you can get."

"You want us in together?" Jordan asked.

"Patrick?" Jackson asked.

"Yeah, I think we'll do well together."

Jackson nodded.

They headed to the conference room where the man was waiting. Like many of the others, he was young. His hair was neatly cut, and he was clean-shaven other than the bit of stubble that had begun to grow overnight. He had been sitting there, staring blankly at the table until they entered. He started to rise but Patrick lifted a hand, indicating they'd be sitting, too.

"Mr. Johnstone, I'm Patrick Law, and this is Special Agent Jordan Wallace."

"How do you do," Johnstone said, and then grimaced. "I, uh, well…" He winced. "I'll say anything you want, as long as Marcia and Rene are okay!"

"Your wife and child?" Jordan asked. "We will do everything in our power to keep them safe."

He nodded. "I mean, I know they're okay now. I heard you two rescued them. I can't thank you enough. I mean… you don't know what it was like," he whispered.

"How about you explain. I believe you love your wife and child more than yourself," Patrick said. "So, how did they get in such a horrible position?"

The man shook his head, close to tears. "I never meant for it to come to what it did, but…with the pandemic and everything, I was out of work. I was at a bar, and a fellow told me just selling pot could get me through any tough time. I never thought pot was that bad, and it's legal in over half the country now, and… I didn't think I'd be hurting anyone. Then I found out the pot we were selling came with other stuff. When I wanted out, they showed me they'd taken Marcia and Rene. And they would die if I didn't do what I was told."

"Who got you into this?" Patrick asked him.

"The guy at the bar?" Johnstone asked. "He's the one I would report to all the time. He said his name was Smith. John Smith."

CHAPTER SEVEN

"There's a lot of life here for a graveyard," Alfie said.

Jordan was amused and amazed a ghost could maintain such a sense of humor. But Alfie's spirit was on fire. He felt vindicated, as if he might make a difference.

And find Susie.

"Oh, and it is a graveyard—a graveyard grows up around a church, and in this case, around the abandoned chapel. A cemetery is freestanding, a place specifically for the dead. Did you know a vault is something dug into the earth, as in an area where there are cliffs? A mausoleum is freestanding."

Jordan arched a brow to him.

Alfie smiled at her. "I have a friend in the cemetery—wife of a cop who died in the 1940s—who was an English teacher for thirty years. She's a sweetie but makes you a little crazy. Don't ever say 'he did good,' unless he did good deeds. You can do good, but you've usually done 'well.'"

"I'll remember," Jordan assured him. They stood on the dirt-and-gravel road between the old Victorian mansion and the graveyard. Matching the grim task of the day, the sky had settled into a dismal gray. The sun wasn't peeking out with a single ray, and the color seemed to have settled over everything around them. Reaching the little cemetery, Jordan thought the gray of the day permeated everything, broken gravestones and the weeds that crawled around through them. Lichen, moss, and simple dirt had created a layer over standing tombs and mausoleums.

They could see Krewe members closer to the center of the graveyard. Colleen Law had a map of the graveyard in her hands and was pointing out something to the others.

Bry-bo started barking excitedly.

"Hey, watch your manners, boy!" Patrick chastised him. He glanced at Jordan and Alfie. "He sees Hugo. The two are good friends."

"Do the dogs know they're cousins?" Jordan teased.

"I guess so."

"Red is out there, too. He's never met Red," Jordan reminded him.

"They are professionals; they'll do fine," Patrick assured her.

Apparently, he was right. As they met up with Colleen, Mark, and Ragnar, the dogs greeted each other with sniffs, woofs, and a lot of tail wagging. As the dogs welcomed one another, everyone acknowledged Alfie, Colleen a little nervously.

"Alfie, she's not going to be here," Colleen said.

"I know," Alfie told her. "I believe Susie is still alive, too. But where? Everyone we've talked to thought there were three holding sites for the captives. You found three. It seems like maybe we had it right all along: Rory Ayers was calling the shots even while he was in jail."

"Possibly," Colleen agreed.

"Hey, is Megan coming here?" Patrick asked.

"No, she's at home, but she's going through the cemetery records. Time and the elements can do a hell of a job. And some of these graves have been here for hundreds of years. We may be comparing bones to bones. And..."

Colleen stopped speaking.

"There may be more than one recently dead man here," Alfie said.

Colleen nodded. "We just don't know. It's been a massive undertaking. So many people have been brought in, and the questioning has been endless. It seems some were roped into becoming criminals, some were threatened, and some were bribed. But I'd guess at least one of the guards at each location was a stone-cold killer, ready to handle whatever needed to be handled."

"Execute a prisoner for causing trouble, or just as an example," Jordan suggested.

Colleen nodded.

"Where would they have taken Susie?" Alfie asked.

"We don't know. But I still don't think she's here," Patrick said.

"We've just planned out a grid. We have three dogs, so we've done pie-shape sections I can show you," Ragnar said. "We figure we split up and walk it, too. Axel Tiger and Bruce McFadden are here, and Kat is on her way to see any remains we discover. She's a Krewe member and medical examiner," he explained to Patrick.

"All right. Where do we start?" Patrick asked.

"Your pie, right across from the house, up to the old chapel."

"Okay," Jordan said. "We'll get started."

"Mark and I are in the far corner, coming in toward the

chapel, and Ragnar and Hugo will be coming in parallel with us. Anyone finds anything, just shout," Colleen said. She looked at the dogs, who were now on their haunches, watching their humans and waiting for orders. "Or bark," she added.

All three of the dogs barked.

"And to think I was a cat person until Red," Colleen said. "I'm learning how quickly he obeys!"

She left for her piece of the grid with Mark; Ragnar waved and started off for his piece of the triangle they had created.

"I don't see any disturbed ground," Jordan said, after they'd separated to cover more ground, though still within earshot of one another.

Bry-bo was trotting alongside Patrick. He would run off to sniff now and then, but returned to his master's side each time with nothing.

"This place looks like something created for a Halloween party—not real," Patrick said. "So many pieces of broken stones…that angel with moss and dirt dripping off her one remaining wing."

"Dust to dust and ashes to ashes," Alfie said. He was closely following Jordan as if he was determined to protect her. Even as a spirit, he was an impressive law enforcement officer.

Except she didn't think she had anything to worry about that day.

Police had set up blocks on the roads that led to the area. Not that it mattered. Apparently, other than the captors and hostages in the old house, no one came out here anyway.

"There is a man here somewhere," Patrick said. "And one of the men here wasn't just a dumb out-of-work guy getting roped into a real criminal enterprise because he'd been laid off. One of them here was a killer. Jackson will sort out who. Whoever has been doing this…"

His voice trailed.

Bry-bo had started barking excitedly.

Jordan hurried over to where Patrick was standing. There was a chipped stone marker by his feet, but the ground nearby appeared to be little more than dirt, unusually clear of old grass and leaves and bits and pieces of the bracken from the growing things in the graveyard.

Patrick looked at her. "Too clean," he said.

Bry-bo kept barking.

Patrick called out to summon the others, and then he hunkered down by his dog. "Go for it, my friend. You'll be sharing the dig spot in a minute." He stood as the dog began to dig.

"We can't let him—" Jordan began.

"Not to worry; we'll just let the dogs take down a layer, and we'll take greater care after that."

They were quickly joined by the others, including Red and Hugo. And just as Patrick had said, the three dogs obediently stopped digging when ordered to do so.

Patrick was down by the growing hole when he commanded Bry-bo to stop. He looked up.

"We need a body bag," he said.

"We've got an ambulance waiting down the road," Colleen said. "Calling now."

Within minutes, a crew had come to remove the body from the ground. Kat Sokolov arrived with them and supervised the removal, telling them that her preliminary estimation was that the remains were male, that they had been in the ground between six months and a year, and that the victim had been shot in the back of the skull, execution style.

Then she was off with the body.

"We could use showers," Colleen muttered.

"But are we done here?" Patrick wondered.

He stood, dusting off his hands. They did need showers. They were all covered with dirt.

But Jordan wasn't worried about being dirty. She was looking toward the old chapel. Alfie wasn't with them; she thought he had wandered off that way.

"Um, not sure where Alfie went," she said, striding toward the chapel.

The place had been little more than one big room with a raised altar, two rows for a small chorus, and at one time, perhaps two dozen pews. Now most of the pews were broken or gone. The floorboards at the altar were broken. The wooden cross once strung above the altar had fallen and crashed into it, and the podium had fallen into pieces as well.

But it was while staring at the broken podium that Jordan noticed the floor was cleaner near it; it appeared something had been dragged around it. Hurrying up but taking care of the floorboards, she discovered the decay allowed her to see there was something beneath, far beneath.

The remnants of a stairwell remained. And the stairs, she thought, led down to catacombs. She turned to see that Patrick had followed closely behind her.

"What is it?" he asked her.

She shook her head. "I don't know. A sixth sense?" she said.

Bry-bo ambled in behind Patrick, looked at his master, and awaited a command.

"The flooring is tricky," Jordan said. "I'm not sure Bry-bo—"

"I'm not sure a human being should be headed down there," Patrick said.

"But someone has been down there. Look at the marks. I believe someone dragged someone else here and brought them down to the catacombs. I'm going down. I weigh less than you, and I can see stairs and a banister, and I can even see where steps are missing. Of course, more light would help, but I have my flashlight and—"

Patrick was already by the stairway to the catacombs, holding up a light. He looked down the stairs and walked away, then called out to the others.

"Be careful," he said to Jordan.

She nodded. "I will be very careful. I'm not looking to break any bones or become a porcupine of splinters."

"I'm here, behind you. Ready for whatever," Patrick vowed.

She started down carefully, holding what remained of the banister and watching her footing. She felt a rush of what felt like air.

It was Alfie.

He passed her and looked back at her, grimacing. "I don't need to fear broken bones," he told her.

"It's okay. The remaining stairs are still solid. You just have to look out for the ones that are missing."

"*You* just have to look out for the ones that are missing," he said.

"Hey, guys!" Patrick said, speaking loudly. "We're all up here—Ragnar, Colleen, Mark, and our canine crowd. I'm going to follow you, Jordan."

Jordan reached the ground. Again she was reminded of a scene out of a bad horror movie. Shrouds covered bodies that were nothing but bones with bits of fabric and metals left behind—belt buckles, buttons, pieces of jewelry here and there, all encrusted with dirt and spiderwebs. The underground burials here were hundreds of years old, Jordan thought. Some shrouds were so rotted that eyeless sockets stared at her from skulls with only bits of linen remaining on them.

Ahead, she saw there was something covered in what looked to be contemporary plastic garbage bags.

She stared for a minute and then started when she felt Patrick behind her.

"Sorry," he muttered. "What—"

"There," she said simply.

Patrick strode forward with her. They looked at one another and worked carefully together to strip away a length of the gray plastic.

Enough to reveal a skull.

This time, with flesh still covering bone and remaining bits of the eyes staring at them.

Alfie swore softly.

Patrick looked at Jordan. "How did you know?"

She shook her head. "I don't know. Logic. We'd looked elsewhere. It's an old chapel, and many people have been buried in or beneath churches."

He nodded, serious as he studied her face. "Good call," he said. "I just wonder, Alfie, have you found any new friends here?" Patrick asked. "Anyone who could help us, tell us how many murdered people might be here?"

"No. No pun intended, but this graveyard is dead. Whatever souls might have been here, they are long gone now," Alfie said.

Patrick walked back to the stairs and shouted up. "Hey, we have a new body down here. We need Kat and a removal team. Stairs are broken up. Everyone must take extreme care."

He moved to the old "shelving" where the murdered victim lay, found an angle, and snapped a picture.

Alfie looked at Jordan.

"Susie isn't here."

"We'll find Susie," she said. "Alfie, I promise, we will find Susie."

"Tight quarters," Patrick said. "Let's see if we can get out of here, and get Kat and a team to remove him and get him to autopsy. We'll have forensics do a thorough search down here, though the way the dead were brought here, it seems apparent we've found the only recent addition. The killers never thought that law enforcement would search a graveyard for bodies. They figured it was a good way to get away with murder. And they might have pulled it off."

Jordan turned. Bry-bo was already trying to make his way back up the broken stairway. She reached down to guide him to unbroken steps and followed him up. By then, members from the medical examiner's office and the forensics team had arrived.

"There's a man down there. But the place isn't big, and none of the old interred are covered. I believe the man who hasn't been there a hundred years or so has been dead three to six months. The catacombs are in a stone basement and the temperature is a constant cool, so I'm not sure about the level of decomposition. Kat will get a better idea at autopsy," Patrick said. He looked at Jordan, made a face, reached out, and pulled at her hair with one hand.

"Hey!"

He opened the hand that had touched her and swept a spider from the top of her head.

"Oh. Thanks," she said, looking at him.

"Any on me?" he asked her.

"Nope. Just a few webs."

"The team will work this. Let's get back outside," he said.

"Sounds good."

Back in the daylight, it was still strangely gray, as if the earth itself had decided it was in mourning because of the evil that had been committed.

Colleen Law was there, talking to one of the forensics team members.

"One man?" she asked.

"That we could see, but we're not sure. Most of the inter-ment slots have bodies that are down to bone with disinte-grated shrouds, so it's easy to see there are no other bodies behind them," Jordan told her.

"But it is a man, right?" Colleen said.

Alfie hadn't come up with them; he was still in the cata-combs.

"It's definitely not Susie," Patrick assured her.

"Thank God," Colleen said, closing her eyes for a minute in relief. "Megan says she'll talk to you later. She's got more information on Susie, and it may help us, though we can't find records on her anywhere. You know Angela; if there was any slip of information out there, she would have found it. No credit cards, which is not a surprise. But they can't find any record of her from the past few years, period. She was born Susan Patricia Anthony in Tecumseh, Washington. She went to grade school and junior high there and disappeared during her junior year of high school. Anyway, Megan will fill you in. I'd suggest we all try dinner, but Mark, Ragnar, and I will finish up here first. I just spoke with Jackson, and he's got Marie Donnell back at headquarters. He wants you there." Colleen grimaced, turning to Jordan. "You two might want to grab some quick showers first. I don't know if you've seen yourselves."

"Do we have time?" Jordan asked her.

Colleen nodded. "Jackson doesn't mind leaving Marie alone in a room to stew. Go ahead and get going. We'll keep up the search here. Kat will see the bodies get to the morgue so she can examine them. Also, Jackson wants a task force meeting tomorrow morning. Including consultants," she said, grinning as she looked back at her brother. "I'd hug you, Patrick, I'm so glad you're here, except, seriously. You are…disgusting!"

"Thanks, sis," Patrick said. "Okay, we're leaving. Hopefully we don't ruin my car in the process. I thought it was just Jordan who was disgusting," he teased. "I guess it's us both."

"Trust me," she responded, "you're disgusting, too."

"Ouch!" he said.

She grinned. He was joking. And Jordan realized she was envious of what he had with Colleen and Megan—and through them, with Mark and Ragnar. They were a family. She'd had a family, of course. She still had her mom and aunt and cousins who lived far, far away.

But the triplets had something special. Maybe their very strangeness had made them even closer; they knew about each other. Knew they shared secrets that had to be kept—except now they were shared with the Krewe.

"Oh!" Patrick said. "Poor Bry-bo. Even he is disgusting. Anyway, I'll drop Jordan off at her place, brush Bry-bo, shower, and we'll get to headquarters. We'll see you later, Colleen."

Colleen nodded.

Patrick took Jordan's arm. It was just in an "escorting" way. He was distracted.

It didn't mean anything. And she decided not to wrench away and inform him she could walk on her own and knew where they were going.

She looked up as they waved to others they passed and headed for the car.

"Yeah," Patrick said.

"Pardon?"

"Such a strange day," he said. "It's as if the sky is in mourning."

Jordan shook her head. "I wish we knew more about John Smith and who he really is. We know he recruited at least one of the guards holding loved ones hostage. And we believed he was Rory Ayers, working from behind bars. But now Rory Ayers is in a coma. He may die. And if he dies, we'll never know the whole truth."

"We will find the truth. We've severed his hold on I don't know how many people. Money lures them at first, but then they can't get out." He hesitated. "I had a case like this in Philadelphia once. People were forced to plant bombs. Mothers and kids, husbands and wives. They were kidnapped and separated. They knew that if they didn't obey every instruction given to them, their son, wife, father, mother, sister, or whoever would be murdered. John Smith managed to take it to a whole new level. And he has been doing it for years, it seems."

"Marie Donnell knows," Jordan said.

"We'll find out just what she knows soon enough," Patrick said.

Jordan smiled at him. And she realized they were truly both disgusting, covered with bits of green from the algae and moss that grew over tombstones, dust and dirt from the graveyard, and spiderwebs from the catacombs.

She hesitated before getting in the car.

He laughed. "You can drive tomorrow—we'll get this guy cleaned!"

Smiling, Jordan slid into the car.

"Do we really have time for the luxury of showers? I mean, you have to drop me off, go home, pick me back up—"

"Or I can go in with you, brush Brian Boru while you shower. Then we can both head to the hotel, where I'll be quick, and go to headquarters."

"That will work," Jordan said.

Then she wondered if it would. She was going to be in her shower. He was going to be in her home. She'd be naked with him just outside…

She felt a rush of blood sweep to her cheeks, and she was oddly grateful for her patina of spiderwebs.

She was being ridiculous. This was a professional relationship. And yet she was liking him more and more. And finding him more and more attractive.

Even in spiderwebs.

She couldn't believe she was even thinking along such lines when they were so intensely involved with such a complex case.

Bry-bo barked from the back seat, as if giving his approval of the plan.

They reached Jordan's apartment, and Patrick found parking on the street about a half a block away. As they started toward her apartment in the row-house complex, she saw one of her neighbors was headed out with his tablet to sit on the porch.

"Hurry!" she told Patrick.

"Okay, why?"

"I don't want to explain how we look!"

He nodded.

Jordan hurried up the two steps to her own little porch and quickly opened the door. Bry-bo and Patrick came in after her so quickly they almost collided. That made them laugh; and with Bry-bo excited and swirling his massive body around, Jordan found herself falling forward and catching herself with her hands on Patrick's chest.

"Oh, sorry, sorry, okay, make yourself at home. I'm going to be fast. Oh! I don't have a dog brush, but—"

"I have one," he said, producing a brush from his jeans pocket. "I keep it in the car."

"Brush him in the kitchen. It's the easiest to clean up," she said.

"Will do."

Jordan quickly gathered fresh clothing from her bedroom and headed into the master bath. She caught sight of herself in the mirror above the sink and paused, smiling and grimacing.

She was disgusting. Her face was grimed, her clothing might need to be fumigated, and her hair was still covered with silver sheens of spiderwebs. She set her Glock and holster on the counter and stripped off her clothing as quickly as possible. With the water turned on hot, she stepped in and felt it wash over her, and the feeling was good. She hadn't known how good.

And she still found herself thinking about how Patrick was there. She was wet and naked, and Patrick was there.

Impatiently she scrubbed her hair and body, rinsed, stepped out, dried, and put on clean clothing as quickly as possible. Lastly, she slid her holster and Glock through her belt again and covered it with the fall of a clean jacket.

Hurrying out, she found Patrick in the kitchen. He'd brushed the dog and swept the floor.

"Well, now I am the only disgusting one," he said. "By the way, I really like your place. These little row houses are great. The size is just right. Your furniture is great, and I want a TV as big as yours!"

"Glad you like it. By the way, I have water, lemonade, and tea, all in travel bottles. We could grab a few before we go."

"Good idea. I'll have some tea, thanks."

She dug into her refrigerator and grabbed a tea for each of them.

"So, no pets, huh?" he asked.

"No, I told you. I'm never home."

"You might have had fish or a bearded dragon."

She smiled. "No pets. There are birds that fly around in the little backyard, but they take care of themselves. Nothing against pets—Bry-bo is the best."

He smiled and headed for the front. She followed him quickly and they were soon back in the car. "Hmm," he mused.

"Hmm?"

"Well, you wanted to hurry to get into your house. Not so easy at a hotel. How bad do I look?" he asked her.

She shrugged. "Bry-bo and I are respectable."

It wasn't long before they arrived at his hotel. When he parked, she reached over, trying to dab the worst of the spiderwebs and dirt from his face.

"Thanks," he muttered. "Should have thought to have at least done that at your place!"

"You're okay. We'll just move quickly," she said.

They did. But at the elevator, there was a woman with two children who were about ten or twelve, and she smiled first at Jordan, saw the kids were excited about the dog, but then looked at Patrick with a confused and wary expression.

"Just a day at work," he said casually. "And the dog's friendly, by the way."

"Uh, okay," the woman said.

When the first elevator came, Patrick stepped back. "You go on, please. We'll catch the next."

The woman and kids went past him.

Jordan laughed as the elevator disappeared and Patrick hit the button again.

"I'll bet they usually gush at you!" she said.

"What?"

"Women. Does it hurt to be icky?" she teased.

He smiled, lowered his head, and shook it. "Nope. Wait, yes. It feels...ugh. But I'm going to rectify that now."

The elevator arrived and they headed up. Patrick collected some clothing and disappeared into the bathroom without further conversation.

Jordan sat with Bry-bo and waited. And she found herself thinking that she was out here now. And he was in there. Naked and wet.

Marie Donnell! They were going to talk to her. They were going to try to find the truth.

Patrick emerged, dressed and ready, drying his hair. She hadn't been able to take the time to dry hers; she had just pulled it into a wet queue at the back of her neck.

"Ready," he said.

"Maybe we'll get to see that lady again and she won't be so horrified," Jordan teased.

He shrugged. "And maybe she's wondering what incredible talent or magnetism I must have to draw a gorgeous—clean—creature like you up to a hotel room with me," he said.

She laughed. "Is that what she's wondering?"

"Hey, what else?"

They headed back out. Jordan hadn't really thought they'd see the woman again, but she was at the lobby check-in counter, paying for drinks from the little concierge area. The kids saw Bry-bo and rushed over, and the woman started to say something but went silent when she saw Patrick and Jordan.

"It's okay, really. He's a good dog," Patrick said.

"Um, thank you!"

"Service dog," Jordan told her.

"Oh, I, uh… You look like…cops?" she asked.

"Agent," Jordan muttered.

"Psychiatrist," Patrick told her, smiling. "She really needed help!" he joked, indicating Jordan.

Jordan groaned. "He is a psychiatrist—just not mine," Jordan said.

The woman smiled.

"Well, you're a beautiful couple, and thank you for letting the kids play with the dog," she said.

"We've got to get to work," Jordan said.

"Of course. Kids, the puppy has to go to work!" the woman said.

They were able to go to the car at last.

"Actually," Jordan noted, "the car isn't so bad."

"No, the dirt and grime stuck to us," Patrick said. "Well, the back seat always has dog hair. But as most dog people know, dog hair is an accessory."

In the car, she grew serious. "Jackson seems unwavering in his belief that Marie Donnell knows the truth about Rory Ayers."

"I think she does, too. And I think she was terrified he would find a way to hurt her if she said anything to us. But she's not the suicidal type. I don't believe John Smith was ever holding someone she loved. In all honesty, she strikes me as a sociopath, if not a psychopath. She loves herself and is unlikely to die by suicide. But that doesn't mean she wasn't terrified, which is why she wanted out, so she could hide. Plus, she's got the kind of ego that would allow her to believe she could pull it off. But there are people being held who are guilty, who did commit murder, and think little of having done the deed. In the general population, she believes John Smith would find a way to have her killed."

"He would," Jordan said.

They arrived at headquarters. Angela greeted them as they entered, shaking her head.

"What? What's happened?" Patrick asked.

"Jackson is in with Marie now. She's decided she isn't going to say anything to anyone. She has a lawyer. She's been in solitude, but says she doesn't care if we put her in general population. We can just spin our wheels."

"Where are they?" Patrick asked.

"First conference room," Angela said. "I'll be watching. Leave Bry-bo with me. Jordan, you might as well join Patrick. You're the one who caught up to her. The two of you together might manage to say something that gets her going."

"Right," Patrick said, following Jordan as she quickly walked to the conference room.

Marie—dressed in a correctional facility jumpsuit—was seated at the table, grinning.

Jackson was across from her.

"Ah, look, it's Barbie and Ken!" Marie said.

"I thought you weren't talking," Jordan said. "That sounds like talking."

"I have nothing to say to you people. And you have nothing to threaten me with."

Jackson stood up. "Welcome," he said. "Marie agreed to come in to tell me she doesn't have anything to say, and she doesn't care what we do."

"I will be out soon, and no, I don't care what you do. I enjoy the company of other women. General population will be fine. In fact, I enjoy the company of women much more than that of men. Sorry, boys, but men are idiots."

"Just good for money, eh?" Patrick said. "I mean, you were a madam, right? Making money off men? So yes, I can see where that would make you think they were stupid. And women, sure, you enjoy them—making them do things for money, right?"

Marie waved a hand in the air. "People choose what they do, right?"

"Not when you're holding them prisoner, and you're about to sell them to the highest bidder," Patrick said.

"I wasn't selling anyone. I was forced. And my lawyer will get me out," Marie said.

Patrick held a chair for Jordan, nodding, and took a chair himself. "So, the lawyer will get you out, and it's general population until then. You're not afraid anymore."

"You don't scare me, pretty boy," Marie said.

Patrick smiled. He looked at Jackson, and then at Jordan.

"She's really not scared, and she really won't talk. That's because she thinks she's in the clear. She knows Rory Ayers is in a coma. So, Marie, that's it, right? There's nothing to be afraid of anymore because Rory Ayers is in a coma?" He leaned close to the woman. "But then again, how did he get to be in that coma? Who got to him and tried to hang him? Would that same person be after you?" he demanded.

Marie sat back away from him.

"I'm not afraid," she repeated. "And it has nothing to do with Rory Ayers."

"And yet everything changed once the man was in a coma," Jordan said.

Patrick stood and shrugged and looked at Jackson. "She's lying. So put her in general population. I guess she thinks Rory Ayers attempted suicide. She thinks she has nothing to worry about. I guess Rory Ayers is the man we've been seeking as John Smith." He turned to Marie and smiled. "So, Marie, bring on your attorneys. You are welcome to be in the general population, and I know you're thinking your expensive lawyers will see that you're released until your trial date. But I wouldn't be so certain of that. Then again, you're welcome to think whatever you want. Enjoy!"

He stood and walked out of the room. Jordan and Jackson followed him.

"You don't have anything on me!" Marie shouted.

Patrick stuck his head back in the room. "Oh, you are wrong, Marie. So very, very wrong."

As she shouted and flew out of her chair, Patrick pulled the door closed. Jackson reached over and securely locked it.

Marie's screaming rant was muffled, along with the sounds of her pounding against the heavy wooden door.

CHAPTER EIGHT

Out of the room and out of earshot, Patrick looked at Jackson and grimaced. "Was that a good threat?" he asked. "Mine—not hers."

Jackson nodded with a grim smile.

"She is as guilty as John Smith," Jackson said.

"At least some of the women we rescued will be able to testify that she wasn't one of them," Jordan said. "She only saw to their health and welfare so they might bring in the highest bids."

"And she has a record," Patrick said. "She won't be out. Still, I've seen defense attorneys do amazing things in courtrooms."

"She won't get out before her trial," Jackson said with certainty. "A repeat offender? She'll have to go to trial. There won't be any deals to get her out of that. But our problem is proving whether Ayers is John Smith. If he dies, does the whole operation die? There's something more. Rory Ayers has been in a correctional facility. Despite everything, no one knows how someone managed to get to his cell. The guards there have all been questioned over and over. We've had different agencies searching for any red flags in their backgrounds. I don't believe any of the guards were involved with what happened with Rory Ayers. We learned the hard way to make sure every guard is thoroughly vetted. But no one knows how he got the belt he used to hang himself or whether he was even suicidal."

"Ayers is not suicidal," Patrick assured him. "Someone got to him somehow. Or there's something more going on."

"He is in a coma," Jordan reminded him.

"He is," Patrick agreed. "I think he worked closely with Marie—really closely. Prisoners do have rights; he has made friends, I'm sure. Or purchased friends or threatened friends. There's got to be a money trail somewhere; that's how it starts out. They find people who are desperate for money. And those who are desperate usually have loved ones they would die for. John Smith has been using that to his advantage."

"Angela has been searching for a money trail, but with offshore accounts, it takes a lot of time and finesse. So many people—captors and captives—are involved in this; but usually, we get the same story. With the captors, they were lured to a life of crime out of necessity, starting with misdemeanors, but then they get roped into felony crimes. And if they refuse, a loved one is taken—loved ones, children... Threaten someone's child and you can control them," Jackson said.

"But still nothing solid on John Smith?" Jordan asked.

"The best lead we have to suggest Rory Ayers might be John Smith stems from Marie Donnell's newfound confidence," Jackson said. "What I can't figure out is the money and how Ayers might've been juggling it all from inside a cell."

"Maybe we should speak to his ex-wife?" Patrick said. "She might have some insight into what he was up to. And I'm willing to bet she'd be happy to oblige us in any way. The man tried to kill her daughter, after all."

"Maybe. But there's someone else you might want to talk to," Jackson said. He handed Patrick a piece of paper with a name on it. "Janice Sloan. You saved her life, Patrick." Jackson nodded toward Jordan and said, "You were both involved in saving her. She was the woman Patrick found shot in the warehouse. Jordan, from the reports that day, I see that you got a shot off before her would-be killer could finish the deed. Anyway, she went through surgery and is on the mend now. She asked to see the two of you."

"I'm glad she's healing," Jordan said. She looked at Patrick. "You saved her life."

"Maybe, but thank God you were there, too, since the guy had another gun," Patrick said.

"That's why we're a team," Jackson said.

Jordan grinned. "No person is an island."

"Shall we head to the hospital?" Patrick asked.

"Let's do it," Jordan said. "If we can do anything…"

"It's all right for now," Jackson told them. "Just remember you can't go without sleep. See her, then knock off for the day. We have people working paper trails and minor leads twenty-four-seven. Get some rest."

"Will do," Patrick promised him. "We'll just grab Brybo from Angela's office and head out. People usually like me better when I have the dog anyway."

"People do love dogs," Jackson said.

He joined them down the hall toward Angela's office. She was at the door with the dog when they reached it.

"I just heard from Mark. They've found another body at

the graveyard. Someone who was killed no more than a few months ago, according to Kat. They must have thought they found a great dumping ground. And they were right—until now. Why not stash a body with more bodies?" Angela said. She shook her head. "Bastards. They have been getting away with murder."

"But we'll stop it," Jackson said.

"Alfie is still with them?" Patrick asked.

"The body was—" Jordan said almost simultaneously.

"Not Susie. Another male," Angela said. "That group will spend the day there tomorrow. You two see if you can get something definitive on Rory Ayers."

"Financials," Patrick said.

Angela looked at him and nodded. "Trust me, we're seeking any connection we can find. But when offshore accounts are being used and money is laundered, it's tricky. But I will not stop searching, I promise."

"We're out of here," Patrick said, and talking to Bry-bo, he added, "Let's go, boy."

"Keep in touch," Jackson said.

Jordan and Patrick left for the hospital.

She was silent and he glanced over at her. "What's wrong?"

She turned to him, smiling. "You can't read my mind?"

"At the moment, no. But let me guess. You don't believe this woman will be able to tell us much about John Smith or if he also goes by Rory Ayers."

"Good guess. Are you sure you're not reading my mind?"

"Doesn't work like that," he reminded her. "Sometimes, yes. But I usually get real thoughts through body language; or if it's just a voice, through the inflection or the words."

"It's good we're visiting regardless. You did save her life."

"Thanks. But I couldn't have kept pressure on her wound

and saved myself if you hadn't—if you hadn't had my back when the guy had another weapon."

"Teamwork," she said. "We're not so bad at it."

"And that surprises you?"

"Well, you did think I was an idiot."

"I was… Okay. I didn't want you or anyone else dead. And backup should have been in place once you were at that hotel."

"Who kidnaps someone in the middle of a swim?"

"These guys."

"Okay, true. But—" she shook her head, turning toward him as he drove "—why haven't we found Susie? We know they had her. Patrick, I'm afraid she is dead, and we'll never find her, and Alfie will never be at peace."

"I don't believe Susie is dead. From what I understand, that girl went through hell. Attacked in her own home by one of her mother's boyfriends, a runaway, turning to drugs to endure the life she was living, with constant death threats. She's scared. Wherever she is, she's scared. And she doesn't trust what she sees, not yet."

"But if she just came to us—"

"Maybe she doesn't see a way to come to us," Patrick said. "Maybe she doesn't know we're looking for her."

"I hope you're right."

"So do I."

They reached the hospital and produced their credentials and Bry-bo's papers even though they had been through the drill before.

Arriving at the floor where Janice Sloan was recuperating, they were glad to be stopped by a police officer at her door.

The FBI and the local agencies were working tightly to see no harm befell those who had been rescued or even those who had been guarding them. Even a hardened criminal could prove to be an asset.

In the room, they saw Janice Sloan was awake and aware. Her coloring remained pale, but she had a smile for them as they entered the room. "Dr. Law and Agent Wallace?" she asked. "Angela said you might come by. I've been so anxious to thank you. Not just for saving my life, but for giving me a life, even if it's in a witness protection program. They're helping me get a job!" She smiled at Bry-bo. "That's a beautiful dog."

Bry-bo whined softly and looked at Patrick. Patrick nodded and the dog padded over to the woman's bedside.

"He's gorgeous. And there's something…"

Her voice trailed. Bry-bo was so big, she could easily pat him even from her bed.

"Something about dogs?" Patrick offered. "Bry-bo is a good boy. Happy for the attention."

"And please, we are the ones who are grateful," Jordan added, walking to the side of the bed and taking her hand. "We're grateful you're out of there, and incredibly grateful you're alive."

"You're a fighter. You helped save your own life," Patrick said.

Janice sighed softly. "I was about to be sent off as part of a harem!"

"That's why you were by yourself in that room?" Patrick asked.

She nodded. "A lot of it happened online. Sales all over the world. If I could have escaped, I would have. I didn't have family or friends who were being threatened. I just got kidnapped soon after I moved to DC. My folks passed away within a few months of one another, and I'm an only child and… I was in Chicago, but I needed to move somewhere, you know? I like people. I mean, I had friends, but…they all knew I had moved to DC. I don't think anyone ever reported me as a missing person unless the company I was supposed to start working for did. But oh, my God! I was so scared and then that monster walked in and aimed his gun at me. I would be dead if not for you, Dr. Law."

"Patrick," he said, and shrugged.

"Jordan," Jordan told her.

Janice had a beautiful smile. She had shiny black hair and stunning almond eyes, but it was her smile that made her exceptional.

"I am so grateful," she muttered.

"How did they get you?" Patrick asked her.

"I've gone through it all with the police—"

"I know. There are hundreds of pages of reports, but if you don't mind—" Jordan began.

"I'd do anything for you," Janice said. "I'm sorry. I just thought… I was still at a hotel, rent paid in advance. I had just gone out to eat, and it was getting dark as I was walking back to the hotel. Suddenly, there was a bag over my head, and then I was in the trunk of a car. It was…so fast. And I tried screaming, and one of them slapped me. Then I was dragged into a cell, and there were other girls in cells and…" She paused, wincing. "Then they came back and ripped my clothes off and dragged me into a shower. I was told to scrub, or they'd do the scrubbing for me."

"These were all men?" Patrick asked.

She nodded. "I didn't see the woman until the next day. She came in and…she was worse than they were. She grabbed my face. She checked out my teeth! She made me stand, walk, and take off the thin shift they made me wear to check for…

blemishes, anything wrong with me. She was pleased, and she warned me if I didn't walk and turn and do what I was told, they'd rip one of the other girls to shreds in front of me. They made videos of us. For the online auctions. The day before you came in, they all seemed pleased with me. I was separated from the others and put in that room. I'd been sold. I'd made them some good money. They gave me something decent for dinner."

"Everyone there was…vicious?" Jordan asked, glancing at Patrick.

How many of the captors had been forced into what they were doing, threatened into it? And how many had relished their roles of torturing captives?

"No, no, not everyone was cruel. Some of them seemed to be in pain when they ordered us to do things. When I spoke with Angela, she said she'd bring a book of pictures, so I could tell her more about each person. I think she's going to bring it in tomorrow. I'm going to be happy to point out the people who were decent and those who were cruel." She gave them another grim smile. "I trust Angela. She's going to make sure I'm all right."

"She is the best," Patrick said. "I've got a question for you, though. We're asking everyone. While you were there, did you happen to meet a girl named Susie?"

She frowned. "Susie? The day you found me, I heard Dragon Lady—that's what we called her—talking to one of our guards. They were talking about a Susie. She was a troublemaker, they had been told. They were to find her, get her, and bring her out to the old Victorian house and deal with her there. I wasn't sure what that meant, but…whoever Susie is, she wasn't going to be sold. I don't know what she did, but someone seriously wanted her…punished."

Though it seemed on the tip of her tongue, Janice couldn't seem to bring herself to say the word *killed*. She was enjoying petting the dog at her side, but when she almost said the word, her hand paused on his head.

Patrick and Jordan glanced at one another. They'd seen what had happened at the Victorian mansion, except it really happened in the graveyard.

But they had searched with Ragnar, Mark, Colleen, and others, including whole forensics teams, and they had only found three bodies.

None had been Susie.

They'd be searching again tomorrow.

"How long before the raid did you hear this discussion?" Patrick asked.

"It was early that morning. Dragon Lady came to trim my hair. It took all my strength to not wrestle the scissors from her. I hated her so much. But I was terrified. I wonder if Susie stood up to them. Maybe she did steal some scissors or maybe she just slipped out a door... I don't know why she was so important to them. I don't think that they thought she'd bring in an amazing bid or anything. When they talked about her, it was more..."

"As if she was hated?" Jordan asked flatly.

Janice nodded. "She did something to someone somewhere along the line," she said softly.

"Thank you," Patrick said.

"No—thank *you*. I'm alive," Janice said. "They told me how brave you both were."

"Part of the job. But it's rewarding when everything turns out okay," Jordan said. "Anyway, we'll let you rest."

Janice smiled and nodded. "Everyone has been so nice.

They've already got me set up with the Marshals office. I've promised Angela all the help I can give her tomorrow."

"That's fantastic. Thank you," Patrick said. He nodded at Jordan, who smiled back at him.

"If you come back, please bring this gorgeous creature," Janice said, referring to the dog.

"He's on the job, too, not to worry," Patrick told her.

As they left the room, Patrick felt his phone buzzing. Apparently, Jordan's was doing the same thing. They looked at each other, and then at their phones.

"Same message?" he asked.

"I believe. 'Come back to headquarters. Judy Greeley is here, and she might have some interesting information.'"

"So much for calling it a day," Patrick said. "Let's go. We didn't really get much of a chance to speak with her before. And the deeper we go, the more we may discover."

"But also food," Jordan said quietly.

"Pardon?"

"Yes, we'll talk to Judy. But after that, food!"

"Food will be good," he agreed.

At headquarters again, they found Angela was hard at work on a money trail. She looked up at them as they entered her office, shaking her head.

"Seems like Rory Ayers did not have much when he married into money. And through records, it appears everything he had was tied together with his wife. After his arrest when she sued for divorce, he lost most of that. There has to be money somewhere," she said.

"If he was dealing in cash, he found a way to get the money out of the country," Patrick said.

"That's what I'm figuring, but I'm still looking for a way to find it. One of us is going to have to take a trip out to see his

ex-wife and the young woman he raised as his own, Deirdre."
Angela grimaced. "Judy Greeley is waiting; she specifically
asked to speak with you. Trust is hard for her to come by."

"That's fine," Patrick assured her. "We're glad to see her."

"First conference room again. I'll have the camera running," Angela said. "Bry-bo can stay with me."

They went to the conference room where Judy Greeley
was seated, staring at the paper cup of coffee in front of her,
running her fingers over the rim. She looked up when they
entered, started to stand, and sat back down when they both
persuaded her it was fine to do so.

"I—I hope I'm not bothering you. I realize you're probably very busy, but…"

"It's no problem," Jordan said.

"I just don't know what I'm saying, really. I may be way off,
but…well, it's hard for any of us to trust anyone these days.
It was hard for us to even trust each other because anything
said or done could hurt someone else, but…"

Patrick and Jordan had taken seats across from her. Jordan reached over the table, taking her hand. "You've been
through a terrible ordeal. Having a gun pressed against your
head is terrifying. We understand. Do you know why they
chose you?"

"Special Agent Crow asked me that," she muttered. She
shook her head. "I don't know why they suddenly dragged
me out. Except that—" she paused, looking at them "—I had
been friends with Susie."

Patrick knew that Jordan was containing her reaction just
as he was.

"There wasn't a Susie with you at the house," he said quietly.

Judy shook her head. "We'd been together first at the mansion. Sometimes, they moved us around. We were there together for a bit. Connie was with Susie first, and she told me to be careful, very careful, because Susie was in trouble. She told me to stay away from her. But I admired her. She stood up to people even when they slapped her around. When we were moved, Susie wasn't moved with us. Connie told me never to mention her, even when we were alone. The walls had ears, she told me. And we didn't talk about Susie, and I don't know what happened to her." She paused again. "I would never make anything harder on anyone else, but... I think Connie knows more. And I think one of Connie's kids is really Susie's child."

Patrick was so stunned he didn't speak for a moment. Neither did Jordan.

"What makes you think that?" he asked at last.

"I always thought Connie cared about Susie, even though she was insistent we didn't talk about her. But I know Connie's husband, Beau Granger, had fallen in with drug dealers, and Connie and her kids were swept up because of him. Beau was at the warehouse; he was killed," she said quietly. "But Beau had almost been in trouble before. Someone had intervened, done something that straightened out the situation. I think it was Susie. And because of it, Connie was pretending all the children were hers, but I don't think they were.

"Connie was grateful to her." She closed her eyes, wincing. "She'd just learned Beau had been killed when we were with the police and social workers. And she didn't say anything, so I didn't say anything. But Connie is so fragile now. I'm afraid for all the children. I don't know if what I'm saying is true, but if it is, I felt I had to say it. Susie might have family out there, if she's not still out there herself. And I'm afraid it's highly likely Susie isn't among us anymore. I heard people talking one time. Susie was kept a prisoner because that was worse than death. It was a longer form of torture, but eventually, they would tire of the torture. If she did have family, her family might find happiness with her child—if it is her child. I think that Connie will be honest with you. Whatever happens with her now, she'll be raising her own kids alone. I'm sure no matter how grateful she might have been to Susie, she will need help now. And one less child is one less child, especially when that child belongs to someone else."

"What's the baby's name and how old?" Jordan asked softly.

"Benjamin. He's almost two. Our keepers were just our keepers. When people were moved around, we were warned to behave and follow orders. Escape attempts could mean immediate termination. And while they wouldn't want to do it, they would terminate a group. That meant children, too, I'm pretty sure. Thankfully, I didn't have a group. Maybe that's why I was a good choice when they wanted a bullet in someone's head. At least they wouldn't have to kill kids."

"Thank you," Patrick said. "That's all very helpful."

"I don't know if Connie will just volunteer any information," Judy said. "I don't think any of us will ever be right again. I wonder if, even with help from all these different agencies, we'll ever be able to live without fear again."

"Time doesn't heal all wounds," Patrick said. "But it does ease them. And hopefully, we are getting to the root of all the bad that has happened."

"Yeah. Hopefully. I found there was never anyone you could trust," Judy said. "And that's why I believe Connie hasn't said anything yet. She's afraid she'll speak and one of the agents or social workers will turn into a goon."

"It's going to be hard," Jordan said. "But we understand."

"Well, I just keep telling myself it's a miracle that I'm alive."

She paused, wincing. "I was taken because of my brother, Austin Greeley. Pot smoker," she said dryly. "Selling a little weed seemed like a fine idea—heck, it's legal in many places now. I had no idea what was going on when they took me. None. At least Austin is alive. He's still in a coma, but he's alive. And I just keep hoping and praying that when we're all relocated, maybe we'll get to be together and start over. Thankfully, our folks are gone."

"I'm sure the doctors will do everything possible for your brother," Jordan said. She was rising. "Thank you, Judy. I know you're afraid; everyone is afraid. But don't give them that hold over you. You are alive, and you are free, and you will have the help you need. So get even. Live. Live well."

Judy smiled at her. "You're right," she said softly.

Patrick rose and joined Jordan standing by the door. "We're going to get on this," he promised her.

They left Judy and went back to Angela's office to get Bry-bo.

Angela had heard everything. "So, Susie possibly had a child. And it sounds like she was at the mansion."

"I think she escaped," Jordan quickly added.

"But if she escaped, where is she?" Angela asked quietly.

"She's either hidden somewhere or she's too afraid to trust anyone. I refuse to believe she's dead."

"Well, I did find something," Angela said.

"What?" Jordan asked anxiously.

"Marie Donnell. I found a Swiss bank account in her name. But the details are fuzzy. The deposits were cash."

"Can the bank provide us with anything?"

"Do you know much about privacy and Swiss accounts?" Angela asked him dryly.

"Not really—never had one," Patrick told her. "But if she

has been dealing with large amounts of money, then it's all the more likely she knows the real identity of John Smith."

"And since she's so certain she'll walk now, and she's all lawyered up and could care less where she's incarcerated, that would suggest that the puppeteer really is Rory Ayers," Jordan said.

"She was in it eye-high with him," Patrick said.

"We need to talk to Connie," Jordan said. "Alfie has been staying out at the mansion. If Susie was there—dead or alive—in that graveyard, Alfie would have found her," she said softly.

Jackson appeared in the doorway to Angela's office.

"Go home," he said.

"But, Jackson, we've just learned—" Jordan began.

"That Susie might have had a child. Even so, that child is fine. I spoke with people I trust with social services and the Marshals office. The children are fine. The parents—or caretakers—are fine. I'll see to it Connie is here tomorrow morning. You can talk to her then."

"But—" Jordan began again.

"Whether we see her now or tomorrow, and find out the child is Susie's, we still won't be any closer to Susie," Patrick said.

"I need you rested and sane," Jackson told her. "Go home. That's an order. The team at the graveyard have been out there all day. I've just ordered them to head home, too. Listen, I know it's frustrating. But this has been going on for years. We keep cutting heads off a hydra. This time, we're going to reach the heart of the beast—and make life safe again for dozens of people. But you need to be well rested to be useful, and you can't ever forget—"

"That the Krewe is a unit, a team, and we all need each other, cover for each other..." Jordan recited.

"And watch one another's backs," Patrick finished. "Okay. Jordan, Bry-bo, let's go."

She nodded, looking from Jackson to Angela.

"Task force here at eight a.m. sharp," Jackson said.

"We'll be here," Patrick promised.

He absently set a hand on Jordan's back to lead her out. She didn't seem to notice; she was deep in thought.

When they were in the car, Patrick said softly, "Susie is alive."

Jordan was silent, shaking her head.

"You're thinking if she were alive, she would move heaven and earth to be with her child. That isn't Susie. She would take herself out of a child's life if she thought she might bring harm to that child. Susie is out there. But people are still afraid."

"We are so convinced the man behind everything is Ayers—and yet, if that was true, why is everyone still so scared?"

"First, fear is an emotion that is hard to let go. And second, we don't know if we're at the end of it or not. We need to find out more from the ex-wife and the daughter who wasn't his biological child. There's money out there."

"But even if he figured out how to get that money moving while he was in prison, if he's in a coma, he can't be conducting any business now," Jordan said.

"That's true."

"So, everyone is afraid of someone under him?"

"That, or he was the second man, or...we're off entirely."

Jordan glanced at him. "Are you mind reading?" she asked him. "Is that how you knew I was thinking Susie must be dead if she hasn't come for her child?"

He shrugged and grinned at her. "Maybe. Or maybe I'm getting to know you. So, what do you want for dinner?"

"You don't know?" she asked him, a half smile on her lips as she leaned back against the seat and closed her eyes.

"I'm trying to be polite. And you want delivery because you're exhausted."

Her eyes flew open, and she stared at him. "You are—"

"Again, I'm getting to know you," he cut her off quietly. He gazed her way, grinning. "Of course, you're also thinking that you want me to stay. I'm incredible, and you'd really love the company," he teased. "Sexy as all hell, right?"

She started to laugh. "Incredible ego!" she accused him.

But she turned toward him, and she hadn't stopped grinning. And he suddenly wished they hadn't worked so hard together, and he hadn't come to know her mind and the beauty of her passion and care for others.

He was falling in…

Desire, of course. She was stunning, agile, and her eyes could play a million tricks on a man's soul.

He looked at the road again.

"Dinner. Delivered. And yes," she said very quietly, "I want you to stay. I don't feel like eating alone and there might be something…"

"Between us?"

She laughed, but that glittering light was still in her eyes.

"I may think of something that has to do with the case and you'll be right there, so we can talk it through."

"But of course!" he said. "All-American. Burgers and fries from somewhere?"

"That will do."

Bry-bo let out a woof as if he approved.

They were all silent again as Patrick drove the rest of the way to Jordan's place. It was a fine silence. A comfortable si-

lence. And Patrick felt something he didn't remember feeling in years.

He felt good. Glad to be in the company of a woman who
knew about him, his family, his "strangeness," and he didn't
need to hide any of it.

Jordan opened the door. The dog rushed in. She turned
as Patrick closed the door and wound up flush against him,
in his arms as he went to steady her. And to his surprise, she
spoke very softly, a silky tone to her voice, and the kind of
sensual smile a man ten times stronger couldn't resist.

"Burgers can wait," she told him.

CHAPTER NINE

She had to be insane.

It didn't matter. She didn't know if their work had just been so intense something needed to break up the racetrack in her mind, or if the impossible had happened. She had accepted the fact she was sexually attracted to Patrick Law; he was a far more decent human being than she had imagined at first. She had found him steadfast, rather incredible, and built, with eyes that were mesmerizing…

What the hell. She was all grown up. Capable of making whatever mistakes she chose.

Because it had to be a mistake…

But the smile he gave her when she said their burgers could wait was enough to send fire sweeping through her. He pulled her closer, body to body, lifting her chin. His mouth covered hers, and the kiss they shared was searing and deep, liquid and wonderful. When he broke away, his eyes were searching hers.

"You couldn't possibly be reading my mind. I can't read my own mind right now," she said.

"I'm reading your body. I'm reading my body, too. Maybe it's just what we both need—and both want," he said softly.

His hand curved over the contours of her face and his mouth lowered to hers once again. The kiss was a little slower, a little deeper. When it ended, Jordan leaned her head against his chest.

"Crazy," she muttered.

"But we are crazy," he told her.

She looked up at him. It wasn't an insult of any kind; it was just what they were.

Bry-bo barked.

"Hey! Burgers in a bit!" Patrick said, and he looked at Jordan and asked, "Mind a bit of a romantic?"

She shook her head. He swept her off her feet and headed toward her bedroom, telling the dog, "Watch the front door, boy."

In her room, he laid her down and stretched out beside her. She smiled and they rolled together, hands now reaching to touch and caress; but something hard slammed against Jordan, and she let out a muffled cry. They realized they were both armed, hadn't thought to divest themselves of anything, and laughed together as they set their guns and holsters on the bedside tables, kicked off their shoes, and started helping one another shed their clothing, touching, caressing, finding new places for wet kisses as they did so.

Crazy, crazy, crazy.

But so good.

She hadn't been with anyone in forever; things always fell apart for her, sometimes because she had been so focused on her studies at the academy, and sometimes, because she was so different, she had trouble connecting with others.

But none of that was on her mind now.

Because Patrick was an amazing lover, tender and yet passionate. His lips and tongue were like a delicious, lavalike fire. He moved against her in a way that seemed to awaken her entire being, and she longed for nothing more than to touch in return, to feel the tremor of his muscles, the strength of his body against hers, and feel him moving against her, lower, higher, kisses falling everywhere, intimate and so sensually arousing she might have soared out of her skin.

But it was too good to be in her skin. To let her mind go, and be nothing but a woman with a man who aroused her to amazing heights.

And when they were together at last, moving at a breakneck speed, needing more and more and more, she clung to and savored each second of the amazing physical sensation, and the release that at last seemed to shiver over her with glitters of light and darkness and pure magic. After, she just lay there, her mind returning as she stared up at the ceiling.

"Hey," he said softly. He was up on an elbow by her side. Their naked flesh still touched. He was smiling when he very tenderly touched her lips. "I am reading your mind right now. Or maybe not. Maybe I've come to know you, and you're worried that maybe we shouldn't have done this. Maybe it's not entirely professional, but I know it wasn't a mistake. Jordan, we work incredibly hard. And we're good at what we do. We can take a minute to enjoy each other's company."

She smiled. "Maybe. I just don't know what came over me earlier."

"My amazing physical appeal?" He winked.

She gave him a quick jab on the shoulder.

"You're kind of cute," she told him.

"Cute?" he protested.

"When you're not being judgmental."

"Hey, I've apologized! And I explained—"

"And you were right. But you were a jerk about it."

"Okay, I was right, but I was a jerk."

"Very cute!"

He winced. "That word again."

"It's a very complimentary word."

"If you're a puppy."

"What were you looking for?" she teased.

"Ruggedly handsome?" he asked hopefully.

"Don't push it." He might be ruggedly handsome, but she refused to give in to it. "Ego!"

"No, just hopeful," he said lightly.

To Jordan's extreme embarrassment, her stomach let out a rumble of protest. "Excuse me!"

Patrick laughed, pulling out his phone. "Time to put the order in. Anything special on your cheeseburger?"

"No cheese. I like cheese, just not on my burger. No pickle or onions. And lots of greasy fries, please. Don't forget Brybo."

"Never. I'd be in the doghouse," he assured her. "Drinks?"

"Tons of tea here."

He put through the order and rolled toward her. "Food is ordered. But you know, delivery time. And they just leave it at the door."

"Right. But—"

"I can be faster than a speeding bullet," he told her.

She started to laugh. "I don't think that's supposed to be a good thing."

"Hey. Only when a delivery person is coming."

She started to laugh, and she rolled into his arms, and they started to kiss again. She had never thought she could feel such a depth of longing from a kiss, or such a sensual hunger combined with such a strange sense of comfort and belonging.

She felt like she soared, like the world, her world, exploded. And she was happy to lie in his arms, feel air fill her lungs again, listen to the beat of her heart grow slower when they lay together after.

When they heard the doorbell indicating the food had arrived—and Bry-bo's barks of confirmation—she looked at him and started to laugh.

"What? Not exactly a speeding bullet?" he teased.

"Close!" she told him, throwing the covers aside to rise. She went to her closet for a robe as Patrick grabbed his jeans.

She started to leave the room to get the door. He caught her arm, and he was serious. "Holster in place, with my gun. In the middle of a case, and even not in the middle of a case, it's always best to be prepared. It's in the silent rules of what we've chosen to do with our lives."

"Gotcha. But—"

He grinned. "Keep the robe. I like it. Easy on, easy off!"

"Hey, now—"

"I can only imagine you with a full stomach and renewed energy," he said.

"Oh, you are ever hopeful," she laughed.

He went to the door for the food, and she moved into the kitchen. Bry-bo followed his master, eager for his burger. Jordan found a dish she decided would be the dog's. It was good to eat together, laugh at the way Bry-bo finished his food in a few gulps and then went on to look at them hopefully.

"He's been taught not to beg," Patrick said. "That doesn't mean he won't look at you with really soulful eyes."

"And since he's not begging, I'm going to give him this last bite I'm not going to eat," Jordan said, and she gave Bry-bo the last piece of her burger. They picked up the trash and Jordan looked at Patrick.

"We have a task force meeting at eight a.m.," Patrick stated.

"Right. Showered and ready."

"And I don't have any clothing here. So, I guess—"

"I guess you'll have to go to the hotel and get it," Jordan said.

He pulled her close to him, in his arms, looking down into her eyes. "Do you want me to come back?"

She couldn't resist a twisted smile. "You're not reading my mind?"

"I can't read your heart or soul," he told her.

"Thank God something is sacred!" she said, but she didn't look away. "Yes, I would like you to come back."

"Okay. I'll leave Bry-bo, then, if you're okay with him."

"Of course. I always like the dog."

"Ah, better than me."

She shrugged, grinning.

"Okay, I'll be back," Patrick said. "Lock up."

She smiled, locking the door when he left.

She was surprised to feel so light, as if the weight of the world had been lifted from her.

And yet, in truth, they still had little information. It would be interesting to speak with the women who had been held at the one house with Judy Greeley and Connie. If Connie had taken on the care of Susie's child, she might well know where Susie could be found.

Or if anything had happened to Susie.

Patrick had been gone about fifteen minutes when Bry-bo began to whine.

"Hey! He's coming back, boy," Jordan told the dog. "He didn't just desert you!"

But the dog's whining turned into a bark, and he raced to the door, barking harder. His tail wasn't wagging, and his bark became a growl. Jordan walked to the door and looked through the peephole. There was nothing there she could see, but the dog was anxious.

Jordan went back to her room and pulled on a pair of jeans and threw on a T-shirt, then grabbed her holster and Glock. She stood at the door and looked out again. The dog was going crazy.

Still, she saw nothing. Then, against the streetlights, she thought she saw a shadow.

Bry-bo suddenly raced through the house to the back door.

She followed the dog, wondering what could have gone from the front to the back of a row house. The walls were flush.

"Squirrel?" she asked.

But as she followed him, she heard something at the front again and turned, Glock ready.

The doorbell rang. She still approached the door cautiously and looked out.

Patrick was back.

"Hey, I—" he began, but broke off, frowning. She still had her Glock aimed at him.

"I'm that bad?" he asked her.

She lowered her weapon, shaking her head. "Bry-bo has me a little unnerved. He's gone crazy, barking at the front and then barking at the back!"

Patrick's frown remained in place.

"Bry-bo doesn't go crazy," he told her. He turned, latching the door and heading toward the back with determination.

Bry-bo was still at the back door, his growl deep in the back of his throat. Patrick switched off the lights, drew his own weapon, and opened the back door, ready for whatever he might encounter. Bry-bo streaked out, barking furiously, racing to the wall at the back of the property.

He barked for a minute as Patrick hurried over to him. The dog sat and wagged his tail.

Patrick turned back to Jordan, who had joined him—literally at his back.

"Someone was here."

He caught hold of the top of the wall and maneuvered himself over it. Bry-bo barked anxiously, and Jordan patted him on the head and said, "Stay, Bry-bo. Guard!"

She had never tried to hop the wall at the back of her place before. It wasn't easy, but she strained and hefted her own weight, finally getting her stomach over the top of it, and swung around.

Patrick had made it halfway down the alley.

He trotted back to her.

"Whoever it was, they're gone now. I tried the narrow break between the row houses, but whoever it was had already gotten through and hit the streets."

"Why would they be here?"

Hands on his hips, he cast his head at a skeptical angle. "Why?" He smiled. "You're underestimating yourself, and that's hard to believe."

"Hey! But—"

"Congratulations. Someone sees you as a real threat. We need to report this to Jackson."

"Maybe it was just a common thief."

"You know it wasn't."

"But I don't want off this case—"

"Not suggesting it. Want a hand?" He indicated the wall.

"Sure. But watch your hands, buddy," she said lightly.

He laughed and joined her over the wall. Bry-bo was waiting patiently for them.

"Bry-bo! Let's go back in. Good boy, good guard duty,"
Patrick praised the dog.

"He is a true guard dog," Jordan said.

"You haven't seen the half of it yet," Patrick told her, grinning and turning to the dog, who was following them back
into the house, tail wagging. "Stay on duty, boy. Front door,"
Patrick said.

The dog padded to the front door, turned around in a few
circles, and lay down.

Jordan walked over to the dog and hunkered down, patting
his head before giving him a hug. "You're the best, Bry-bo.
Best pup ever. Thank you."

He whined and gave her a sloppy kiss, and she grinned and
wiped her face. He was a big dog.

"My hero," she said.

"We're calling this in and letting the local cops know.
They'll probably do a drive-by now, keep an eye on the place,
look for cars that keep coming around, that kind of thing. We
should go to bed—early meeting, remember? We can sleep
with our Glocks handy. Plus, we have something even better
to warn us if anyone comes near here."

"Bry-bo?" Jordan asked.

He nodded.

"But you're calling to report this to Jackson?"

"Of course."

"No, you're not."

"Jordan—"

"I'll do it," she said.

She headed into the bedroom and found her shoulder bag
and phone. Patrick came in as she was talking to Jackson.

She suggested it might have been a common thief just testing the waters.

But, like Patrick, Jackson didn't buy the theory.

"Someone thinks you're close."

"If only!"

"Maybe we're closer than we know. You, specifically. You and Patrick. I'll see your place is watched. I can send an agent—"

"I have Patrick Law and Brian Boru," she said.

"All right, then. In the morning." Jackson ended the call.

"We need sleep," Patrick said.

"Right!"

They undressed and crawled beneath the sheets. Patrick pulled her to him. He lay easily next to her, his arm around her, holding her close. He closed his eyes.

She stared at the ceiling, trying not to move. If he could sleep, good.

But in a few minutes, his eyes opened. She looked at him.

"I can't sleep." She felt the heat of his body next to hers. Felt muscles tense, and the response her soft whisper had wakened in him.

It was good.

"Maybe we need to tire one another out," he suggested.

She smiled.

"Hey. Who knows? It just might help."

Later, tired out, she did sleep. It had been a late night. Still, when the alarm rang at seven, she was awake and alert. She wanted to get the day going.

Maybe they were close. Closer than they knew. Maybe she knew something she didn't realize she knew, or had access to someone who knew...

Connie.

Maybe. Connie had taken on the care of Susie's child. If

anyone knew anything, it might well be the woman who had
custody of Susie's greatest love in life.

The meeting was held in the Krewe's largest conference
room. Arriving, Patrick greeted Colleen, Mark, and Ragnar, as he expected them to be there. He was surprised to
see Megan was there, too. Of course, he'd known both his
sisters had become friends with the ghost of Alfie Parker,
and he'd been waiting to hear from Megan to see if she had
learned more than Angela had garnered about Alfie's last
stand or Susie.

Naturally, the dogs were there—all three of them. Red,
Hugo, and Bry-bo. They were happy to greet each other and
accept whatever attention and appreciation they might from
friends and strangers alike. But when the meeting began, they
sat at attention as if taking in every word.

There were a few representatives from local area police as
well as other FBI agents. The case, of course, was far-reaching, though Alfie Parker himself was not in attendance.

Jackson and Angela both spoke. Jackson brought the room
up on the case history. Both police and FBI had been involved
when a complex of houses had been raided; much of the information that had led them down the right path had come
from Sergeant Alfred Parker. He had gained his information
through a young woman he had arrested—and then helped
into a halfway house. At the time, they found a massive stash
of arms and documents that detailed crimes related to murder for hire, drug trafficking, and more.

Alfred Parker and two other officers had been killed. So
had the majority of the gunmen who had preferred death to
capture by law enforcement. Those they had in custody in-

formed them that John Smith had been at the head of the operation.

John Smith had not been found. Susie had disappeared; she had not been at the complex.

Angela stepped in to speak. She had researched Alfie's notes on Susie and the discoveries he had made through her, and she got everyone up to speed on the details. While the case involving John Smith and Susie had grown cold, they had come to theorize the man known as John Smith was still active and was recruiting a small army of gunmen to manage his criminal enterprises, including the recent Embracer murders and those involved. The name John Smith had come up in recent interviews and they had an image of a man calling himself by that name.

"We had suspected Rory Ayers, incarcerated for attempted murder in the Embracer case, to be this man," Jackson said. "It's possible he was, but at this time, he's in a coma. One of his lieutenants, Marie Donnell, has changed her tune about being protected, which indicates he might be the man we're looking for. We are seeking money trails, still searching for victims, and since we don't know if Rory Ayers is John Smith, we're on high alert. We have found large sums in offshore accounts, but since Rory Ayers has gone into a coma—presumed suicide attempt, though under suspicious circumstances—we know he's not manipulating the money…not anymore, at least. And here is where we need to be hypervigilant on getting the complete truth. If we don't get the real head on this hydra, the murders, drugs, and human trafficking will pick up again, and we'll be back where we started."

"What now has you convinced all of this is related? That wasn't so back when you first brought in suspects on the Embracer case?" one of the officers asked.

"Witness testimony as we've moved forward through the past months," Jackson said.

He hadn't blinked. Krewe members never mentioned a dead man had come to them for help.

"What's the suspected motive?" someone else asked. "I mean, I understand money as a driving factor, but this guy seemed to be recruiting others to kill—the whole Embracer thing. No one made any money on that. Assaulting victims and then burying them alive? That's just sick."

"Yes, I agree. Someone's fetish. That may have begun with a dead man, Ralph Carver, one of the first 'Embracers' the Krewe got onto. This John Smith appears to be happy to encourage the sickest behavior possible—anything that brings the criminal element under his control. We don't have the full picture yet, but we know we're dealing with drug and human trafficking and murder for hire. Those are the moneymakers. And to have control—real control—you must have control over what drives a person. That's where keeping loved ones as hostages comes in."

Another man spoke up. "Have all the hostages been found?"

"To the best of our knowledge, we've found their three sites. At the graveyard by the Victorian mansion site, we also found several victims buried. They used the old graveyard as a disposal site. We don't know the full extent. We are still working through interrogations. Our sketch artist, Maisie, created a sketch of John Smith based on a witness account; there's a copy in the briefing going out to law enforcement across the country. Of course, John Smith is most probably a chameleon and may not resemble the sketch now."

"What about the fellow in the coma? If he is John Smith—"

"Then we must get to the root of the money, and make sure whoever has been dealing with it while he's been in prison is stopped," Jackson said. "But we also don't definitely know Rory Ayers is John Smith. We're still digging into information on Marie Donnell. As many of you know, she went to prison years ago for running a prostitution ring under the guise of an escort service. We need to be on the lookout for any activity connected with this enterprise. Drug deals. Murder for hire. Most importantly, abductions. They made a good deal of money trafficking humans to the highest bidder, sometimes for sadistic purposes. Everyone here is responsible to their units, getting information in, making sure it's all out there. Thank you all for your diligence. A monster might still be out there. We're going to stop him this time."

The meeting was over; police officers who had worked with different FBI agents greeted them and vice versa. Patrick felt a hug from behind and turned to see Megan.

"Hey, big bro!" she said.

"Big bro? We're triplets," he reminded her.

Megan grinned, green eyes dancing a bit. "You were first out. That makes you the oldest by several seconds, at the very least. Not to mention—you're physically bigger than me."

"Thanks," he told her dryly.

Her smile suddenly faded. "I know Jackson wants you and Jordan to talk to Marie Donnell again, with me listening in. After, I would like to see Alfie at the cemetery where he's buried. To talk about Susie."

"You're still consulting?" he asked her.

"No, I'm editing a book right now called *The Revenge of the Star People*. Don't laugh—it's an excellent sci-fi read. But," she added, wincing, "the book everyone wants me to work on is one about becoming a victim of The Embracer. Hard to work on when we still have so many questions! But as far as anything connected to finding Susie for Alfie Parker? I'm available."

He nodded. Colleen, Mark, and Ragnar were coming over to join them. Colleen seemed to be hiding something of a secret smirk.

"What?" he asked her.

She grinned. "I'm going to love it when you're in the academy," she told him.

He arched a brow.

"Oh, come on. We're all going to pressure you. And you're going to realize just how good it is to work with people who are as weird as you are," Colleen said. She laughed softly. "Besides, it seems you're getting along just fine with Jordan. I thought you might."

"We're working together well," he said flatly. Leave it to siblings—no matter how much you love them—to tease a man about his social life.

For all his abilities, he hadn't realized Jordan was right behind him.

"So, I was just talking to Jackson," she said. "Megan, it seems you're headed out with Patrick and me to the correctional facility to attempt a conversation with Marie Donnell. I thought she'd refuse to see us. But apparently, visitors help to alleviate the boredom. It's worth a try."

"I'd wanted to talk to Connie about the kids, find out if she has been watching Susie's child," Patrick said.

"Jackson will have Connie here this afternoon," Jordan said.

"Okay, so onward to Marie Donnell."

Megan nodded. "I'll be in the observation room."

Colleen looked at him and said, "Mark, Ragnar, and I are going to take the dogs and head out to the woods. We keep searching the areas between the Victorian mansion and the graveyard and the other two sites where hostages were being held. So far, nothing. But Susie has to be somewhere."

"I believe we'll find her," Patrick said.

"Alive, I'm hoping," Megan added.

"If they had 'punished' her along with the men they killed, she would have been hidden in the graveyard, I think," Patrick said. "They were so sure no one would ever find the bodies there. From what we have learned, Susie is clever and resilient. She's a fighter. But she doesn't know who to trust. And even if she does trust someone, I think she's afraid no one can protect her. Anyway, are you ready, Megan? Is Hugo with us?"

"No, he's going to the woods with those guys," Megan said. "He's good; he can help."

"Bry-bo will be disappointed," Patrick said. "But he'll get over it."

Megan laughed. "We have to give the dogs a playdate."

"Definitely," Mark said. "Okay, then, let's move."

They headed out with the dogs, splitting up to reach their cars. It was a given that they would keep in touch; they all waved and said it anyway.

"Hey, Bry-bo!" Megan said, crawling into the back with the dog. "Aren't you glad to be here? You get to play with Hugo again, and it seems you get along great with Red."

"Three males, alpha pups, and they all get along," Jordan noted, looking out the window.

"They're all well trained. And Bry-bo and Hugo have had plenty of playdates," Patrick said. "Maybe we have weird dogs to go along with being weird people."

"We're not weird," Megan argued. "We're uniquely cursed!"

Jordan smiled at Megan's words. But it was time to focus on getting Marie to talk. He was certain she had no intention of doing so. She just wanted to keep playing with them to get out of her boring circumstances for a while.

At the facility, Bry-bo headed into the observation room with Megan, and Patrick and Jordan entered the interrogation room where Marie Donnell was waiting for them.

"My, my, my!" Marie said. "I knew agents were coming, but I didn't realize I'd get to see Wonder Woman again." She smiled. "Sweetheart, I know you think you're tough. And I'm so sorry, but that so-called toughness of yours *is* going to pay. Pay *me*. My lawyer is already preparing my suit against the federal government for the bodily injury you caused me as a victim."

"That will have to go through court, won't it?" Jordan said, smiling as she took a seat opposite Marie. "Who knows? There are so many young women ready to testify against you. Curious that you were given that extremely expensive suit to wear, while they were clad in scraps of fabric."

"I don't have to talk to you. I agreed to come here just to get a bit of time. But I have an attorney, a good one. And when you're discredited and I'm vindicated, oh, honey, you are going to be so sorry. Oh! Dr. Law, I don't mean to ignore you. It's just that she manhandled me so horribly," Marie said sweetly.

"Good luck with that," Patrick said. "I don't care how good your attorney is. The facts stand against you."

"I don't have to talk to you. I have rights. And by law—" Marie began.

"And yet here you are," Jordan told her softly.

"Maybe I'm John Smith," Marie told them. "Did you ever think about that? You're Miss Tough Guy. Didn't it occur to you that the main man might be a woman?"

"Yes, it did," Jordan said.

"Again, I don't have to talk to you."

"I'm going to say that by not talking—by threatening us, by trying to get the judge to release you until your trial date, by wanting to be in the general population while being held— you're telling us that Rory Ayers is John Smith," Patrick said.

She smiled.

And her mind seemed open to Patrick. Yes, she was feeling good. Because they were right. Rory Ayers was the man who had taken on the pseudonym of John Smith. But Marie had been in his hierarchy.

"She was his top lieutenant," he said quietly, glancing at Jordan. "But that didn't mean she wasn't terrified of him. She didn't know he still had the ability to pull all kinds of strings even while incarcerated. But if he's gone, well, there you have it. She's on top of the world. We can go now. Marie, thank you for the information." He rose with the last comment and Jordan followed.

"I didn't give you any information at all!" Marie cried.

They ignored her and left the room.

"I didn't know what she was thinking," Jordan said after they thanked the guard. "But it was more obvious than ever that she was terrified of Rory Ayers. I think you're right, though. She had to be like his right-hand woman. His top lieutenant. Angela says she has money in offshore accounts, and it's starting to add up—"

She broke off. Megan had just come out of the observation room, Bry-bo at her heels.

Patrick looked at his sister. Her face was pale.

"What is it?"

"So much for Rory Ayers being in a coma!" she said.

Jordan's mouth fell open. "But the doctors—"

"Dr. Larkin, who was his main caregiver, is dead," Megan explained. "Angela called me, not knowing how you'd want to deal with Marie Donnell and the news. Ayers apparently came to, faked that he was still out, and killed Larkin with a scalpel. He also killed a guard, then escaped the premises in Dr. Larkin's clothing."

Jordan shook her head and looked at Patrick.

"So, he's out again—out there killing again!" she said. "The question is, do we tell Marie? Or let her get the information in gen pop?"

CHAPTER TEN

Jordan turned to Megan, disbelieving such a thing had happened and wondering where they went from here.

Would Marie Donnell now feel forced to give them information because she had a new potential target on her back? Especially if they convinced her Rory Ayers believed she had given out information on him or had taken his money and power as her own?

"How the hell did this happen?" she asked Megan. "They knew that Rory Ayers was dangerous, suspected of far more than he was being charged with. How—"

"Was Rory Ayers not chained to the bed?" Patrick asked.

"I don't know exactly. Jackson is heading to the infirmary now to get the details. But Ayers was to receive a test and he was being prepped for it. He got his hands on a scalpel. He also attacked a guard and two nurses, who were critically injured—blood loss—but have so far survived." Megan shook her head, looking from Patrick to Jordan. "He had to have been awake for a while; he planned what he did. He took the doctor down, got the nurses, put the dead doctor on the table after stealing his coat and mask, and then called the guard in and got behind him, swiping the man's throat from left to right." She winced. "Jackson was told the place looked like a bloodbath; he can't figure how Ayers managed to casually stroll out as a doctor. But then again, it seems the only time the man messed up was when he attempted to kill his own daughter and pretend that she'd been a victim."

"He messed up when he went after Krewe members, too," Patrick reminded her. He looked at Jordan and asked, "What do you say? Marie is still in that interrogation room. It sounds as if Jackson left the ball in your court."

"We still have Connie waiting for us at headquarters," Jordan said, worried. "I know the Marshals Service is excellent at what they do, and police are involved, but, Patrick, now that Rory Ayers is out, all those hostages are in extreme danger."

Patrick nodded grimly. "Rory Ayers is the worst kind of psychopath. He has no empathy for anyone. I believe he condoned and orchestrated the Embracer murders because it was entertaining for him to help others assault and kill their victims. He would kill anyone for the fun of it and not feel a thing. But I'm not worried about those who are being protected."

"You're worried about Susie."

"We all are," Megan said. "That's one of the things I wanted to talk to you about. I do believe she's hiding out in the area. I managed to find an old friend of hers from when she was a teenager. Susie was hurt and broken, she told me. When she left, she said that she'd never come back. It would always be a place where terrible things were done to her, and where the one person who should have defended her betrayed her. Susie's life has been cruel, to say the least. And I believe we haven't found her because she just can't bring herself to trust anyone."

"All right. Let's get back in with Marie Donnell," Patrick said, looking at Jordan. "We'll plant a few seeds and see if we can't get something out of her. Then we'll check in with Connie and see if she can provide us any clues at all."

"Let's do it," Jordan said.

"Come on, Bry-bo. Time for us to watch and listen again," Megan said, returning to the observation room with the dog.

"You start, Wonder Woman," Patrick said, teasing and yet serious.

Jordan nodded and walked back into the room.

"What, you're back? Oh, tough girl. This is the United States of America. You can't force me to speak against myself. I do love those Founding Fathers!"

"I didn't come back to force you to do anything," Jordan said, pulling out a chair. Patrick did the same.

Marie was quizzical, frowning as she looked at the two of them.

"We're glad you have an attorney and feel comfortable. That is the American way," Jordan said.

"And, of course, in general population, you have friends," Patrick said.

"Then again," Jordan said, looking at Patrick and nodding, "you probably also have enemies."

"Not when your friends are stronger," Marie said complacently.

Jordan looked straight at her. "It's amazing what can happen in prison. Like, take Rory Ayers... The man was found hanging, barely alive. He was in a coma."

"Did he die yet?" Marie asked.

Jordan shook her head. "No. He's very much alive. And out

in the world again, I'm afraid. He has already murdered two more people. You know, Patrick," she said, turning to him, "I'm willing to bet Rory Ayers faked that whole hanging. Not as a suicide attempt, but to get into the infirmary. Maybe he knew from the beginning exactly what he was going to do."

"Definitely possible with Rory Ayers," Patrick agreed. "That's the thing about him; he is capable of real long-term planning."

Jordan was glad to see Marie Donnell was silent and white as fresh-fallen snow.

"You're lying. Rory didn't get out!"

"He appeared to be such a devoted family man," Patrick said, shaking his head as he looked at Jordan. "He was a pillar of society, a businessman. And all the while, behind the scenes, he was orchestrating not just his own deviant crimes, but serving as a puppet master." He looked from Jordan to Marie. "That was it, right? He has one of the sickest minds out there. Now, I'm going to suggest he got you out of your last legal troubles, and in exchange, you became his lackey."

"I was never a lackey!" Marie spit.

"Yes, you were. He engaged you, I imagine, by coming to you at first as a man simply infuriated that anyone had a right to say who could and couldn't buy sex. You provided women with a living and men with entertainment," Patrick said. "I'm sure Ayers was convincing with the things he said to you. They had no right to shut you down. Laws weren't fair, they weren't smart, and they didn't make sense. And when he suckered you into it, you quickly realized he wasn't just dealing with prostitution, but with human trafficking. But that didn't really bother you, because, in your case, he showered you with money. You endeared yourself to him; you became one of his key people. Not a lackey—of course not. But you oversaw a lot of the money—most of which is in offshore accounts. And, though you found out just how quickly he would kill—I believe you paid the hit men—that was okay. But now he's out, and he might just suspect the rumor out there is true; you intend to be a witness against him in court for a plea deal. I mean, you are an accessory to murder. That could command a death sentence since you'll face state and federal charges. Of course, unless you are pro-tected, I'm not so sure you're going to have to worry about a death sentence, since, well, we all know what happens…"

"You—you can't let anyone get to me," Marie sputtered.

"We can't do much. You told a judge yourself that you were innocent, a victim like all the others we rescued from various places," Jordan said.

"I was a victim!" Marie cried. "Rory Ayers came to me. I didn't know what I was getting into."

"When you did, you didn't care," Jordan said tonelessly.

"Don't you understand?" Marie demanded. "Once you get with Rory, there is no way out. Except death. There was no way out."

"Well, the problem with that is, according to the women we've interviewed, you were cold as ice," Patrick told her.

"I can help you!" Marie said.

"So," Jordan said, leaning forward, "let's make sure we have this straight. You are telling us Rory Ayers has been the head of a major criminal enterprise for years. Even behind bars, he managed murder, drug and human trafficking, and a dozen other crimes."

Marie let out a sigh. "He had the warehouse where you found me and the others for years."

"And you were managing everything for him. How did you receive your orders?"

"I would just check in with his attorney," Marie said. "No, the attorney isn't dirty. Rory and I had worked out a code a long time ago."

"Are you the only one who knows Rory Ayers is John Smith?" Patrick asked.

She waved a hand in the air. "There were a few others. They were killed in the shoot-out." She stopped, staring at them, shaking her head. "Look! You must protect me, really protect me! I—I mean, maybe he doesn't know anything. I didn't talk! But…"

"But?" Jordan asked. "Ah! But what if he does think you talked? If he thinks you were the reason we found the houses and the graveyard and all those people he was holding hostage? I mean, seriously, you were the one who knew everything, right? If I were Rory, I'd be wondering how anyone found out the way that we did. And since he escaped, killed a doctor and a guard, he knows he isn't going to find any mercy when he's caught."

"*If* he's caught," Patrick said. "He is as slimy as an eel. That man spent years pulling off this charade. Even in trouble, he managed to get out."

"I will give you everything," Marie said. "Everything. But you have to promise—"

"I'm going to call Jackson Crow down here. You'll give him everything," Patrick said. "He will then see you're protected."

Patrick stood and Jordan did as well. Marie jumped to her feet. "But…what about now? You can't put me with other people. You can't just leave me. You can't. Listen. There's a place I own—under an alias, of course—where I hid a hard drive. You'll only ever find it if I tell you where it is. I mean, forensics could find something if they're tearing apart the warehouse, but you'll never find the hard drive. Please! You can't just leave me here."

Patrick and Jordan started for the door.

"No, no, don't leave me without someone making sure I'm protected. The hard drive is in a little nook in the bathroom wall. It looks as if it just holds toiletries. There's a spot you hit directly behind the toothbrush. Don't leave me. There's so much I can tell you!"

Jordan glanced at Patrick. Marie had gone from being cool as a cucumber to someone on fire with fear.

Because she knew Rory Ayers.

He nodded to her. "All right. Jordan, give Jackson a call, will you? He should get here quickly."

Jordan stepped out into the hallway, nodding a quick thanks to the guard, and stepped into the observation room with Megan and Bry-bo to put the call through. Jackson told her he would be there as soon as possible. The Marshals Service had seen to it Connie Granger arrived safely at Krewe headquarters and Angela would stay with her until she and Patrick returned.

"Angela can talk to almost anyone. But I think Connie will feel best with the two of you. She knows Ayers is out. Angela has been working on assuring her we won't let the man get to her, and she won't be paying for her husband's criminal involvement with him. Beau Granger paid the ultimate price after falling for easy money."

"Thanks, Jackson," Jordan told him.

"I'll need Marie to reach her attorney," Jackson said. "When I get there, I'll see we keep her alive while he arranges for a plea deal for her. She'll still go to prison—a federal prison. But we can see she is protected. Until we get Rory Ayers. I kept figuring she was deeply involved. It's horrible Ayers is back out, and that people died for us to get to that truth."

"Agreed," Jordan said quietly.

"Is our civilian all right?"

Jordan glanced at Megan. She couldn't have heard Jackson's words, but she arched an amused brow to Jordan.

"Please tell Jackson I'm fine."

"Megan is fine," Jordan said. "Besides, her big bro is protecting her," she added, glancing Megan's way.

"Right. I'm on my way as we speak," Jackson said, ending the call.

"You are good, right? Anything you're hearing I'm not?" Jordan asked her.

"I'm good. Special Agent Wallace, I have seen you in action. I feel safe with you and my brother. And as for what I'm hearing, I don't know if my presence has made any difference. We all knew she was lying at the start, and we all know she's terrified and desperate now. To stay alive, she'll give Jackson anything he asks for. She won't hold back."

"That's good to know," Jordan muttered.

"Watching you two, you are great partners," Megan said. "I don't know if you realize you look at each other at just the right time. You have the right attitude—not exactly good cop/bad cop, or not good cop/bad cop at all, just the right way for finding the right words. Now that Rory Ayers is out there, well, I hear someone was at your place last night—if someone is after you, it's because Ayers has come to think of you as a threat. I'm glad Patrick has your back."

"Hey, I'm trained. And like you said, I'm not alone."

"No, you're not," Megan said. She was wearing a little smile that made Jordan uncomfortable. Megan knew she and Patrick had become more than partners. But were they really? He had seemed a bit distant that morning.

Maybe they weren't more. Maybe she had started something that had seemed—enjoyable—to Patrick for the moment. She had needed him when she had instigated their bout of love-making, but maybe he didn't need her. He had his family, his sisters, Mark, and Ragnar—and the dogs. He had parents who had protected and nurtured their children.

She reminded herself she loved her own mom. But she missed her dad—and she'd never known what it was like to share life, relationships, and love with a sibling.

As if he was a mind reader, Bry-bo whined softly.

"It's all good, boy," she said, patting him. She managed to speak lightly. "Megan, we're all going to be okay. And we are going to find Rory Ayers. And Susie. Though the Krewe has tried for years, we will finally find justice for Alfie."

"We're going to do it," Megan agreed.

Jordan smiled and left her, nodding her thanks to the guard again before she rejoined Patrick and Marie Donnell. Patrick was listening to her while writing notes into his phone.

He glanced at Jordan when she entered. "Marie is being true to her word," he said. "We've got a few bank accounts frozen already."

"Great," Jordan said. "Jackson will be here soon. Marie, he needs you to reach your attorney."

"She's already done so. He'll meet Jackson here so they can outline a plan to present to the judge."

"Perfect," Jordan said. She realized Marie was staring at her.

"He knows about you," she said.

"What?"

"Rory Ayers. He knows you're the agent who infiltrated the college pack and ultimately brought down the warehouse."

"And how does he know about that?" Jordan asked.

Marie inhaled, closing her eyes, then opening them again. "Me," she said softly. "I've been in contact with his attorney."

"You told the attorney that you had been arrested because of me?" Jordan asked.

"Code," Marie reminded her.

Patrick stood. "You keep your end of the deal, Marie, and Jackson will keep you alive. He'll deal you out of the death penalty, and he'll see to it that you don't wind up dead of a suspected suicide in your cell either."

"I just want to live," Marie whispered.

"You could tell us more about Susie," Jordan said.

"Susie?" Marie said. She shook her head. "I assume she's not with us anymore. The order was put out to see she was… taken care of."

"Why? And how was she even swept up into this?" Patrick asked.

"How else? Kid was working the streets. You work the streets, and you wind up on drugs. She first got swept up in it before my time, but Rory suspected she was up to something back when the first shoot-out occurred. He thought she had died that day, but he was furious with her and he had people trying to verify her death. Finally, someone found her. Dragged her back. And she hated Rory with a passion, though I'm not sure she ever met him face-to-face. She knew of him as John Smith. He liked keeping her imprisoned. He liked it when he heard that one of the guards had slapped her down for helping someone else. He took his time ordering her death, because she was such a little spitfire, and he wanted to see her fire go out. Then…the order came down."

"How did you hear about that?" Patrick asked.

"Because I'm the one who gave it," Marie said.

★ ★ ★

Connie Granger was visibly shaken. The woman had dark hair, almond eyes, and a strained, but pretty face. Jordan thought she was in her late twenties or early thirties.

Angela was with her when they arrived back at headquarters. She jumped out of her chair when Jordan opened the door to the conference room.

"Oh, my God, I will never feel safe again. I will never sleep again. They say the man known as John Smith has escaped. It was all over the news! I don't understand. My husband…" She stopped talking, choking on a little sigh. "He died, he wouldn't surrender to the police because he'd put us at risk, and now I'm so scared. What if he retaliates against everyone? On the news, they talked about the doctor he just killed and…"

Jordan walked over to the woman and put an arm around her shoulders.

"It's all right, Connie," Jordan said gently. "You're protected now. You and your children are protected. No one will let him come near you. Local police, the Marshals Service, and the FBI are all on this, and we will find him. But until we do, you know you are in a protected facility with guards and cameras. Any little thing someone sees on a camera will bring a small army to protect you. It's going to be okay. But, Connie, we do need your help."

"I'll leave you all to talk," Angela said. "Is Megan in my office?"

"She is," Jordan said. Angela nodded and slipped out the door just as Bry-bo and Patrick entered. Bry-bo woofed softly and padded over to Connie, anxious to provide what comfort he could. Connie took her seat, winced, and looked at

them with tears in her eyes as she hugged the dog, grateful
for the canine affection.

"We will find Rory Ayers, Connie," Patrick said, his tone
calm but filled with something that was solid and determined.
"Every law enforcement agency in the country will be looking for him." He sat down across from her and folded his
hands on the table. "Connie, you're safe. I swear it. But Susie
isn't safe. And we believe you're looking after her child for
her. You pretended her little boy was yours because you care
about Susie, because she cared about everyone else."

Connie sat back, staring at Patrick.

"I…"

"It's okay," Jordan said. "What you did was heroic and wonderful."

"I'm not heroic. I'm a complete coward."

"But one of your children really does belong to Susie?"
Jordan said.

Connie let out a long breath. "We…we were both at the
mansion. One of the men threatened me because I moved the
wrong way or did something else that they considered wrong.
They aimed a gun at me, and Susie swirled around and pretended she was going to run. The attention was off me, and
they were yelling about her having been there before, trying
to write notes on the gravestones out in the old graveyard.
I just grabbed Benji, and they thought he was mine. Susie
looked at me, and I knew she was afraid for herself. And because of that… I don't know if any of those men could have
killed a toddler in cold blood, but…"

"Connie, I'm serious. You think you're a coward, but what
you did was brave. Very brave," Patrick said. "What happened with Susie?"

Connie looked at them hopefully. "Is she—alive?"

Jordan shook her head.

Just because Marie had given an order, it didn't mean it had been carried out. They'd been all over in the past few days, raiding places, interrogating those who had been hostages and those who had been their keepers; they didn't know the order had been carried out. She kept telling herself that over and over.

"We don't know," she said honestly to Connie. "Can you tell us about the last time you saw her?"

Connie nodded. "We were at the house where you found me and the kids. But they were talking about bringing Susie back to the mansion. I never knew what it was about her. She didn't have any personal connections who were working for John Smith—at least, not that I knew of. She was just a prisoner, and a challenge. She'd get in trouble, they'd knock her around, and she'd get right back up. But she was with us, and it was great, because she's wonderful with kids, including her own child. She was such a help to us with the others. I was so afraid at first someone would find out we were lying; but she had taught Benji to call her Susie, and we were surviving. She almost got a note out with a deliveryman who came to the wrong address, and our guards were talking about the fact she had to go back to the mansion—to a very special place at the mansion. We all knew what the special place was— the graveyard. She told me she was going to have to take a real chance, and she might not make it. And she begged me to love Benji, which I do. If we don't find Susie, I will continue to love him like my own. But she loved him so much. He was everything to her. We were talking in the attic room, and then she was gone. I didn't know if they had taken her to the mansion. I didn't want to believe it, and I told myself she got away. Maybe she did because none of our guards left that day, and no one came to the house. I don't think they discovered she was missing until the next day, and I don't think they told anyone because they could be just as scared as we were."

"Connie, we believe Susie is out there. And we hope to find her," Jordan said.

"We will find her," Patrick added softly.

"Quickly," Connie said. "You have to find her before John Smith—Rory Ayers—does. If that man gets his hands on her, he will kill her this time. I think he had fun torturing her and threatening her. You must find her!"

"We'll do everything in our power, I swear," Patrick promised.

"Thank you so much for talking to us," Jordan told her gently.

"And you will be safe. They would need a small army just to challenge the protection services you're being given," Patrick said. "We are so sorry. Please, keep being brave. Right now, you need protection. But the time will come when you'll have a new life, when there will be a decent future for you and your children."

Connie nodded, tears in her eyes. "Maybe, if you find her, Susie and I could get a house, an apartment...whatever. A place to live together. The kids all love each other, so maybe..."

"Maybe," Jordan said softly.

One of the marshals, a tall, solid man with a serious face, looked in. "Agents, with all due respect, we'd like to get Ms. Granger back to the safe house."

Connie looked at Patrick and Jordan worriedly. "Why? Could something happen here?"

"I sincerely doubt it," the marshal said, smiling. "But with the recent news, we'd just like to have you there with the others, instead of on the road."

"We're all set here," Patrick said. "Connie, we promise, we'll keep you advised every step of the way. And thank you. You're a true heroine."

Connie gave them a weak smile. She was obviously still terrified. And broken. Fixable, but with the loss of her husband and the fear with which she was living, it would take time, Jordan thought.

They all stood. To Jordan's surprise, Connie rushed to her and hugged her tightly. She returned the hug and told the woman, "I won't tell you that anything is all right, Connie. I'll just promise we're all going to do everything we can to make it get better."

Dabbing her eyes, Connie nodded and left with the marshal.

"You were good with her, great with her," Patrick said, studying her.

"Thanks. I guess…"

"I know," he said. He moved closer to her, studying her still. "You're upset with me," he said.

"Um, no—"

"Yes."

She shrugged, and to her surprise, she suddenly smiled and said, "I'm envious. You and your sisters are unique, and you had such support, and you still support each other. I've never known anything like that."

"My sisters are great. That's not why you're upset."

"I'm not upset. I'm glad we're good partners."

He grinned, surprised. "Okay, so I'm not much of a great mind reader today. I said we worked well together or whatever out of respect for…well, for what you might want."

"I don't know what I want," she admitted. "I've been nothing but focused for so long, getting through the academy, making it to the Krewe, finding others like myself, others I can work with…"

She fell silent as Angela, distracted, walked back into the room. "You two were wonderful with her, and with Marie. Jackson just called. They've gone to the address Marie gave us. They found the hard drive Marie talked about. They've been able to freeze lots of accounts now—frightening how many—and…" She paused, shaking her head. "We know where to find more bodies we didn't know we were looking for. But, Jordan, apparently Rory Ayers believes you are the cause of his downfall. I don't know how he thought he might beat the courts, but he did. At least, until we raided the warehouse. Given the involvement of Mark, Colleen, Ragnar, and even Megan in his previous trials, Jackson wants you all together at the safe house. Three dogs, the locks, the alarms… It's the best place for you to be now."

"The safe house?" Jordan said.

"It's where you're safest. Anything happens, and alarms go off everywhere; local police, SWAT, agents can be there in seconds," Angela said.

Megan was right behind her. "The house is really great; I should know, having stayed there before. The kitchen is stocked. It's comfortable and the dogs love the yard. I don't mind going back there at all." She paused, grinning. "It's going to be fine. You'll like the place, Jordan."

The place might be just fine, but…

All of them? Under one roof? Two couples—and her and Patrick. They were great partners! But just how many rooms did the safe house have?

"I—I'm glad we're going to be safe," she said. "But we

need to keep up the search. Now that Ayers is out there, and Susie possibly alive—"

"I'll keep Megan here with me for now," Angela said. "You two go collect what you'll need. And be careful. Now that Ayers is out there, we don't know what he will do, even if we are getting control of his main source of power—his money. Until Ayers is caught, no one is really safe. Jordan, it could have been anyone outside your place last night, but we can't take chances. That's part of being who we are—a team, watching out for one another."

"Of course," Jordan said, trying not to appear shell-shocked.

"I'll get Bry-bo. We'll stop by Jordan's house and my hotel room." He glanced at his watch. "All right. I didn't realize how late it was getting."

"I don't think Ayers keeps nine-to-five hours," Jordan said.

"We have a night team out there. Tomorrow, the six of you—the nine of you, with Red, Hugo, and Bry-bo—can head back out again. I know this is intense and personal. I understand. We are all so fond of Alfie, and hopeful for him. But we need rested, functioning agents, too," Angela said.

A few minutes later, with Bry-bo in tow, they were in the car. Jordan sat awkwardly silent.

"Hey," he said gently. "It's all right. We can keep our distance if you wish. We can forget last night ever was, if that's what you want."

"You're not much of a mind reader," she told him.

He smiled and stopped the car. "Jordan, trust me. I know where you're coming from. I've spent my adult life chasing my vocation, because getting close to someone usually results in me just being awkward. You're beautiful, funny, brave—and let me add extremely sexy. You do know what I see, feel, and know. We will play this however you wish, but I will never regret last night, and I truly hope that you won't either."

She laughed softly. "I don't regret last night in the least, and I never will, my dear, brilliant Patrick. If anything, I regret we're not going to be alone at my place."

He leaned back, smiling. "You know, my sisters are not the kind who judge. And they both think the world of you."

"Your sisters are great. And Mark and Ragnar are super, too. Still—awkward."

"Only if we let it be," he said. "And I don't intend to let it be awkward in the least. But, Jordan, this is all up to you. We'll go wherever you want to go."

"Again, I say, you are apparently not reading my mind."

"Sometimes, I can read minds. But I can never really read another heart."

CHAPTER ELEVEN

Jordan was skilled, Patrick determined, when it came to packing what might be needed for a stay of unknown duration at a safe house.

She was ready to go within ten minutes. He wasn't sure *he* could collect his belongings from a hotel room as quickly.

"They teach that at the academy?" he asked.

She grinned. "I'm sure they'll teach you all kinds of things you never knew!"

"Like packing."

"No, that was my mom," she told him, grinning.

Bry-bo rushed ahead of them, as if he knew they were leaving the house. Jordan took a look around before they stepped out, seemingly hesitant to leave.

"Hey," he said softly.

She looked at him curiously.

"It's going to be all right."

"I know. And it is what it is. So, onward to your hotel."

Patrick saw there was a police car down the street as they

locked up and left. He was glad to see Jackson had spread the word, and others were keeping a watchful eye on the place. He still found himself being especially vigilant as they got back into the car, something that probably wasn't necessary, because if anyone was within a threatening distance, Bry-bo would have let them know.

He was wary as he parked at the hotel, too.

When they entered, he was surprised to see Karen Crawford talking to a clerk at the reception desk. She turned as they entered, smiled broadly, and said, "Never mind. There he is!"

Of course, Bry-bo hurried to her, his tail moving a thousand miles an hour.

"Hey!" Karen said, walking toward him. "I lost my phone! I had to get a new one with no numbers in it. I was leaving you a message to please call me so I could have your very exclusive number again." She smiled at Jordan and extended her hand. "Hi. I'm Karen Crawford, Patrick's neighbor and friend."

"Nice to meet you," Jordan said, extending her hand with a slightly weak smile. "I'm Jordan Wallace. I've been partnered with Patrick on this case." Her smile broadened. "I can tell you two are friends. Bry-bo is crazy about you."

"I'm the pup-watcher when Patrick is out of town. He feeds my cat, Jilly, when we're away. Anyway, I just wanted to keep in touch in case Patrick had time while we were both in town for dinner, though, of course, I understand he's here on a heavy-duty case."

"Hopefully, we'll get to the bottom of it soon," Patrick said.

"Hope so. Not to worry; I was just getting your number. And no pressure if nothing works out. See you back in Philadelphia. Jordan, a pleasure. Be safe, both of you!" With a final pat for Bry-bo and a wave, she started toward the exit.

"Karen!" Jordan called.

Karen turned back.

"You forgot to get the number!"

"Oh!" Karen hurried back, grinning sheepishly. "Thank you. Patrick—"

"Give me the phone. I'll put it in and call myself right away and know it's you," Patrick said.

She handed him her phone after keying in the password, and he called himself, then handed Karen's phone back to her. "Good to go. Just make sure you put my name with it in contacts."

"Ha ha," Karen said. "Thanks for the reminder." She looked at Jordan. "We can see why I'm not in your line of work!"

"But you are an incredible artist," Patrick told her, smiling. "I'll pull up some of your work for Jordan to see." He gave her a kiss on the cheek. She hugged him, then waved again and left.

"A good friend," Jordan said as they continued toward the elevator. "That's a big dog you have; nice to have a friend take care of him."

"Yep, she's great," Patrick said, hitting his floor number. He walked ahead of Jordan to his room, slightly amused. "Friends are something we all need to cherish. Anyway, I need to be ready in ten minutes to keep up with your pace."

"You didn't grow up with my mom," she said, taking a seat at the foot of the bed. Bry-bo sat on his haunches at her side and waited as well. She set a hand gently on the dog's head. "And you're down to nine minutes."

"I'm moving, I'm moving!" he said.

Luckily, he was good at living out of his suitcase. And he was packed and ready within six minutes, something he decided to tease her about.

"Being one of triplets," he said, shrugging as she glanced at her watch.

"That is so interesting," she said. "What was it like, being a boy with two sisters the same age? Were you the odd man out? Were you all equally close? Did you ever fight? Don't tell me you never fought. I'd hate you and I wouldn't believe you."

"Oh, no, we fought. And triplets are odd. We're obviously not identical, though it is possible to have identical twins and another fraternal child in the womb at the same time. But each of us was a different egg. I happened to push my way out first."

"I'm not surprised."

"Ouch! Being a boy was different, yes. And we fought, yes. Not horribly, but like any kids. Then we found out we were weird—"

"Talented!" Jordan interrupted with a grin.

"Talented, cursed, weird, lucky, not sure."

"I refuse to be weird. Even if we are weird. But you're weirder."

He laughed at that, loving the way she was looking at him.

"Anyway, I guess our folks set the pace. We learned to be a team, which is probably why we work so well with law enforcement now. We were aware there were things we couldn't share with others, and we had to trust and lean on one another. By the time we were in separate colleges, we didn't get to see each other as often, and we grew closer when we were together. I guess, in a way, Megan was the odd man out. She supported us, but had no plans to go into law enforcement. In truth, other than sharing what most people only get to share once they're with the Krewe, we're normal siblings. We pursued our goals in different places, but even Megan wants to help when she can. She just doesn't want to be law enforcement day in and day out."

"But she's fine with Ragnar."

"Yep." He grinned. "And honestly, I think Ragnar is happy to be an adoptive father to the dog. Red was great with Ragnar, but Red was Mark's dog. Now Ragnar has his own."

"So, Ragnar gained a significant other and a great canine!"

"There you go."

"Did you have big brother moments worrying about your sisters?" she asked.

"Sure. But I also respect them and their choices. Megan loves books, and she can be amazingly brave when she needs to be. As far as partners in life go, as it happens, I think they made great choices."

"Ah," she muttered. "Well…hmm. Still…"

They were getting close to the safe house. And Jordan was looking more uncomfortable.

"Trust me," he said softly, "they think you're an excellent agent."

"Still a bit of a newbie," she muttered. "Anyway…"

They had reached the house. Patrick hit the call box; Jackson had told them they would have key cards for the gates, but he hadn't gotten his yet. He could see two cars were in the circular drive that fronted the house. The others were already there, and they would buzz them in.

He pulled the car in and glanced at Jordan.

She just shook her head. "Awkward!"

"Again, only if we let it be," he said.

He collected their bags from the back of the car as Jordan stared at the house. But when he joined her to walk to the front door and knock, it opened before they could reach it.

Megan was there.

"Renovations! Since I've been here, and that wasn't that long ago. It's great. They turned the office into a third bedroom. We're all set," she said happily. "But we didn't set up anywhere yet. You two have been lead on this phase of the case, so you should get to sleep where you choose."

Jordan was staring at her blankly.

"Oh, man, I'm sorry," Megan said. "We made assumptions. We should have asked. There's also a sleeper sofa in the back. I can't believe we misread things so badly. And I'm supposed to read between the lines!"

"You didn't misread anything," Jordan said, surprising Patrick. "I mean, we don't know what we're doing, but whatever. I don't care where we are—it's a safe house. Hopefully, we won't be here long. I mean, hopefully, we'll find Ayers. We'll stomp out his criminal enterprise, round up anyone still in his employ, and find Susie soon. We will find her," she added.

"You guys are the best," Megan assured her. "You will find Susie."

Colleen came out of the kitchen then. "We're going to find Ayers. The man is truly a monster. Jackson saw to it a detail has been sent to protect his ex-wife and her daughter. Marie Donnell is also being protected. Hostages are all in the hands of the Marshals office, and they know what they're doing. Now we just have to find Ayers and stop him. The man kills as easily as most of us swat away gnats."

"We need to find Ayers *before* he finds Susie," Patrick emphasized.

"That, too. So, the house. We didn't do anything as far as unpacking because…" Colleen looked at Megan. Megan shrugged and looked at Jordan.

"We don't care where we sleep," Jordan said.

Patrick slipped his arm around her.

"And yes," Jordan said, surprising Patrick again. "We just need one room."

"Cool," Colleen told them. "I mean, there is a sleeper sofa in back, though it's not the most comfortable ever. Still, anything is better than being unprotected. Being together here gives us strength."

Jordan grinned. "Remind me in my next life not to get tangled up in a situation like this."

She grinned at Patrick, and easy laughter rose among them that brought Mark and Ragnar to welcome them as well. Megan suggested they might like the newly renovated office/bedroom. It was on the right side of the house, while the other bedrooms were on the left. "The entry here is wired, the windows are wired, there are cameras that show everything on the street and to the left and right. It's quite a feat of planning, but Adam Harrison and Jackson were in on it from the beginning, and they knew what needed to be done. Why don't we all unpack and then have dinner. Ragnar found ingredients in the kitchen for his family's famous Norse salmon preparation."

"Shouldn't we be out there tonight? At least one team?" Jordan asked.

Patrick glanced her way. Jordan was an exceptional agent, but Ragnar, Mark, and Colleen had seniority, with Mark and Ragnar having the greatest experience with the Krewe. Protocol dictated that Jackson would be communicating his orders to the most senior agents when it appeared they'd be working as a team.

"Mark, Ragnar, and I are leaving as soon as we're settled and we've all eaten. You guys and Megan get to do dishes. And as I'm sure you know, we've had agents out searching from Virginia, West Virginia, DC, and Maryland since Ayers maneuvered his escape. Not to mention the fact that every law enforcement agency in the country has been notified.

You'll head out in the morning, so get a good night's sleep," Colleen said.

"I'll be in our room tracking what I can on the computer," Megan said. "We're trying to get accounts frozen, but finding them all—and finding most in foreign countries—has been a nightmare. Anyway, research is my contribution, and I am happy to say I have made a few discoveries." She shook her head. "Money. It's always the lure." She grimaced. "Let's sit down and eat, and then these guys can get moving."

Without much chatter, they split off, selecting rooms. The dogs ran about, checking each room, the hallways, and one another.

Mark suggested the dogs all needed to run around in the yard.

Ragnar called from the kitchen that dinner was being served. As they sat to eat, he explained his family counted salmon as a staple.

"Besides, most people like it better than sheep's heads," he told them. "Another Norse specialty."

"So the great marauding adventurers were galloping gourmets as well," Jordan teased lightly.

Ragnar shrugged, setting the food on the table. "Marauders, yes. And yeah, the Viking age was pretty brutal. But guess what? They settled places, too. Olaf the White was the founder of Dublin, Ireland. And don't forget Bluetooth!" he said.

"Bluetooth?" Jordan asked.

Megan, having just rinsed down a bite of her fish, explained. "Harald Bluetooth. Mid 900s. King of Denmark and Norway. He introduced Christianity to his people and was known to be a pretty cool fellow. The 'Bluetooth' option we use today is named for him."

"I did not know that!" Jordan admitted.

Ragnar grinned. "Yes, the Viking age was rather ruthless. But there were a few good things in there as well."

"And heading into the Middle Ages," Patrick said, "people tortured their enemies in dungeons, and in some places, hanged so-called witches or burned them at the stake. We— as human beings—are not known for being the kindest creatures out there."

Megan wagged a finger at him. "All right, brother dearest, I'll have you know I believe most people are good and intend to be kind to others. You have simply spent far too long dealing with those who are depraved."

He grinned at his sister. "Maybe I can become a writer!"

"No. You'd write horrible things."

"Like massive space creatures who live on blood?" he asked.

Megan rolled her eyes and looked at Jordan. "He must be great to work with."

Jordan laughed, looking at Patrick. "Believe it or not, he is. And, Ragnar, the salmon is great."

He thanked her.

Patrick was glad to see Jordan slowly relaxing. Megan talked about the year they talked their dad into going to a tree farm to cut down their own Christmas tree, and how, one by one, they'd deserted him to sit with their mom by the fire in the little office. Colleen reminded them they'd gotten into trouble when Patrick accidentally knocked the Easter Bunny into the mall's fountain in his excitement to ask for special Easter chocolate.

Jordan laughed and glanced at him now and then; she seemed at ease.

But that had to change when dinner ended and Mark, Ragnar, and Colleen grew serious as they prepared to head out. The discussion turned to a decision on whether they should go ahead and take Bry-bo, too, allowing each agent a dog. But Colleen determined he would be better than any alarm system if someone dared think about attacking those in the house.

"I believe we're safe in the *safe* house," Patrick told his sister.

"I'll just feel better," Colleen said.

Patrick nodded. "Okay, then."

"Jackson is sending us all a grid for the search, though Ayers could have eyes on us, too, and move when he believes an area has been searched. But we won't have the only canine crew out there," Mark told him. "Anyway, we'll update you in the morning or send a message if we have anything new."

"Thanks," Patrick told him, with Jordan echoing the word.

Megan kept chattering a little nervously as the three of them picked up dishes and cleaned the kitchen. Then she excused herself and headed to her room, ready to get back to work.

Patrick saw Jordan was grimacing, looking at him as Megan made a point of closing her bedroom door.

"I…"

"Hey, don't worry. We can get a good night's sleep. Fully clothed, no problem," he assured her, grinning. He understood; she might be the Krewe member, but this was his family.

She smiled. "Maybe," she told him.

But they hadn't reached the door to the room they'd decided on before Megan came bursting back out with her computer in hand.

"Something is happening," she told them.

"What is it?" Jordan asked her.

"I don't know. There's suddenly movement on an account. There's no reason money should go out like that unless… I'm not 'reading between the lines' or anything like that. It's just pure logic."

"Megan, please," Jordan said quietly. "What are you talking about?"

"Okay, so, I've been watching Amelia Ayers's money movements as well, just on a hunch," Megan said. "She was his wife, he hated her when she divorced him, and her attorney managed to cut him out of her family's money. She just wired money—several hundred thousand dollars—into an account in the islands. I think I might know where Rory Ayers is. I think he must have gotten into his house."

"They've been watching the house," Patrick said, frowning. "And I'm sure Amelia had the alarm codes changed. I don't see how—"

"I'm afraid if police or agents stormed the house and he is in it, he might kill her. Then again, he might have gotten her to transfer money and intends to kill her anyway. I mean, the man tried to murder his own stepdaughter."

"Let's go," Jordan said to Patrick. "We'll call Jackson on the way."

Megan looked worried. "But, like I said, if you just go up to the house—"

"We won't," Patrick said. "We'll get through to Jackson. We'll get what we can from him about the house and Amelia. Don't worry."

"What about Bry-bo?" Megan asked.

Patrick was about to say they'd take the dog. But he didn't. He suddenly felt as Colleen had earlier.

Bry-bo would be the best alarm system in the world for his sister, and she'd now be at the house alone.

"We may be better off on this one alone," he said.

Jordan had her phone out and nodded to him to indicate they could leave while she was talking to Jackson.

They left Megan, and as they got into the car, Jordan told Jackson she was putting him on speaker.

"Megan believes Ayers is somehow back in his old house," she told him. "There was a sudden money transfer. I don't know how he could have gotten in. I mean, didn't she get a new alarm system for the house and aren't there police and agents watching it?"

"Yes," Jackson replied. "But I think Megan could be right. Ayers was bitter after the divorce stripped him of his easily available income. I'm afraid if we go in guns blazing, he'll take her out first. And if he got in there, he's got a way to get out."

"I think I should just go to the front door," Jordan said. "Ayers has never seen me. I can pretend to be an old friend of Amelia's daughter, Deirdre, and pretend I hadn't realized she wasn't still staying with her mom. If I can get her to the door—"

"You'd have to get through the gate," Jackson said.

"Or over the gate and then pretend the intercom wasn't working?"

"Risky," Jackson said.

"We can't just let him kill her!" Jordan protested. "Jackson, I can pull this off, I swear it. Because Patrick can be seeking a way in while I distract Ayers. I think he'll let her get to the door. He'll be afraid someone might use force to come in if she isn't seen. And I will know right away, Jackson, if something is or isn't wrong."

"I can't see another way to do this," Patrick agreed, listening to her.

He didn't want Jordan taking any risks. And yet he knew if she were a male agent, and a plan to use subterfuge had arisen, he would have weighed the situation and believed it was their only recourse.

He knew he had to let Jordan be the agent she intended to be.

"Jackson, we can do this. I'll be right there." He glanced at Jordan. Her jacket, he knew, covered the Glock at the back of her waistline. Her hair was loose, and while her appearance was businesslike, it could also be considered casual enough. Something she wouldn't have bothered to change before stopping by to see if a friend was available.

And, he thought dryly, she was wearing pants. So much better for scaling walls.

"I'll inform our agents and the police captain of what you're attempting and why. They've had a constant check-in here. No one has approached the house from the front, and we've had agents circling the property as well. It is in a heavily wooded area, so of course, they've made a point of circling the perimeter throughout the day.

"The man managed to fake a murder attempt. He was willing to play Russian roulette with his own life. And he had no problem murdering the doctor trying to save his life. I'm sure no matter how agreeable she is—transferring money to save her life—he'll kill her when he's gotten all that he wants. He loathes her; she was his charade for years. Now the charade is over. Jordan, we protect and save, but I'll be damned if I want to lose an agent to that man."

"I've played it close before, Jackson. I'll be fine," Jordan said. "Again, I'm not alone. And maybe—" She broke off, staring at Patrick. "Alfie! Alfie could help. Is the cemetery on the way?"

"Close enough. Let's go pick up a ghost," he said.

"Keep me caught up on every step," Jackson said.

"Yes, sir," Jordan assured him, ending the call. "Night again. One of these days, we will get arrested for trespassing at night in the cemetery."

He grinned. "Alfie will hear us, and when we ask him to jump in, he'll do so. We can explain on the way."

He was glad to be proved right. Alfie had been chatting with a friend, a man whose ghostly uniform suggested he had protected and served back at the beginning of the 1900s. He saw Patrick and Jordan heading toward him—having hopped the wall again—excused himself, and hurried over to them. He was anxious. "Something? Nothing?"

"We need you to walk through a wall," Patrick told him. "Come on; we'll explain on the way."

They did. When they pulled up near the Ayers house, they all left the car quickly. Patrick paused only to grab his bag of tools. Both Jordan and Alfie looked at him curiously.

"I learned a lot from some of the criminals I've encountered," he told them with a shrug. "Break-in tools."

When they reached the grounds, Alfie grinned and walked through the wall and fencing system, leaving them to carefully crawl over toward the rear, where they could find the cover of several old trees.

"I'll be right back," Alfie promised.

He slipped into the house. Patrick and Jordan remained hunched down by the trees and waited.

"You were right. How the hell he got in there, I don't know," Alfie said. "But he's got Amelia downstairs in her office. He has a gun to her head. He believes she's terrified and addled enough to be having trouble finding numbers and accounts."

"Amelia has a housekeeper who has been with her forever; she's a part of the family, really," Patrick said.

Alfie nodded. "Whatever the plan is, execute it soon. The housekeeper is on the floor by the stairs; she's been knocked out. Blood trickling from her forehead. She's going to need medical assistance ASAP."

Patrick frowned. "You're sure she's alive?" he asked.

Alfie nodded. "I know the difference between the living and the dead," he told them dryly.

"I'm ringing the bell," Jordan said. "Alfie, get back in there. Maybe you'll get a chance to trip the man. Patrick—"

He pointed. "Give me a minute. I'll get in through a window in the rear."

"You might set off an alarm," Jordan warned.

"And if I do, it will throw him off. And you will be ready. Alfie—"

"I can't shoot anyone," Alfie warned quietly.

"No, but you can throw him off, too. I need to get in there. He'll probably start worrying about getting out in whatever way he came in. Which means he won't dare kill a hostage; he could be shot down if he is seen and he'll know that. He's not a stupid man. He's been playing everyone for decades. When he realizes he may be apprehended, his first thought is going to be to get away. Jordan, give me a minute to get around and figure out my entry. Then ring the bell."

"I'm going in," Alfie told them.

Heading around the house, Patrick found a large bay window. He *had* learned a great deal from the criminals he'd worked with. He opened his bag and found glass cutters and a grip. He wanted to keep the glass from crashing, to avoid any sound until they were ready.

He heard the doorbell. He'd managed to remove a good-sized sheet of the glass when the doorbell sounded. The glass opened to the parlor; the small office was one room over.

Patrick could hear Ayers talking to Amelia.

"Who the hell is that?" he demanded. "I know you didn't call the police, even if they're out there. Get up. Now. I want to know what the hell is going on here. You open your mouth, say the wrong thing, I'll be happy as hell to put a bullet through your head."

"You're going to kill me anyway," Amelia Ayers whimpered.

"But you're going to live on hope until the last minute!" Ayers told her. "Let's both pray it's not a cop ringing that bell."

Patrick kept at it with the glass as the two walked away. He had cleared an entry when he heard Ayers say, "It's some woman. A pretty one. Maybe we could have some fun here tonight. Who is she?" he demanded.

"I don't know. I've never met her," Amelia said.

"Open the door. Find out what she wants. Invite her in. Wait a minute. Why didn't we hear her at the gate?"

"Maybe the alarm isn't working. Maybe she jumped the fence. I don't know. I didn't call her. I didn't call the police, I swear it!" Amelia said.

"Open the door. She's my type. Gorgeous. And young. Much younger than you, bitch. All the money in the world couldn't make you attractive to me! Of course, you weren't for years, but you were a good old girl when it came to making me look good."

Patrick heard the door open. And he heard Jordan's cheerful voice.

"Hi, Mrs. Ayers. We haven't met, but I'm a friend of Deirdre's, and I had heard she was living back home for a while?"

"I'm sorry, dear. Deirdre isn't here now. She's back working."

Ayers must have shoved his gun into his ex-wife's head, because she seemed to choke before speaking again.

"But come in, come in!"

It was time to move. Patrick jumped over the sofa and started for the hallway.

But as he did, he heard Amelia Ayers suddenly scream, "No!"

And a shot went off.

CHAPTER TWELVE

Two things happened that saved the life of Amelia Ayers.

Alfie was there. And while he was nothing but spirit, something of that spirit moved the air and Rory Ayers's hand just to the left.

And Jordan had a choice. Catapult herself through the air and bring Amelia down where she'd be out of the range of the bullet, or...

Let her die and take Ayers.

There were all kinds of arguments that might be made. Amelia needed to die so that others could live. But they might get Ayers before he managed to kill again; he was on the run. And with Amelia alive, money could be transferred back, and he wouldn't have the funds he needed to keep up his reign of terror.

In the split second in which she had a choice to make, Jordan knew she had to save the life of the woman who had just been willing to die to warn her to get out.

And so, Jordan flew at Amelia, bringing her down, rolling as quickly as she could before Ayers regained himself and shot them both.

His bullet went astray and killed a lamp.

Miraculously, he didn't take aim again. Because he heard someone coming. He knew someone was in the house. Someone lethal.

Coming for him.

Ayers turned and ran. He jumped over the body of the prone housekeeper and disappeared across the parlor like a streak of lightning.

But Patrick was there, ready to take up flight, except just as he reached them, Amelia began to seize violently on the floor. He stopped briefly with a pained expression before falling to his knees and yelling for Jordan to find something, some kind of a stick, something for Amelia to bite down on lest she take out her own tongue and choke on it.

"There!" the ghost of Alfie Parker said.

There was a small newspaper stand by the door. Jordan slammed it violently on the marble entry floor and handed him one of the narrow legs. He quickly rose and caught hold of Amelia Ayers's violently flopping arms and secured her against his form while getting her to bite down on the stick. He didn't have to tell Jordan to get on the phone and get help there fast.

Because law enforcement was watching the house, help arrived quickly. A police medic first, and then emergency services. Amelia was quickly secured in an ambulance, the seizure being brought under control.

Medics also confirmed the housekeeper was alive, though she had taken a heavy crack to the head and might have a skull fracture.

Jordan had also alerted the officers on the scene, and Jackson, to the fact they'd had Ayers. While teams searched the grounds and surrounding area, others scoured the house top to bottom.

Every room, every closet, and every nook and cranny was searched. They couldn't find Ayers. One of the officers broke down the space beneath the stairs, but there was nothing there except for dirt and spiders.

Officers reported there had been no time when the perimeter of the house hadn't been watched; they even had security footage.

But then, the security footage never showed the man entering the house in the first place.

As Jordan and Patrick listened to Detective James Parker of the county police, Patrick shook his head. "It's impossible. He got in somehow, and he got out somehow. We just haven't figured out how."

"My men have gone crazy in there. They've broken walls and found nothing. Hell, I can't figure it out either," Parker said. "You'd think the man was a ghost."

"An insult to all ghosts," Alfie muttered, standing behind Patrick.

"It's there—he has a secret entrance in there," Patrick said.

"But we would have seen him in the yard," Parker said. "I swear to you, we have been on this. The FBI has had your fellow agents on it. We would have known if he'd approached the house, and we would have seen him fleeing, for sure!"

"He was real," Patrick said. "Flesh and blood," he added dryly, aware of Alfie's words, though, of course, Parker hadn't been.

"We'll keep at it," Jordan said.

Parker looked at her, shook his head, then looked at Patrick.

"Kudos to you both. From what I understand, Ayers wanted to kill that woman and you kept her alive."

"And let him go," Jordan said regretfully.

"But we serve and protect; you saved her life. We'll keep looking. We'll have crews out here until we do know what the hell happened—"

"We're here to help, too," Patrick said. "And when we hear she's stable, we'll bring a computer to the hospital. Mrs. Ayers is going to want her money back."

"Right." Parker nodded. "Well, we have crews who can do this, and you surely deserve the rest of the night off, but if you're determined, knock yourselves out."

"Thank you," Patrick said. He grinned. "We'll do that."

When Parker had walked away, Patrick turned to Jordan and said, "He headed toward the kitchen. Basement stairs, I believe. He got in and out that way, I'll bet."

"Megan," Jordan said.

"What?"

"Patrick, we have to get the money back. The money he forced her to transfer to his accounts. Is Megan good enough to get in there and get it transferred back?"

"Megan is good with this stuff, but we should call Jackson. They have people at headquarters who can get on it."

"Right! If anyone can manipulate anything, it's Angela."

"I'm headed down to the basement." He paused, looking at her. "That was amazing, by the way. You really did save her life."

"With a little help," Alfie said. "Still, you did move like... a speeding bullet."

"And thanks to you, Ayers murdered a lamp!" Jordan said. "But now he's out there..."

"We can never second-guess," Patrick said. "Jordan, just pat yourself on the back for once, okay?"

She grinned at him. "I wasn't too reckless?"

He groaned and turned and headed for the kitchen. She looked at Alfie and then hurried after Patrick, remembering the house was now crawling with officers and agents and forensics crews.

The door to the basement stood open and Jordan hurried to it; Patrick was already going down the stairs.

He stood on the concrete floor at the base of the stairs, and she joined him.

It was a basement. Just an ordinary basement: pipes were visible throughout, the water heater stood against one wall, gardening tools were in a corner. Another section housed a washer and dryer, plus an ironing board. Folding tables were in another. The walls all looked like old brick. Structural elements of the house were clear and evident.

Jordan shook her head. "I don't see anything!"

"But we know he is flesh and blood," Patrick said, his hands on his hips as he studied the place, slowly.

He walked to the wall in the laundry area and crawled over a basket to reach the wall.

It was a large house.

That meant a large basement.

But Patrick wasn't giving up. He went by the laundry, the gardening tools, and the water heater. Old bikes were stacked up in one area, probably not used for years, Jordan thought. Patrick walked behind them, and searched for any sign of a break or oddity in the wall. He walked past the little area where the water heater was, looked at it curiously, walked back. He stepped behind the heater and began running his hands over the wall again.

"Patrick?"

"Come over here. It's made to look as if it's just where bricks join. But look, it's too smooth—too clean-cut—even where the bricks are different sizes."

"Right," Jordan muttered. "No grout!"

He kept pressing the wall in different places. Jordan took a step back as he did. She frowned and noted there was a strange handle near the floor that didn't seem to be connected to the water heater.

She stepped over to it. It was metal, the same as the water heater. But she stooped down and pulled it and then jumped back at a strange grating sound. The wall was opening behind the water heater.

There was, however, no one there. Instead, there was a tunnel that led into darkness.

Jordan hadn't realized Alfie was standing behind her until he spoke quietly.

"I should go first," he said.

"Alfie—" she began.

"What's he going to do, kill me?" Alfie asked.

"No," Patrick said. "You have to give us a chance to tell the cops and warn whoever is out there in the forest that Ayers has a tunnel here and he might be anywhere by now. I'll just run up, and Jordan—"

"I'm already calling Jackson," she said.

A minute later, Patrick was back. "Let's go." He switched on a heavy light he had apparently obtained from his bag of tools.

"Alfie, feel free to lead," he said.

Alfie nodded and started into the tunnel. Jordan followed, and Patrick—keeping the beam of light high and clear above them—followed behind Jordan.

At the beginning, the tunnel was brick, as if it had been in place for hundreds of years, perhaps part of an earlier dwelling or building. But they were no more than a hundred feet or so when the brick structure began to disappear, and they were traveling along walls that were composed of nothing more than earth.

Jordan stopped suddenly, realizing that, behind her, Patrick had as well.

"Patrick?"

He flashed the light upward. "Exit—or entrance—there," he said.

And looking upward, with the light trained high, Jordan saw there was a section of the "earth" ceiling to the tunnel that was square and supported with wood. He beckoned to her, lifted her, and she pushed on the area of the square.

It opened to the moonlight.

She hopped out, lay flat, and reached down for Patrick. No easy task, but he gave himself enough of an impetus so her hold allowed him to gain the traction to hike himself out. Alfie followed behind.

"Alfie," she muttered.

"I can't fly, but… I can do strange things," Alfie said. He was standing right behind her.

"He's had this secret entrance for decades, probably," Alfie said. "I think this tunnel is the lock on Ayers being the puppet master all those years. Running everything. He made a confession of sorts to Ragnar before, but now we know he was John Smith when we raided his complex. He moved on after the loss because he was never caught!"

"And then after the compound," Jordan continued, "he was quickly able to recoup his losses because he just went home every night like a good family man, slept in a warm bed, and lived the life of a businessman and husband. No one was the wiser as he put his empire back into play."

"And then he thought it might be fun to play 'Embracer' himself and bury his daughter alive," Alfie added.

"He was so cocky he exploited his wife's philanthropy to get Adam Harrison and the Krewe involved," Patrick said. "A mistake at last."

"And now he's out there somewhere," Alfie said.

"Again, every agent and officer in the area is looking for him. Alfie, we will get him," Jordan said. She looked around. The woods here were thick. And in this area of Virginia, they seemed to stretch forever. All that was beautiful about the north of the state now seemed to be working against them.

"Most important thing," Patrick said, "we have to stop the flow of money. Marie Donnell's accounts are all frozen, so he can't touch any of those. That must be why he was willing to risk entering his old house to force Amelia to transfer money to him."

"All right. So where are we right now?" Alfie muttered.

"In the woods," Jordan said dryly. She smiled at Alfie. "I don't know exactly where we are."

"Okay," Patrick said. "Let's call it in. They can coordinate our position from our phones in a matter of minutes and get agents out here. We need to get to the hospital and get with Amelia as soon as she can safely speak. We have to reverse the money flow, and our only opportunity is going to be while he's still on the run."

Jordan nodded. "You're right," she said.

She pulled out her phone and called Angela at headquarters to explain they had found Rory Ayers's escape tunnel and were in the woods perhaps a hundred yards or so from the house, in a westwardly direction, she believed. The forest was dense. Ayers was ahead of them, and might be anywhere.

Agents were on it. Angela, Megan, and the tech team would be doing everything possible to inhibit any flow of money while they waited for Amelia to be able to reverse any transactions.

"I had to stop Ayers from killing her," Jordan said.

"Of course! Jordan, if he had managed to do so, he might have shot one of you, too. Then he'd have the money and be on the run. This way, he's on the run, and we can stop the money. Jordan, never be sorry you saved a life. That's what we're supposed to do—preserve life."

"Thanks," Jordan said softly.

"Of course. And we will get him."

Jordan thanked her and ended the call, looking at Patrick.

"I suggest we take the tunnel back. I'd like to think I'm a manly man who can find his way through any forest and I'm not ready to disprove that."

The ghost of Alfie Parker chuckled. "I say we take the tunnel, too. It's important you get to the hospital and we not pretend we can read every broken branch on a tree. Besides, teamwork. Agents will be scouring the woods for Ayers. You have to get to Amelia, and the car is at the house."

Jordan found she could smile. "The tunnel it is," she said.

The three of them started back. Several agents remained at the house. Mark and Colleen had arrived, working out a grid for the search and looking for isolated neighbors and businesses in the area where Ayers might hold hostages or resort to murder to find a hideout.

"We're trying to get agents and officers out everywhere, get a warning going," Mark told them. He shook his head. "The man murdered people, orchestrated murder, and much more for years and years—and not even his wife knew what he was doing. He is the worst of the worst. It amused him to encourage others to follow their fantasies and commit murder. But here's the thing—he had finances all the while."

"And we didn't know a thing about him when I was involved!" Alfie said.

"You were amazing, Alfie. And are amazing now, still helping others."

"Hey, who knew I could be more helpful as a ghost?" Alfie said.

"You're the best," Jordan said.

"The more we're able to cut off Rory Ayers's resources, the closer we'll come to ending his reign of terror," Colleen said. "Ragnar is out there now with Red and Hugo. Jackson has a team of twenty, including the McFadden brothers, who know the area well, hunting him down."

"We'll get to the hospital," Patrick said. "We haven't heard anything more, but we'll sit and wait until Amelia can talk."

"I'll hang here, back out in the woods," Alfie said. "If he's out there, he's listening, and he'll hide. But he won't see me."

"Good plan," Patrick said.

They left. In the car, Jordan realized it was about three a.m. She should have been exhausted. She probably was, but adrenaline and anger seemed to light a fire within her. She felt as if she were wide-awake and wired with electricity.

"Hey, we're doing everything we can, and we're not alone," Patrick said.

Jordan nodded. "I can't stop wondering, what if he kills someone else?"

"You did what you had to, Jordan. Besides, he's still just one man and he knows we're looking for him. We will get him."

She smiled. Patrick was confident.

She shook her head. "What makes a mind like his tick? I mean, this guy goes beyond being horrendously ill. He is entertained by the suffering he encourages others to cause?"

"For him, it's like watching a show and believing he financed and produced the entertainment. He is a psychopath. He has absolutely no empathy within him whatsoever. But we will get him."

"I want it to be soon."

"I want it to be yesterday, but that's not the way the world works."

They had reached the hospital. After checking in with security at the entrance, they went up to speak with the doctor and nurses in the intensive care unit.

"I'm going to be moving Amelia out within the next hour or two," the doctor told them. "She's doing exceptionally well. She's a lucky woman. Fear really can cause death. But by the time she got here, her heart function was doing well again. We've done all kinds of tests. Her mental status is fine. We had her lightly sedated, but she's awake and aware now."

"We can see her?" Jordan asked. "Without endangering her health?"

The doctor nodded with a small smile. "She told me you saved her from being shot. I know she wants to see you."

They thanked him and went into the room where Amelia Ayers lay quiet and pale against the sheets.

But when she saw them, she pushed up, smiled, shook her head, and reached out.

Patrick gave Jordan a little shove. She walked to the bed and accepted the warm and almost desperate hug Amelia gave her.

"You saved my life!"

Jordan managed to ease back. "Hey, you're a beautiful life worth saving," she assured Amelia.

"But we need your help," Patrick said.

"Money," Amelia said.

"Money," Patrick agreed. "We need you to get back everything you transferred."

"I don't think it's going to be possible. Haven't you ever transferred money? They warn you that a transfer is final—"

"Not necessarily," Patrick assured her. "We're going to put you on speakerphone with Krewe headquarters. We'll get you working with Angela Hawkins Crow and my sister and the whole tech team. They'll get it back. Of course, if you're up to it."

"Oh, yes!" Tears suddenly filled Amelia's eyes. "How was I such a fool? How could he have done all those things…and I really never knew? It wasn't here or there. He was orchestrating horrible cruelties on others…and I would welcome him home, and I slept in a bed with him! I was such an idiot."

Patrick took a seat by her on the bed, taking her hand. "Amelia," he said quietly. "You are not an idiot, and you are not at fault. Your ex-husband's sickness is the kind that allows him to pretend that everything is ordinary. Killing a man is as easy as swatting a fly, except more entertaining. He has no feelings for others, and that allowed him to maintain a convincing cover. You are not at fault. But we need to move quickly now. Are you okay? We won't risk your health."

Amelia sat up straighter, showing tremendous dignity in the lift of her chin. "Get that speakerphone going. I can be strong, especially since that monster nearly killed my daughter, nearly killed me, and worse. He cost so many others their lives! Just tell me what to do!"

They set up the call.

Jordan glanced at Patrick and they both stood back, waiting as those at headquarters worked on computers, going back and forth with sign-in information and codes.

It took half an hour.

And when they were done, Amelia was elated.

Somehow, they had gotten back every cent she'd been forced to transfer to Rory Ayers.

It had been an effort for her.

And yet Amelia's coloring was improving.

Her eyes were bright.

"One should never wish evil upon another," she said. "But I pray he is caught. I pray he gets the death penalty, and it is carried out in his case. I hope there is a hell and he burns there for eternity."

"We could get some sleep," Patrick suggested. He didn't think his suggestion was going to do any good. Jordan was so determined, she almost appeared to be wired with crackling electricity.

He wished he could do something. He could almost see her mind spinning; and if he couldn't, he would have understood.

She had really been quite the heroine that night.

"I don't know about you, Patrick, but I feel like I've got to be out there with the others," she told him. "I don't think I could sleep now. But of course, you're probably worried about Megan being at that house alone. I understand—"

"Megan isn't at the house alone anymore. I just got a text from Jackson. He went and picked her up himself. They dropped Bry-bo at the Ayers house with Mark and Colleen. Megan is at headquarters and safe and sound. She was already there when they were on the phone with Amelia, entering her info into their computers, getting the necessary codes, et cetera."

"Right. Of course. I didn't realize. I mean, with the internet—"

"You can be anywhere. So, Megan is safe. We can pick up Bry-bo and get out into the woods with the others, if that's what you want."

"Thank you," she said softly.

He laughed. "You're the one who is 'Special Agent Jordan Wallace.' I'm just along for the ride."

She glanced over at him and grinned. "Patrick, I can't imagine you ever being 'along for the ride.' It amazes me you do understand a mind like the one belonging to Rory Ayers. You were wonderful with Amelia, assuring her she wasn't a fool, because he is just, by his very sickness, a skilled actor. I may have saved her life, but I think you gave her back the belief it could be worth living. Well, that and getting her money back."

He nodded. "That's going to force him to lie low until he can figure out a way to get financing."

His phone was vibrating, and he glanced at it on the console. "Jackson," he said, nodding for Jordan to answer the call.

"Hey, Jackson, it's Jordan, putting you on speaker," she said.

"There's a ranger station out in the middle of nowhere, closed at night. But it has an ATM and Rory Ayers just used a credit card belonging to the doctor he killed to escape," Jackson told them. "Not a big amount—the doc kept limits on his withdrawals. But video footage confirmed it was him. Ayers is walking around with a few hundred dollars now. The doctor was a man in his early thirties, so Ayers can't easily use his ID, being older; it's unlikely he could check into a hotel or even a bed-and-breakfast without one. Not to mention there aren't many places open at… What time is it now? About four thirty a.m. He'll be in the woods for a while, I believe. The rangers are on high alert, police are on high alert, and we've informed every main and satellite office in our own agency. He's just one man. Yes, he's pulling off an ungodly amount of carnage for just one man, but we are an army."

"That we are. We will find him."

They ended the call.

He realized Jordan was watching him.

"Not much you can buy from an oak tree or a blackbird," Patrick said. "But he went to the ATM. He had to know he would be seen on the camera."

"Right. So, hmm. What does one do in the woods with, say, four hundred dollars?"

Patrick didn't answer Jordan right away. He put in a call back to Jackson.

"Jackson, hey. Ayers is running. He broke into his ex-wife's house but didn't steal anything, didn't sit down to dinner, but rather threatened her to transfer money. Of course, he always intended to kill her. He risked a camera at an ATM. I think we need eyes on any food or drink machines by any of the ranger stations, those closed and those not. He's hungry. He's going to be looking for a snack machine or soda or water. He didn't intend to find himself stuck in the woods with nothing."

"On it," Jackson promised.

Jordan was still watching him. Then she turned away and her fingers moved feverishly over her phone in her hands.

"You're looking for snack stations out here in the state and federal lands?" he asked.

"You bet."

"Okay, as soon as—"

"Patrick, the road we're on forks up ahead. Right would

take us back to the Ayers house, left takes us to a ranger station with outdoor vending machines!"

"All right. We'll leave the car halfway and move in."

As he'd said, Patrick followed the road to the left up ahead. The road became nothing but rock and dirt quickly. It was by no means a main entrance to the wooded area. Trees and brush were thick along it, and he knew why Ayers was so fond of the forest. He could find a position. He could watch. And he could hide, and observe others, and never be seen.

And if he'd judged Ayers right, the man would be amused by any chance encounter he was able to evade. He'd enjoy laughing at law enforcement.

"Parking here, and we'll move in on foot," he told Jordan. She nodded.

When they exited the car, they both closed their doors as softly as possible.

They should have gotten Bry-bo. They needed his extra-sensory nose.

But they didn't have the dog; and while they were working a long shot, it was one that made sense.

Jordan motioned to him. She'd use the cover of the trees to the right; he would use those to the left. They both had their weapons drawn and moved along at a similar pace.

Up ahead, he saw the wooden ranger station, and to the left of it was a bank of soda and snack machines.

Someone was there. Someone carefully studying the machines.

They were still too far. They couldn't be sure the someone was Ayers; and if they shouted a warning, whoever it was could streak off into the darkness and be lost again.

Jordan looked over at him. He could barely see her; the

sun had yet to come up, and the moon offered some light but not much.

But while darkness could hide many sins, it could also be their friend.

They kept moving toward the machines.

As they did, someone else started streaking toward the person at the machines.

Someone brandishing a gun, visible because it caught a ray of moonlight and seemed to shimmer a deadly warning in the murky darkness.

"No!" Jordan shouted.

They had both taken aim at the body with the gun.

The explosions from them firing their weapons seemed as loud as a chain of fireworks in the still darkness of the forest.

CHAPTER THIRTEEN

They'd been too far away for anything accurate.

Their shots didn't go wild, though; Patrick believed they'd struck the figure with the gun, and at least, they'd scared the person enough that they tore back into the darkness and the cover of the trees.

In front of the machines, the first figure proved to be a woman. She cried out as she fell to her knees, but at least she was safe. Her would-be shooter had raced into the woods, instantly swallowed by the darkness.

And could be moving in any direction.

Jordan had already started running toward the woman. She looked back at him.

"Susie?" she wondered.

Susie? Yes, it could be.

Patrick hurried after Jordan. She reached the kneeling, wailing woman first and was already down on her knees as well.

"It's all right, it's all right. He's gone," Jordan soothed. "He's gone. You're safe. I'm with the FBI and Patrick is consulting FBI. We're here to help you. Are you Susie?"

The young woman looked up, stunned. She had huge hazel eyes and a headful of waving, auburn hair, and a thin but pretty face filled with fear and now surprise.

"I… I… Um, who are you?" she asked, as if uncertain she had heard Jordan properly.

"We're FBI. We're here to help. Was Rory Ayers trying to kill you? Are you Susie?" Jordan asked.

The young woman just stared at Jordan.

Patrick hunkered down as well, adding softly, "Susie, we're friends of Alfie Parker."

That really startled her, but she seemed to be more accepting of them. "Alfie is… Alfie is dead. And it's my fault!"

"Alfie is dead, but it's not your fault," he said. "You have helped bring down a reign of terror."

"He tried to shoot me. I knew someone was still out there. I've been in hiding, but I catch the news here and there. I knew the police were still hunting for someone, and I know he's the same someone who tried to shoot me. His name is Rory, I think. I heard Marie Donnell say the name one day. I…"

She started to sob. Jordan glanced at him and drew the young woman into her arms.

"Susie, we know you've been through hell. You somehow managed to escape, but we've also heard from others that you helped them. You took the blame for things. Susie, be proud. And trust me, Alfie is proud of you. He just wants to see you alive and well and happy."

Susie inhaled on a sob, trying to smile. "You believe he can see from above? I like to think so. But…" She shook her head. "He's still gone. And that awful man… He got away because of me."

"Susie, we have agents covering the woods, and we've cut off all his resources," Patrick assured her.

Susie smiled bitterly. "I know Alfie thought he could stop it all once. He paid with his life. And now that man is still out there." She laughed nervously. "Friends were nervous when I said I could hide in the woods. The woods are full of dangerous creatures. But there is no more dangerous creature than that man. He snaps his fingers to order death and destruction. He delights in others killing for him. There is no bear, snake, coyote, wasp, bobcat—you name it!—no animal in the woods more dangerous than that man."

Patrick straightened, looking around. "We need to get Susie to safety," he said.

"There is no safety," she whispered. "He hates me; he'd risk anything to kill me."

"There is safety, trust me. We're going to get you to our headquarters. No one has ever breached our headquarters."

Patrick realized he had used the word *our*.

Of course, he was going to stay. He didn't regret the time he'd spent working in Pennsylvania; he'd saved lives, he knew.

But he also knew it was time for him to come here. The work was just right, and he was just right for the work.

And he meant what he said to Susie.

"Come on. Let's get back to the car," he said.

"He'll follow us. If he sees you're with me, he'll take shots at you from the bushes. You won't know he's there," Susie said worriedly.

"He can try," Jordan said. She drew Susie gently to her feet. "I don't think he's particularly fond of me either, or Patrick, for that matter. We kept him from killing his ex-wife, which meant we kept him from his money. Hard to hire people to terrorize others when you're broke."

"But—"

"Susie," Patrick said firmly. "We're going to be fine. Trust me. You'll be between Jordan and me, and we are pretty good at slipping through the woods. Not to mention he took off when we shot at him. He's not stupid. He knows they can track a location through our phones, and we've already called it in to our headquarters. There are agents, police, and rangers racing here now—not to mention we'd already told others about this bank of vending machines. Ayers will be heading as far away as he can get."

"All right. We should hurry!" Susie said.

Patrick nodded to Jordan over Susie's head. They both drew their weapons, secured Susie between them, and started at a brisk pace to the car. They kept a sharp lookout all the while.

But nothing happened. They reached the car, and Jordan slid into the back with Susie while Patrick flicked the ignition and they started out of the woods.

It was a few minutes before Susie let out a sigh of relief.

"You—you were right," she told them.

"Why does he hate you so much?" Jordan asked her.

Susie shrugged. "Many things. Of course, he thinks it was my fault—which I guess it was—when Alfie got everyone to invade the compound. Then..." She paused, wincing. "He had just kidnapped me and taken me back to that compound, but the fellow watching me was shot. I managed to get away and hide for a very long time, but then I was snatched again because I tried to get near one of the compounds. Then they started transferring people around." She hesitated. "At the old mansion by the cemetery, he found out I was writing notes on headstones, using rocks to etch words. I don't know why

I wasn't killed then. But he did kill people there, or had them killed, for any small infraction. Or because their loved ones in his 'hire' didn't do what they were ordered to do. If they failed to obey, to perform, to kill for him, he had them killed. It's crazy. He's one sick, sick man."

"Yes," Jordan agreed softly.

"But, Susie, never blame yourself for anything," Patrick told her. "His sickness is not your fault. We told you—others have told us you've saved them from retribution. You've been incredibly brave and resolute."

"Maybe not brave enough," she murmured. She cleared her throat. "You have invaded a number of the places where he was keeping people?"

"Yes. And we have your child," Jordan told her. "He's safe."

Patrick was driving, but he saw Susie's expression through the mirror. She was stunned at first, and then she burst into tears.

"I had to ask Connie to claim him. I was… I was always in trouble, always afraid."

"But how did you hide with the baby?" Jordan asked her.

Susie's sobbing stopped long enough for her to let out a bitter laugh. "Very carefully! And when I was swept up again, I had to pretend I'd just been watching him. All of the people Ayers lured into service were not the brightest! No one questioned it when we were being shuffled around. I can't tell you how hard it is to deny your own child when you have to because… You have to know what went on! It wasn't past Ayers to kill a child, even a toddler."

Patrick glanced back, aware Jordan was looking at him.

Aware of her feelings.

They had to stop Ayers. Neither of them had come across

a greater monster. Ever. And with a prayer, they never would again.

"Jordan, we need to let them know we're almost at head-quarters," he said, glancing back at her.

Jordan nodded, took out her phone, and quickly called. He could hear she reached Angela, and he knew Angela would have someone meet them in the parking garage.

In no time, they were there. And, as promised, Angela, Axel Tiger, and Bruce McFadden greeted them.

Patrick knew there was no way anyone might have breached the security of the Krewe parking garage, but he'd wanted Susie to feel safe enough to get out of the car.

"Agents I'd trust with my life anytime," Jordan assured Susie as they stopped at the office entrance from the garage and saw the waiting team. "Come on," she said, as she stepped out of the car and reached for Susie's hand.

Susie accepted it and stepped from the car, where she was greeted warmly and with gratitude.

Ayers was still at large.

But Susie was safe. They could tell Alfie she was safe.

She could be reunited with her child.

Not a victory for them, but not a total loss. Two loves snatched from the deadly intent of Rory Ayers.

He left the others to park the car. When he made his way back to the offices, Susie was already in with Angela and Jackson.

Arrangements were being made for Connie to bring her child to her.

Susie would be calling Krewe headquarters home until Rory Ayers was brought in. There was no possibility of an "if" in the case of Rory Ayers.

He had to be apprehended. Had to be.

Meeting up with Jordan as she leaned against the wall by Jackson's office, Patrick saw the exhaustion in her eyes and he smiled.

"Home. Not home, safe-house home. Sleep. For real, we have to trust others, and get some sleep," he said.

She smiled at him. "Not yet."

"Not yet?" he asked.

"They're bringing Connie here with Susie's little boy, Benjamin. He'll get to stay here with her. Patrick, I have to see the two of them together again!"

He nodded and agreed to wait because they had found Susie. And Susie's child was coming for an amazing reunion.

"Well, let's sit down somewhere. Before we fall down. Did you call Colleen, Mark, or Ragnar yet?"

"Oh, my God! We've been so busy, I forgot. They're still with Alfie. We have to let them know right away," Jordan said. "Alfie has to know right away."

"On it," Patrick said, pulling out his phone.

He called his sister. Colleen quickly answered and he explained everything that was going on. Colleen was incredulous and grateful and thankfully still with Alfie. He could hear the excitement going on all around her.

"One of us will bring Alfie in so he can see her for himself."

"How late do you think you can stay out there?" he asked her.

He could hear her soft sigh over the line.

"We're probably going to have to give it up. We're getting so tired we're pretty useless. Jackson has a ton of people working out here. We have local police, and still, nothing. Here's the problem—Rory Ayers spent half his life in this area, killing and supervising murders and carrying out every illicit business known to man. So he knows the terrain. And as good as many of us are—including the dogs—the man knows how to evade capture. We may be at this awhile."

"That won't matter—we will get him. It's a matter of time."

"Time with that man is scary. He kills without blinking. Anyway, we'll be in soon. And what are you doing? You should be sleeping. Some of us have to be functioning again soon!"

"We're just waiting for Connie to bring Benjamin here. They're being escorted by US marshals and we want to see the reunion."

"Of course!"

He ended the call and suggested they wait in one of the conference rooms, which they did. Jordan was startled when he suddenly swept her off her feet and laid her out on one of the tables.

"Hey, you can kind of rest this way."

She laughed. "How about a pillow?"

"How about a chair cushion?"

"That will do."

He found a chair cushion for her and one for himself. Taking a seat in a chair near her head, he rested his own.

They both fell asleep.

He woke when the conference door opened, and Susie rushed in holding her toddler in her arms, with tears streaking down her face.

Jordan woke, too, blinking furiously as she rolled off the table and to her feet, ready to accept the crushing hug she received from Susie with the little boy between them.

Patrick was next.

"Thank you, thank you, thank you! I didn't dare believe. I've lived with fear and loss for so long, I don't think I even remembered what this kind of wonder could feel like!" Susie said. "Thank you, thank you—"

"Susie, Susie, we're delighted," Patrick said. "This work… what we do. When we see someone alive and well and as happy as you are, well, that's the greatest reward in the world."

Jordan, still blinking away sleep, smiled at that. "And Alfie will be…"

She was still half-asleep, Patrick thought, speaking without realizing how what she was about to say might be perceived.

But she caught herself quickly. "I mean, Alfie would be so happy. And we've talked, so I… I believe…"

"I believe maybe he is with us still, in some way," Susie said softly.

As if on cue, the door to the conference room opened. Patrick had to wonder if Alfie had learned to open that kind of a door and was going to appear in an amazing physical manifest.

It was Colleen, happily greeting them all, seeing Susie, her son, and saying just how happy she was.

Alfie was there also. He stepped in behind her.

If a ghost could have cried, he would have been shedding copious tears. Patrick felt Alfie's hug of appreciation before he moved on to Jordan and then just sat to stare at Susie and her little boy.

A few minutes later, Jackson stuck his head in the room.

"People, it will be light soon. We've got teams out, cops have teams out, you name it. But I think you'd better get some sleep if you want to get back out there tomorrow yourselves— sorry, more like out there *later today* yourselves."

"Right," Jordan said. She turned to Susie. "We'll see you sometime tomorrow. You will be here and you will be safe. We'll be back looking for Rory Ayers in a few hours. Susie, we will find him," she said with assurance and determination.

Susie hugged her again, and then threw her arms around Patrick and then Colleen. Patrick went out to the hallway first; someone had to make the move.

Alfie was behind him.

"I'll be here tonight," the ghost told him. "I... I'll be watching over her. I know she's safe here. I just... I worried for so long. But now she's here. And she's okay. And you are... well... Just thank you. Thank you. How did you find her?"

"She was hiding in the woods and trying to get water out of a machine." He hesitated. "Ayers found her first. We were a fair distance away, but when we fired shots, he took off. We saved Susie, but we missed Ayers. We're grateful, of course, to have found Susie. That she's alive. But we'll be more grateful when we get Rory Ayers."

Alfie shook his head. "If ever evil was personified, it's that man. This is years and years he's gone on. It's almost as if he's a demon straight from hell. Maybe he'll go on forever."

"He isn't a demon. He's a man. Flesh and blood. And this time, we've stopped his money flow. Alfie, we'll get him."

"Susie won't really be safe until you do. Not to mention the dozens of others he may hurt or kill," Alfie said.

"We are all aware. Alfie, between Jackson and the police and other agencies, people are searching for him around the clock. We will find him."

"What about Amelia Ayers?"

"She's at the hospital. And she is being guarded. Alfie, I know things happen. But Jackson is on top of this. I promise you Amelia Ayers is being guarded by the best."

Jordan came out to the hallway, smiling at Alfie and then at Patrick. Her smile was beautiful, but she looked exhausted.

"We have to get some sleep," Patrick said quietly.

"Oh, right. Yes, of course. Go. Please, go, sleep. I will be here," Alfie said. He shrugged with humor. "Okay, not that I can do much, but, at least around here, I can warn people!"

"All right. We're out of here," Patrick said. He slipped his arm around Jordan's shoulders and led the way down the hall and out to the parking garage.

"Well," Jordan muttered in the car, "that was a long day."

"And that's an understatement."

"I know, and still—"

"You're going to tell me you don't think you'll sleep until we find Ayers. Trust me. I have a feeling you're going to fall asleep in the car."

"I will not!" Jordan protested. "But—"

"We will sleep. And when we wake up, we'll be in better shape, and we'll get back out there on the hunt."

She shook her head. "How does he do it, Patrick? He seems to have the ability to disappear when it should be impossible. Yes, forests are huge. But they've had the dogs out looking for him—Red and Hugo and others. And he eludes everyone—"

"He has hiding places," he said.

"In forestland? Some of it state, some of it federal?" she asked.

"Ayers has spent his life bribing people and threatening them. He's also a smart man and overly confident—which sometimes works. The forests are old, and through the years, Ayers has made a point of finding out everything about them. Exploring them, if you will, for his personal body dumps."

"And yet Colleen and Mark were able to rescue Deirdre," Jordan muttered. She sat up suddenly. "Deirdre! Is she—"

"Under police guard, I can assure you," he said. "Jackson and Angela would have seen to that right away."

She had her phone out.

"Don't trust me, eh?" he teased.

"I'm just going to make sure!"

He listened, smiling, as she called Jackson. She spoke with him briefly, thanked him, and ended the call.

She looked at Patrick.

"Guess what? Deirdre is being protected."

He smiled. "Oh, ye of little faith," he teased.

"Okay, okay."

"Remember—"

"We're a team. No man is an island. Yada yada yada."

"Exactly!"

She leaned back, closed her eyes with a slight smile on her lips.

He drove in silence and didn't realize until he reached the safe house that she had fallen asleep. He hated waking her.

He couldn't leave her in the car.

He did his best to reach in and lift her out without waking her. He managed to get her seat belt off and her into his arms, but then her eyes opened. She just smiled, tightening her arms around his neck.

"I wasn't really sleeping. Just too tired right now to walk in," she said.

"Hmm."

There was a car parked down the street. He could see there were two people in it. The man in the driver's seat saw him looking and lifted a hand.

Police presence, he thought. He lifted a hand in return, mentally determining he would still verify it was officers outside the house.

Of course, when he keyed in the entry to the gate and then the door, Bry-bo greeted them.

The best alarm that could be had at any price, he thought.

Megan was still awake as well.

Seeing the dog and Megan, Jordan slipped out of his arms, embarrassed.

"Hey, I'm so proud of you all!" Megan said, hurrying toward them, oblivious to the position Jordan had been in or any embarrassment she might have felt. Megan hugged Patrick and then Jordan, saying, "You people are incredible! I feel like—"

"Megan, what you do is every bit as important as being in the field. Plus, you're an editor. And a writer, too, of course."

"Hmm. Not so sure about writing a book on this. It's aged me a century, I think."

"Maybe fifty years," Patrick teased.

"Well, I can't wait to meet her. You found Susie! Alfie must be overjoyed."

"He is happy, yes, of course," Jordan said. "But—"

"Ayers is still out there," Megan said, pursing her lips and shaking her head. "I know. He can't stay out there forever, but I think he might stay that way for a while. I'm sure he has stockpiles of supplies in different places deep in the woods, and he'll lie low now," Megan said. "It will be hard for him, but think about it. In one way or another, he's been an active criminal for years and years. He had his wife to hide behind and he doesn't have that now. His deeds are known. But he's a survivor."

"He is," Jordan said. "But is he capable of lying low and hiding that long?"

"And how many innocents might he encounter who disappear only to be found years from now buried in a marsh?" Megan added.

"We have to get him and we will," Patrick said with determination. "But now we have to sleep. Or our minds won't function at all."

He shrugged, gave his sister a quick hug, patted Bry-bo and assured him he was a great dog, then followed Jordan into the bedroom.

She had fallen on the bed, fully dressed. Her eyes were closed, and he found a blanket to throw over her. Her eyes opened.

"Hell of a romantic, huh?" she asked softly.

"Go to sleep." He gave her a quick kiss on the forehead and told her, "You'll be better at *everything* after some sleep."

He crawled in beside her, thinking that as tired as he was, he was going to lie awake staring at the ceiling.

And he did stare at the ceiling for a few minutes.

And then he wondered what he could do that might help them fathom where to find one man in endless acres of trails and trees.

It was true. If he were just close to the man...

He slept.

He woke suddenly, aware the day was full-on. At his side, Jordan had awakened.

"I think I've figured out what to do," she told him. "I may have a plan—a plan that can trap Rory Ayers!"

CHAPTER FOURTEEN

Patrick frowned and looked at Jordan. She smiled.

"I think my plan could work," she said. "But first, if we suspect Rory Ayers is something of a master of disguise, we should have Maisie do some artist sketches, creating some of the many looks the man might try. Bald, a ton of hair, glasses, nose putty... If he's ever going to come out of the woods, he won't want to be recognizable."

"Okay, we can do that. I was also wondering if she should maybe talk to Alfie again," Patrick said. "About Susie—and her little boy."

"You think Alfie might know who the father is? It could be anyone, Patrick. Maybe Susie doesn't even know. That poor girl. The trouble she got into, and the trouble she escaped."

"True, but still, I can't help but wonder if maybe..." His voice trailed.

Jordan stared at him with horror. "Oh, no. No, no, no. You think Rory Ayers might be the father of Susie's child?"

He shrugged. "I don't know. We know Ayers hates Susie

and wants her dead, but we don't know just what their relationship might have been. She escaped and was headed toward a decent life with Alfie's help. But Ayers dragged her back in, or had her dragged back in. Clearly, there was something about her. I don't think she had the boy in captivity—and I don't think Ayers ever found out she had a child. Maybe with how often she was shuffled around, her captors lost track of the fact that she had a kid with her, lost track of who the kid belonged to. Otherwise, Connie wouldn't have gotten away with covering for her to keep Benjamin safe."

"It's possible. We can look into it, talk to Alfie, and maybe Connie again. Maybe she knows who the boy's father is."

"But back to your plan to capture Ayers," Patrick said. "What do you have in mind?"

Jordan smiled. "I pretend to be Susie."

He shook his head. "Jordan, I don't know…"

"Patrick, listen, we can't jeopardize Susie. We can use her as bait, but I'm an agent. I've been undercover several times. I'm good at it and you know it."

"I know you've done it. And yes, you're a good agent. Still—"

"That's where you come in." She smiled. Megan can stay on top of the money trails while you, Colleen, Ragnar, Mark, and the dogs work the search area. You will have the dogs. The gift of scent. And you'll have Colleen—the gift of hearing—and yourself—that of mind reading."

"And where will you be?" Patrick demanded suspiciously.

"I'm certain Ayers knows Alfie is dead, and I believe he knows the connection Alfie had with Susie, and that Susie would probably visit his grave in the cemetery. That might even be where they got her the second time after she'd been in hiding so successfully." She took a deep breath because he was frowning so fiercely, clearly not yet convinced. "We carefully let Marie Donnell know we have found Susie, and mention that she goes to the cemetery often, and we tell Amelia. I don't think Rory can get to her at the hospital, but I'm willing to bet he'll make a try," Jordan explained.

"If he steps into the hospital, he'll be arrested on the spot."

"Not if he's changed his appearance. If we're assuming he has hideouts in the woods, we have to assume his little caches are well stocked. He could have face putty, all kinds of materials to change his appearance. Or maybe he'll find some other lackeys to do his bidding. It's possible we haven't found every house where he's been keeping prisoners."

"There are a zillion 'maybes' to everything you're saying," Patrick said firmly. "And if you think I'm going to be somewhere else while you're standing there at Alfie's grave like a giant target, you're crazy."

"But you're the mind reader!" she said. "You have to be out there—"

"You just said it yourself; he might be at the hospital. Jordan, he might be anywhere!" Patrick said.

"I think this could work. I think he still wants Susie, and if I pretend to be her, I think we can trap him," she said, her determination just as strong.

"All right, here's the deal. Ragnar, Mark, and Colleen get out into the forest with the dogs. They'll talk among themselves about Susie saying she needs to come in, we'll help her, we're afraid she'll go back to the cemetery. If he overhears, he'll go there. And at the cemetery, he won't have the cover of his tunnels and the trees, though neither will we. But we will get Amelia Ayers to talk about how she heard us talking about a Susie, and how sad it all was, and how Susie had loved and admired Sergeant Alfie Parker. We also let that information get to Marie Donnell in case she does still have a way of communicating with him. She's afraid for her life as long as he's out there, and she might want to redeem herself somehow. Still, none of this is a guarantee."

"But it's worth a try," Jordan said.

"But I will be with you. That's not up for debate."

"Well, you can't be seen with me…"

He smiled. "I don't need to be. I'll be close by. And I'll be searching for the sick and demented mind of Rory Ayers," Patrick said. "If he shows, I believe he will try to kill you. He'd kill you just as quick as Susie if he were to see through the ruse. I'll have to know if he's close, because he might take a potshot. Though, honestly, if he had the choice, I think he wouldn't just shoot at Susie; I think he'd like to make her suffer. He's bitter about her. And bitter about you, too," he reminded her.

She shook her head. "He won't come anywhere close if he thinks I'm the one there. He knows I'd be accompanied by other agents and police. But if he believes Susie has refused or eluded our protection and is back out there, determined to pray at Alfie's grave, well, it's possible he'd take that opportunity to kill her. Patrick, we don't have anything better," she said. "Trust me. Trust me as a capable agent."

He was silent a few minutes and then he smiled, reaching out to touch her face. "I do trust you," he said softly. "And everything about you is why…" He paused to take a breath. "Why I've fallen in love with you. And that just makes me want to do everything in my power to protect you."

"You *will* do everything in your power to protect me," she vowed, touching his cheek in turn. "You will be with me."

He pulled out his phone, and she wasn't sure what he was doing at first, but to her surprise, he was putting her plan into motion by calling Jackson and then Colleen. He waved a hand in the air to her and covered the phone for a minute, saying, "Hop in the shower. I'd love to join you, but I don't trust myself in the shower with you and we're in a hurry!"

She smiled and then rushed to shower as swiftly as humanly possible. He showered as she got ready, and in a matter of minutes, they were dressed, armed, and ready to go. In the hall, Megan met them with two thermoses of coffee.

"Jackson called," she explained. Her hand was on Bry-bo's head. "I'm back on money; Colleen, Mark, and Ragnar have already left for headquarters. Jackson has Maisie working on sketches of how Rory Ayers might disguise himself. They have maps of the area of the forest all the way north through the city to the cemetery. Once Maisie has produced her sketches, she'll help turn you into Susie," she said.

Bry-bo barked.

"This dog is staying right here, Megan," he said.

She smiled. "I knew you'd say that. And I'm fine with it. I know there are agents outside. Don't worry. I'm good."

"No, you're incredible," Jordan replied.

"I don't know about that, but thank you—I'll take it!" Megan said.

"We're out of here," Patrick said, giving her a quick hug. "Bry-bo, guard Megan."

Bry-bo barked his agreement.

They were quickly in the car and on their way to headquarters.

When they arrived, Angela told them Colleen, Mark, and Ragnar were back searching the forest area where Rory Ayers had last been seen. She suggested they head to the first conference room, where Maisie was using a basic computer image of Rory Ayers and showing the different ways he might change

VOICE OF FEAR   241

his appearance using longer hair, a bald look, beards and mustaches, and even prosthetics for the cheeks and nose.

Her work was wonderful, and they thanked her, as did Jackson, who was getting the images out to law enforcement as they were completed.

"We need to speak with Alfie," Patrick said.

"Maybe I'll go speak with Susie while you're speaking with Alfie. Time is of the essence."

"Susie is in the first guest room with Benjamin," Angela said. "Alfie was in my office, helping me search records."

Patrick thanked her and started for Angela's office. Jordan went ahead and moved past the conference room to one of the two guest rooms they kept. The rooms were sometimes used by agents when they were working around the clock, and were kept ready for those guests who needed the utmost protection at all times.

Like Susie.

Jordan tapped on the door, and Susie answered it quickly. When she stepped in, Susie hugged her fiercely. "Sorry! Still can't help myself."

"A hug is never a bad thing to me," Jordan assured her. She saw Benjamin on the floor, cross-legged and playing with a set of large plastic blocks.

"I can't believe I'm back with him," Susie whispered.

"Susie, I don't want to jerk you around or play games," Jordan told her. "But you know and we know we must stop Rory Ayers, and to do that, we need to know about Benjamin's dad. Specifically, we're wondering if his father might be..."

"Who? Rory Ayers?" Susie said. "I might have slit my wrists had that been the case. Oh, Jordan, no. I think his dad was a young British fellow who thought his American friends had brought him to an upper-class establishment. I assume he happily returned home to Britain shortly after. I know he was the father because I knew I wasn't pregnant before him. I'd just been dragged back in. And soon after, knowing I was pregnant, I made my escape."

"Where did you have the baby?" Jordan asked.

"In a hospital—with fake ID procured through a friend. When I left, I spent time working and at the halfway house until I was scooped up. But I'd met Connie before and she had Benjamin. He was safe even though I knew I was walking on thin ice every day. No. Benjamin's father was nice, kind, funny... He came and went like a blur. Feels like a lifetime ago."

"In some ways, it was. And now you're safe—you and Benjamin," Jordan said. She gave the young woman another hug. "We will find Ayers," she vowed softly.

"I believe you," Susie told her, a smile on her lips and tears in her eyes.

Jordan left her and hurried back down the hall to the conference room where Maisie had just finished with her computer images.

"Want to help turn me into Susie?" Jordan asked her.

"Sure," Maisie said, grinning. "Wig first, and that's the easiest. We'll need clothing that belongs to Susie. I don't think we need to worry about contacts. No one is going to let Ayers get that close. I'm not sure what disguise materials we have on hand. I may have to pop out for a few minutes to find the right hair—you definitely need the right hair!"

Jordan smiled and thanked her, just as Patrick walked into the conference room.

"Alfie doesn't know who the father is," Patrick said. "But I did tell him about our plan. He's worried about you, Jordan. As am I."

"It's not Ayers," Jordan confirmed. "Susie thinks it was some British guy she was with. Nice fellow, by the sound of it, probably back overseas. And I appreciate Alfie's concern, but I'm a trained agent. This isn't my first undercover assignment."

"Maybe I should be someone else, too," he said. "That way, if he is watching, if he has others watching…nobody will recognize me."

"Not a bad idea," Jordan said. "Maisie thinks she needs to find me really good hair if I'm going to play Susie."

"I'll head out right now," Maisie said. "Be back in thirty—the shop is close by."

"Maybe we can look at their online catalog and have something rushed over," Patrick suggested.

"Good idea," Maisie said. "That way, I can get started on makeup."

She saved the last of her pictures on the computer and keyed in the shop. She quickly found the wig she wanted and pulled out her phone to call and ask about delivery.

"I'll go get something of Susie's for you to wear," Patrick said. "Maisie, see if you can get me a funky, old rock-star wig and beard. Might as well have some fun with this."

"Of course," Maisie said.

Patrick left the room and Maisie looked at Jordan. "Will this work?" she asked.

"I don't know. I know several times, Susie managed to just disappear into the woods for months. But we know Ayers is capable of almost anything, and he's been killing for years. Our best shot is to lure him out. Hopefully, it works."

"It will as long as you don't give up," Maisie said. "Jordan, you've played roles before, and you've done well. You can do this. I know that you can."

Jordan grinned. "Let's hope. I believe I can be Susie. And

we can make Ayers believe he can find her if he ventures into the cemetery."

Jackson stepped into the room. "Maisie, your images are already working. We just got a call from the hospital. He appeared there as a doctor with his hair pulled under a cap and a mask on his face. One of the officers on duty went to question him, and he managed to disappear. He'd walked into Amelia's room, but was stopped before he could get to her bedside. He pretended to need to answer a Code Red that was being called. They got close to him quickly, so we're not sure if he would have heard anything Amelia had been saying at the time."

"We're sure it was Ayers?" Jordan asked.

"Not certain," Jackson said. "But a car was stolen off one of the hiking paths in the forest near Amelia's house. It was found abandoned about a block from the hospital. Maybe—just maybe—this crazy plan of yours will work, Jordan."

She winced. "He's out of the woods, then."

"Or back into them. The hospital, Amelia's house, acres and acres of woods—all are within an hour's drive even in this area. Hospital security is checking the lot and employees are being asked to confirm their vehicles haven't been stolen."

"Anything missing?" Jordan asked.

"Not from the hospital. But there's plenty of on-street parking near enough, so…"

Jackson shrugged, studying her. Patrick reappeared, carrying a small pile of Susie's clothing, what looked to be jeans, a T-shirt, and a hoodie.

"You do not have to do this, Jordan," Jackson told her, eyeing the pile of clothing. "We have people everywhere. While you've been right about the man changing his appearance to get where he wants to be, there's no guarantee we can lure him to the cemetery."

"I know. But as long as he's out there, so many lives are in danger. This is a wild card. But I think we need to play it," she said.

"Besides, you won't be alone. I'll be there," Patrick said quietly.

"All right, then, go forth and conquer," Jackson said. He turned and left them.

Patrick handed the pile of clothes to Jordan and told her, "Susie knows what you're going to do."

She shrugged. "I guess asking for her clothing might have been a giveaway," she said dryly.

"She's not happy."

"No one is happy. But we must stop Ayers. Come on, Patrick. You know as well as I do that lives are at risk every moment he's out there."

"I know. You're right. I'm going to see what spare clothing we have in back, anything to go with my cool wig," he said, smiling at Maisie.

"You're gonna love it," she told him.

He laughed. "No doubt I will. And, Maisie, amazing work. You may have already stopped the man from killing his ex-wife."

"If so, I'm grateful," she told him.

Patrick nodded and left the conference room.

"My lovely, take a seat," Maisie said. "Let me see what magic I can create while we wait for your hair!"

Jordan sat as Maisie directed her and waited for the artist to retrieve her makeup chest from her office. She wouldn't need a lot of makeup. Susie didn't wear much—at least, not at this point in her life. But she would work with little things, and change the shape of her features with contouring. Jordan's brows had an arch; Susie's were more rounded. Maisie's artistic eye would pick up on the little things that hers did not.

Maisie returned with a makeup mirror and her box of magic. She and Jordan chatted while Maisie made subtle changes to Jordan's appearance.

There was a tap at the conference room door, and Jordan turned slightly to see as Maisie went to answer it.

"Wig here," a man said.

For a minute, Jordan frowned. There was something familiar about him. He had curly brown hair beneath a baseball cap and a neatly trimmed beard and mustache.

She gasped, rising from the chair.

"Patrick?" she said.

Maisie laughed. "Hey, that is good, my friend!" she told Patrick.

"Thanks," he said, grinning and producing a large hatbox. "But that's because you are darned good at selecting. And here is Jordan's 'Susie' hair."

"Perfect," Maisie said. "We're about done with makeup. Let's see what the hair will do."

She took the wig from the box, secured Jordan's hair with the net provided, and set the wig on her head.

"Good, good, good!" she exclaimed.

Jordan stared at her own reflection. Up close, she was still Jordan. But from a bit of a distance, anyone might mistake her for Susie. And she knew she was right when Patrick came to stand behind her. "From a distance, yes," he said.

"That's all that we need," Jordan reminded him.

"Jackson and Angela both have to see this," Maisie said proudly. "Hang on just a minute."

She left the room, and Patrick reminded Jordan, "Don't forget, Ayers is also a master at playing this kind of a game."

"Well, I don't intend to get up close and friendly with anyone at the cemetery. Dead or alive," Jordan said, trying for some levity.

Except she hadn't realized Maisie had left the door open, and Alfie was standing there.

"You know, Jordan, he can still take a shot at you from a distance," Alfie warned her. He sank into a chair at the conference table, looking at her. "I'm a ghost. I can't really help anyone. But I can tell you I'm worried sick."

"So am I," Patrick said.

"Oh, come on, guys!" Jordan protested.

"Good thing you're being provided with this," Jackson said, appearing in the doorway with Angela right behind him. He produced a wad of material. "It's the latest in body armor. Material is thinner than most, but just as protective—or so say the reviews."

"And as always, we have to hope a man with decent aim doesn't go for the head. We have nothing for that," Angela added dryly. "It's something, anyway."

"Thank you. I know you'll have a pack of agents in addition to Patrick nearby," Jordan said. She looked at Patrick. "We should do this thing."

"Patrick, you look like you lost your rock band," Jackson told him.

"That's what I was going for," Patrick said. "Secretly, I always wanted to be a rock drummer."

"There you go," Jordan said. "Read the minds of the audience—and duck before the tomatoes fly!"

"Hey," he protested, grinning. "Anyway, we look good. Thanks to Maisie. But we should get going."

"I'm coming, too," Alfie said. "I know these guys will take good care of Susie."

"By the way, we had another report on a man who resembled one of Maisie's images," Jackson said.

"Hospital? Forest?" Jordan asked.

"In between—and near a stolen and abandoned car," Jackson said. "I've sent the location to your phones. No telling which way he's going now if he is, indeed, Rory Ayers."

"Let's do this," Jordan said.

"We're on our way," Patrick said. "And we're not taking my car; we'll do a company vehicle and keep it far from the cemetery."

Jackson nodded. "Patrick, stay in contact. I already have people in the cemetery. We had the proper people unlock a few society mausoleums so they can be completely discreet. We'll let the operation go until closing hours. And we'll try it again tomorrow if need be. After that—"

He paused because his phone was softly ringing and vibrating in his pocket.

Jackson answered, listened grimly, and then thanked the caller.

They all looked at him.

"Go. Get out there. Jordan is right. Whatever it takes, we must bring him in. He just hijacked another car, but this time he threw the owner out of the passenger's seat. The man is clinging to life in a hospital just south of the Beltway."

Alfie swore softly.

"I have Axel Tiger and Bruce McFadden at the cemetery. They are situated in mausoleums already, and I have a place set for you, Patrick," Jackson said. He handed them tiny earbuds and mics. "Keep in contact. I have others in cars nearby on the street."

"I have a feeling this is going to be close and intimate, but all support is appreciated," Patrick said.

"Will do," Jordan said.

"Operation Susie under way," Patrick said, and he preceded Jordan out of the conference room and into the parking garage.

They were playing a wild card.

But it had to be played.

Alfie had followed them, and as they reached the car, he said, "This needs to work! Anyone living and breathing is at risk when Ayers is around. It's time we stop him for good!"

He crawled into the back seat of the car.

Jordan glanced at Patrick and he nodded as they both climbed in.

It was time for the charade to begin.

CHAPTER FIFTEEN

There was something about a cemetery as the day passed by, as the sun fell in the sky and the colors of the sunset turned from streaks of pastel beauty to deeper shades of mauve and gray.

The place was old, dating back to the early days of settlement, with many a grave remaining for a Revolutionary soldier. That allowed for the feeling of the past to have settled in and over everything. Tombs and mausoleums were covered with all manner of growth, and different manners of funerary art—from skulls and crossbones to angels and flowers—were scattered here, there, and about.

The Virginia Division of Capitol Police was the oldest department in the nation, having its beginnings date back to 1618, formed in Jamestown. No graves dated back that far, but there were stones—almost illegible—that dated to the early 1700s.

Patrick and Jordan entered the cemetery during opening hours. Still, the sun was falling, night was coming, and an eerie aura seemed to have settled over the place.

He was surprised to note the strange, creepy feel that had settled over the graveyard; he saw and talked to ghosts on a daily basis and dealt with something far stranger—the hauntings of many living minds. He had spent his life in law enforcement. He didn't tend to be afraid of much, and he wasn't afraid that night.

Maybe it was just the coming night here. He felt the weight of history, of all those who had lived and died, struggled with the problems, the pits and perils of life, and finally, moved on.

The cemetery still had a smattering of visitors as it edged toward closing time. A tour group was standing around an area that contained the graves of Revolutionary soldiers. A few couples were moving about. A family was at the grave of a fallen police officer, laying flowers on the stone.

"I don't like this," Patrick admitted.

Jordan glanced at him. "Night is coming. Ayers won't be obvious. We have contact with support at all times."

"The problem with Ayers is we don't know what to expect."

"And that's why we have faith in each other, remember?" she asked him.

He nodded. But he couldn't help thinking they'd somehow missed something.

Rory Ayers was a survivor. He would do whatever it took to get what he wanted.

He felt something on his shoulder—nothing real and solid, but rather a sensation. Alfie. He'd set his arm around Patrick and there was just a feeling. Patrick was never sure if it was a feeling of hot or cold, but something alerted him to Alfie's touch.

"You're not afraid of ghosts, right?" Alfie teased.

"Nope. But I *am* afraid of Ayers," Patrick said.

"I'm sorry you two have to split up. He's not going to try to kill Susie if she's hanging with a cool rocker."

"I'm not so sure that's true. He will kill anyone. Won't bother him in the least to kill a cool rocker right along with Susie," Patrick said.

"It could be a long time," Jordan said softly. "I plan to just kneel at the grave."

"And I have a mausoleum to hang out in," Patrick said. "Jackson has made arrangements. And don't forget there are other agents in the area. We're well covered."

"Wonder if you'll be hanging with any of my friends," Alfie said.

"I'm in the Manville mausoleum. There's a stained-glass circular window in the rear right over the altar. Hopefully, nobody minds me standing on the old altar to keep my eyes on 'Susie' as she kneels at the grave."

"I'm not so sure Henry Manville will like it," Alfie teased.

"Hey, I heard no one has been interred there since 1892," Patrick said.

"I believe that to be true. Doesn't mean Henry isn't hanging around. But I'm kidding, of course. Henry would be pleased to aid in the capture of a criminal in any way. He was a cop."

"Thanks. I'll try to have a conversation with him," Patrick said.

"I'll introduce you," Alfie said. He glanced at Jordan as Susie and shook his head. "Actually, no, I won't. I may not be a bulletproof vest, but I'll be right next to Jordan, stopping whatever the hell I can."

"Thanks, Alfie," Jordan said. "Well, we should split up," she told Patrick.

"All right. I'm in the Manville mausoleum; Bruce McFadden is in the Nicholson mausoleum, and Axel Tiger is in the Mountjoy mausoleum. You are surrounded."

"Hey, I've got the best watching my back. I'm going to be okay," Jordan said.

"Hey, yourself. I have agreed with all this—doesn't mean I have to like it," Patrick said.

"Right," Alfie said. "So, act like you are friends saying goodbye to one another. Give Jordan a friendly hug. Don't get carried away—give her a *friendly* hug."

Patrick gave Alfie a frown and did as instructed—first giving Jordan a hug, then moving across the cemetery as if he was approaching the western gate.

Jordan moved toward the section dedicated to the police officers who had served in Virginia from early times to the present.

It was easy to slip around and into the mausoleum. Jackson had seen to it the iron bars closing the burial chamber had been left open after having arranged with the cemetery management to stage his people throughout.

The Manville tomb had wall niches for the dead on either side of the entry and an altar toward the rear. The stained-glass window rose above the altar and looked out over the position where Jordan would be waiting.

"Need to do this," Patrick said aloud, and he wasn't sure if he was speaking to the Manville ghosts laid to rest within the tomb or to God.

He had to hope that any of the once living or the Greater Power would understand.

He crawled up on the altar and looked out. They were approaching closing time. The sun was on the horizon, sending streaks of color to shoot through the soft web of gray that seemed to settle over the place, with alternate shades of mauve.

Every now and then, a bright ray of the sun broke through, as if the sun set in protest and had to prove the last of its power.

"McFadden here," a voice said through his earpiece. "In position. I have a clear view of Jordan."

"Axel Tiger," came a second voice. "I'm here; I can see clearly."

The family was leaving the grave of their police beloved. The tour guide, a young woman in her twenties, was telling a story. Two of the couples who had been wandering through appeared to be heading toward the front exit.

It was then that spoken words suddenly sounded in his mind.

Not in his *ears*. It wasn't Tiger or McFadden. The words did not come through his earpiece.

"They will not expect this!"

And Patrick knew. Ayers *was* out there. He was out there already.

He searched the area again.

Two couples, pausing now on their way out. The family, leaving the grave of the police officer. The tour group, consisting of the young female guide and a group of nine: five men, three women, and a girl of about fourteen or fifteen.

The gates would be closing soon. And whoever didn't leave was Ayers.

Instead of looking for a moment, he focused his mind on Ayers. He could feel the man's amusement; he was certain he was in control.

Ayers had seen Susie—or Jordan as Susie. And he believed Jordan was Susie.

Patrick quickly studied the people still in the cemetery. The one couple were both too young, no matter how good the makeup. The second couple...no. The young woman was only five feet tall, and the man with her was only five-six or five-seven.

He studied the family, but they were already leaving, doing so in a straight line.

He looked at the tour guide, closing his eyes, focusing on her.

The young woman's mind seemed to be on fire.

With fear.

Because one of the men in the group was Rory Ayers, and she was terrified because she knew she was speaking to a crowd that contained an armed man, one ready to shoot her if she failed him in any way.

Patrick spoke softly through his microphone to Axel and Bruce—and Jordan.

"Rory Ayers is here. I'm not sure if anyone else is working with him or not. I do know he's part of that tour group. He slipped in somehow as a paying tourist, and the guide knows. She knows he'll shoot her if she doesn't do as he's ordered her to do. I'm going to slip out; I'm going to join the group."

Jordan remained at Alfie's grave, on her haunches, ready to leap to action at any time.

"Careful!" she warned Patrick.

Patrick was good. He came around the edge of the tomb as if he'd been in the cemetery all along, studying graves and history. He appeared to just notice the group. As Jordan watched, he lifted his hand to the guide and said, "Hey, cool. I couldn't find a tour. I know it's late. I don't mind paying the whole fare. Could I latch on for the last few minutes?"

The guide stared at him, not knowing what to do.

"I—"

"None of us cares," one of the men said.

"Thanks!" Patrick told him. "Oh, hey, man, cool tat!"

Cool tat.

Jordan lowered her head for a minute. Patrick had mentioned the tattoo for a reason. It was probably a prison tattoo.

Ayers probably had someone working with him on the
tour. Did he know yet which of the men might be Ayers? She
studied them herself.

There was the man Patrick had indicated who had the tattoo, but he wasn't Ayers. Even at her distance, Jordan could
tell he was young, in his late twenties, tops. Another of the
men was hovering by a woman and the teenage girl. One had
a full, thick gray beard and wore a baseball cap and glasses.

That had to be Ayers. And she was certain he was holding a weapon, the way his arms were wrapped around his
own body, as if he were cold, his hand hidden by the jacket
he was wearing.

Two. There were at least two, including Rory Ayers. And
there were five Krewe members in the cemetery.

They could easily take Ayers out, except...

He could too easily take out several of the civilians before
going down himself.

"I'm making a move; see if he'll follow," Jordan said.

Patrick would have protested, she knew. Except he couldn't.
He would give them away.

She rose, stretching.

Alfie, at her side, asked, "Jordan, what are you doing?"

She answered carefully, her head lowered. "Alfie, we have
to make him split off from the group. There's a kid on that
tour. Not to mention the others. Patrick won't be able to stop
him from killing before he goes down. You know what he
meant by his comment regarding the tattoo."

"He could be wrong. Ex-cons like tours sometimes, too!"
Alfie said.

"We can't let Ayers grab someone as a hostage!"

She started walking toward the mausoleum where Patrick had concealed himself. And as she had expected, she could see, glancing idly toward the group, that the man she suspected of being Ayers had watched her go.

He nodded toward the man with the tattoo.

The man with the tattoo nodded barely imperceptibly in return.

She walked around the corner and stepped into the mausoleum with Alfie at her side. She backed away from the door and waited.

"Hold positions, please," she muttered into her tiny mic. "I've got this."

A second later, the gate screeched as the tattooed man entered, blinking against the suddenly shadowy darkness in the tomb.

Jordan didn't want to fire a shot; that would have alerted Ayers. But she didn't want him calling out either.

When the man stepped in, she moved with speed, strength, and determination. She slammed the butt of her gun against his temple.

To her relief, her aim and force were true. He stared at her a single second before going down without so much as a whimper.

She ducked down by him, securing him with the flex-cuffs she always kept on her person whether she was officially on duty or not.

With the man secured, she smiled. Alfie was still by her side.

"Good job!" he told her.

"Thanks. At least—"

She fell silent and stared at Alfie in horror as they heard the explosion of a shot.

She leapt up on the altar to stare out the stained-glass window above it.

Rory Ayers had his gun out; he was holding the teenage girl against him as he aimed his gun around the crowd.

"One of you is a cop!" he roared to the group. "Which one?"

Jordan couldn't let Patrick give himself away, not while he had a chance of wresting the girl from Ayers.

She tapped on the stained-glass window and then jumped down from the altar, leaving the mausoleum to look around the corner, certain Ayers was studying the mausoleum.

He was.

She hoped she was still at enough of a distance for her disguise to be working.

"Ayers? Rory Ayers?" she demanded, as if stunned and heartsick. "Let her go, please. You must have come here for me. Please, let the kid go. Let these people go!"

"Move and you're dead!" Ayers warned the crowd. "And don't get any ideas. Buddy there is with me."

Buddy was young. Maybe in his twenties. He had a pained look on his face, but as Ayers spoke, he produced a gun from beneath his jacket.

Dragging the teenager with him, Rory Ayers came toward the tomb. As he neared it, he warned, "Susie! Always trying to be the superhero. You're back in the tomb. A fitting place for you to die. Try to attack me in there, and she dies. You got it?"

The nose of the Smith & Wesson Ayers carried was against the girl's throat. And Jordan believed he would kill the girl before he went down. But what he didn't know was that Patrick could now identify who his last accomplice was.

And that Axel Tiger and Bruce McFadden were ready to move as well.

"No, no, come on in," she said. "I won't touch you. You have a man with a gun out there. Let the girl go when you come in, and I swear I will not touch you. You can see my hands and push her out! I'm the one you really want to kill, right?"

She inched backward, leaning against the side of the tombs where he could see her when he came to the gate.

And he did come to the gate and look in. He saw his man where he had fallen on the floor.

"Ass," he muttered, dismissing him. "He dead?"

"I don't think so."

"He's still an ass!"

Jordan left her Glock in its holster at the base of her back and lifted her hands so he could see she held nothing.

"He's going to do it. I don't believe it," Alfie muttered. "He—he really wants Susie dead! But he's going to know you're not Susie any minute!"

Rory Ayers stepped into the tomb. She heard the girl screaming and crying as she realized she was free from his grasp, but her family was still being held hostage by another man with a gun.

It was shadowy dark in the tomb, but Jordan's eyes had adjusted while Ayers's eyes had not. He smiled for several seconds before saying, "At last. I wanted so badly to toy with you, maybe even skin you inch by inch before killing you."

"You could have killed me before," Jordan said.

"Ah, but I heard you had a kid. I had to find out which kid, though I did consider killing all of them. I wanted to kill your kid in front of you," he said, his eyes narrowing as he studied her.

"He's realizing you're not Susie," Alfie said. He stepped around Jordan, as if he could protect her from a bullet.

If he aimed at her chest, she'd take a blow, but she was wearing the vest Jackson had given her.

"You're not Susie. My God, you're that damned catlike agent. You think you have nine lives? Oh, girlie, you are so wrong!"

"Kill me and you'll never get to Susie."

Ayers stared at her, frozen, his face tightening with anger.

"You're a cop. Or an agent. Whatever. An undercover agent. I know you, and you need to die."

"You really want Susie dead," she said. "Why? I mean, poor Susie. She ran from an abusive home to work the streets and got hooked on drugs. Only Sergeant Alfie Parker helped her and she cleaned up and found legitimate work. And you swept her up again. And I guess you did find out about her child, but she gave him up to protect him. In your sick mind, you want Susie dead because she beat you. She beat you at every turn. Susie's friendship with Alfie is what brought the first raid down on you that nearly cost you an empire. And then the clever girl caused you nothing but trouble. So, why is she still alive? Maybe you wanted to kill her yourself, and after you were incarcerated for attempting to kill your own daughter—"

"Not my kid!"

"Oh, and I will bet Deirdre is grateful for that!" Jordan said. "Thing is, you couldn't kill her yourself while you were behind bars. Oh, yeah. Clever. Attempt to kill yourself, feign a coma or maybe really be in one, and then murder the doctor saving your wretched life," Jordan said. "When we found Susie in the woods, we ruined your first real chance to kill her yourself!"

"You want to ruin everything! But no more," Ayers said, taking aim again.

"Hell, no," Alfie whispered, throwing himself at Ayers.

And Ayers felt him—or seemed to. His arm wavered, and

the nose of his gun dipped just as they heard an explosion from outside, along with screams and cries.

Ayers stepped toward the iron gate and pushed it slightly open.

This time he took aim at someone beyond the gates. Dark was almost fully upon them, but Jordan could see a man was hurrying toward the mausoleum.

"No!" she shrieked, throwing herself at the man.

His shot exploded into the ground, but she'd lost her balance and her wig flew off in her attack; and he rebalanced by wrenching her into his arms by the hair.

Her vest wouldn't help her.

He had the nose of the gun pressed to her throat. He held her in the same way he had the teenage girl before. But even as he gripped her, he jerked around as if feeling something.

It wasn't Alfie. Alfie was at her side, grabbing with futile determination for the gun.

"Let her go, now! Maybe spare yourself the death penalty!" someone shouted.

It was Bruce McFadden. And, undeterred, he was walking toward the mausoleum.

He was alone. But he didn't seem worried about anyone around him. Patrick had apparently taken down the last of Rory Ayers's accomplices.

Where were Patrick and Axel Tiger?

"I will never face a death penalty," he told Bruce. "And I can shoot you—"

"You can shoot me—or my friend Axel over there. And whichever of us you don't shoot, the other will shoot you. And if you try to hurt Jordan—" Bruce began.

"Try to hurt her? I'm going to kill her!" Ayers roared.

Even as he held Jordan, he started twitching again. And he

shuddered as if feeling things from different places. Jordan realized Alfie was behind him, hitting him over and over again. And while he couldn't budge Ayers, Ayers could feel him.

But someone else was pushing him. Slamming at his legs. Jordan could barely see the ghost, but he was dressed in an old manner of uniform, and despite her current situation, she realized he'd been in the Union Navy during the Civil War.

Neither he nor Alfie could grab the gun. But they could torment Ayers.

And he was unnerved.

Of course, that might mean he'd shoot faster and…

"What you're feeling is Sergeant Alfie Parker," she said, swallowing—and feeling the hard, cold steel of the nose of his gun against her throat. "He died fighting you. He died trying to save Susie and countless others. And I know you believe me, because I know you're feeling him!"

"Not possible! Ghosts aren't real!" he shouted. "Ghosts can't—"

She didn't feel the steel anymore; he was suddenly shooting at the air where Alfie stood.

And as he did, she was stunned by another explosion of sound, but not a gunshot this time.

It was an explosion of glass.

Patrick Law came flying through the stained-glass window. The impetus of weight and force brought him flying down on Rory Ayers's back.

The man's gun flew into the air, hit against the tombs to the left of the gate, fell to the floor, and slid toward the altar. Patrick grabbed the man's wrists and secured them swiftly in cuffs.

He looked at Jordan. She nodded, smiling. "I'm fine. And that was—"

"One hell of a leap!" Alfie said. "How did you manage that?"

"Some help from a grateful dad out there," Patrick said. He looked up at Alfie. "Thank you," he whispered, and rising, he added, "And thank you, Lieutenant. We might not have done it without your help."

"Quit it," Ayers screamed. "There are no ghosts. You're idiots, talking to dead people. There are no ghosts!"

Axel and Bruce were quickly at the entry to the mausoleum. "Everyone's alive and well. I call that a good night," Axel said. He grinned at Patrick. "Keep up the moves and if all else fails, you can join Cirque du Soleil!"

"Thanks," Patrick said, then turned to the ghost of Henry Manville. "Sir, I will see that the window is repaired as soon as possible."

"That is not a worry, sir," Henry Manville said. "Glad to have been of service tonight."

The night was suddenly flooded with light as agents stationed just beyond the gates arrived. The tour guide and her group were meeting with them, all speaking at once, talking about the way they'd begun the tour, only to discover they were hostages.

Headquarters was alerted, and Jackson arrived; soon after, Colleen, Mark, and Ragnar with Megan and all three dogs arrived as well.

Rory Ayers started raging again about them all being crazy, talking to dead people.

"Then you're pretty crazy, too," Patrick called after him. "Since you're afraid of them. Think about it, Ayers—you'll be incarcerated forever, and guess what? Ghosts hitchhike! They'll be on you like flies on a bad tomato after this!"

His words either enraged or terrified the man—or both. He suddenly spun with a vengeance, backhandedly grabbing a gun from the agent escorting him.

He never fired.

Because at least five agents fired at the same time.

And Rory Ayers went down.

And this time, it was obvious he would never rebuild his criminal empire again.

Jordan had no idea what time it was when they returned to the safe house that night. As always, there had been debriefing and paperwork. They'd taken time to talk to the members of the tour group who were also being questioned and getting the events of the night down.

The teenage girl Rory Ayers had threatened thanked Jordan and Patrick and the others again, telling them she'd never been so scared in her life.

They discovered the two men Rory Ayers had brought with him to terrorize the tour group in order to allow him entry to the cemetery had wives and children who were still being held. They were in a house in West Virginia.

Agents would head there that night. Neither of Ayers's accomplices would suffer any permanent injury, though both would be spending the night in the hospital for observation.

At the end of the evening, Jordan and Patrick made a point of thanking Alfie again—and Lieutenant Henry Manville. Apparently, Manville had known all about Ayers and Alfie's search for Susie. He was grateful to have been a small part of the evening.

At last, Jordan and Patrick were able to leave the cemetery. They arrived at the safe house just after Mark, Ragnar, and Colleen, and found the three of them, along with Megan and the dogs, outside, awaiting their arrival. The three dogs were running around as if celebrating—as if they were fully aware the night had borne a success for all involved.

"We can sleep!" Mark said.

"Or not," Colleen laughed. "Anyway, we had to bring Megan up to speed. I'm so glad your 'Susie as bait' plan worked."

"I think Alfie stayed at the cemetery tonight," Jordan said. "I don't think he went back to headquarters. Maybe he needs time to realize he has found Susie, and she will be all right."

"If we don't see him at headquarters," Patrick said, "we can all head to the cemetery tomorrow. With Susie."

Jordan smiled. "Yes, tomorrow. For now, let's get to bed!"

The couples broke apart, heading to their separate rooms for their last night in the safe house. Jordan remembered how awkward she had felt at first. But, she realized, no more.

"I think," she muttered, as Patrick closed their door. "I think…"

"Yes?"

"I think your sisters like me enough to…maybe accept me as part of the family?"

He took her into his arms. "My sisters definitely respect and admire you. As far as I can tell, they like you very much."

"It feels great being part of a family," she said softly, stroking his cheek and looking up at him.

He grinned.

"Even better when there is a closed door between you and family," he said lightly.

He kissed her. Sleep was going to wait. They were flying high on adrenaline.

And it just had to be defused somehow. Besides, Jordan knew that she—and the Law clan—deserved a day off.

EPILOGUE

It was a few days later when Jordan, Patrick, his sisters, Mark, and Ragnar headed back to the cemetery with Susie.

All three dogs came along, too.

Those few days had been busy. Patrick had decided it was time for him to join the Krewe of Hunters officially. That meant he had to attend the academy, but he was all right with that, even though Jordan had warned him she was going to tease him relentlessly about being his superior.

Colleen and Megan were thrilled. And a call to their parents had been amusing. But they were proud of their children even if they were a bit frightened for them at the same time.

"Cheaper for us," Patrick's father reasoned. "We only have to visit one city now. Thankfully, Mark has a nice place for us all to stay!"

Patrick's conversation with his parents had made Jordan want to call her mother.

"Oh, sweetheart, it sounds like you found a good guy! I've worried so much because you've always kept your guard up and have so seldom dabbled in dating. I've hated to think of you all alone. I'll be back in DC soon, sweetheart, and I cannot wait to meet this guy!"

The conversations had been wonderful. Jordan felt a bit anxious about meeting the Law parents, but Patrick told her they would love her and be excited to spend some time together.

Personal business aside, they had been very busy with paperwork. And some time spent with the therapist after having fired their weapons. Bizarrely, Jordan had been a little worried about that aspect after that had happened.

Had she wanted to kill anyone? No. But officers and agents alike were taught when a gun was pointed at one of them, or a colleague, and they were in imminent danger themselves, it was necessary to shoot.

But did she feel bad? Did she feel regret?

She was honest. No regrets. Dozens, if not scores, of others had died because of one man. Lives had been ruined.

And there had been no choice. She'd gone with honesty. Apparently, it had worked. She was back on full, active duty.

Except that day, both Jackson Crow and Adam Harrison had insisted they and the others who had been so active in the fall of such a far-reaching criminal empire should take the day to spend with Susie.

To visit the cemetery with her, to visit Alfie at his grave.

"I wanted to come here for so long, but I was so afraid. With good reason, as it turned out. I always felt it was my fault Alfie died. I loved him so much. He was a father, a big brother, the one person I had met who wanted nothing from me and just really wanted to help me," Susie said as they walked toward Alfie's grave. "He was amazing."

"Alfie was all that," Jordan said.

"And still is," Patrick added.

Susie glanced at Patrick. "He—he's still here, isn't he? It's as if I could feel him." Susie stopped walking and looked from Jordan and Patrick to Ragnar and Megan and then to Colleen and Mark. She smiled. "You guys do have a reputation for being 'ghost busters.' But it's real, isn't it? You know when the dead are still around? I mean, it must be. I felt Alfie. I felt he was there, trying to comfort me. And then it was as if I could feel his fear because he knew danger was on the way. But you do more than *feel* Alfie, don't you?"

Jordan looked around at the others. And oddly, at that moment, she felt she was really an accepted part of the group. She suddenly had the siblings she'd never had before. Family was being surrounded by those who loved you, and you loved in return.

And she felt okay to take the lead.

"Yes. We, the Krewe, are...weird. Special. But we'd appreciate it if you don't post that on social media."

Susie smiled, shook her head, and suddenly threw her arms around Jordan.

"I swear on my life, I would never betray any of you. I have a life because of you!"

"And others were spared injury or possibly worse because of you, Susie," she said.

Jordan heard a noise as if someone was clearing his throat behind her.

Alfie. They were standing just feet from his grave.

"He's here now, isn't he?" Susie asked.

Jordan nodded. Susie stepped past her and made her way to stand in front of the ghost.

"I love you so much!" she said. "I always will. And I will thank you forever and ever. You didn't just do everything in your power to save me—you made me strong. You enabled me to fight and to flee—and to know when to do both. Alfie, they're going to set me up in a distant city with Benjamin, far away, just to make sure no danger lingers here. And I promise you, I will live a good life because of you. I will teach my son all the kindness and generosity and courage you taught me. I love you."

Jordan was shocked to feel something drip down her face. A tear.

Agents didn't cry!

But she thought she heard other sniffles. Colleen and Megan—and maybe Mark, Ragnar, and Patrick had slightly damp eyes, too.

Alfie gently wrapped his arms around Susie. Jordan thought the young woman could feel his touch.

Alfie looked over Susie's head. "Please, tell her she has made my life worthwhile. She has made me feel I did make a difference. And…" He paused, shrugging. "Please tell Jackson and Angela I'm sorry. I won't be hanging around the office with any tips anymore. I'm feeling light as air, like sunshine…like moving on. It's time. Susie gave me the closure I needed and I'm excited. I just needed to know she was all right. Thank you for seeing me and believing in me."

"Alfie, we all love you," Jordan whispered. She repeated his words to Susie, who listened with a smile and tears. When Jordan looked back at Alfie, he waved, and he turned, and in a trick of the sunlight streaming down through the trees, they saw flashes of beautiful, glittering gold as if the sun had shifted in the sky.

And Alfie was gone.

"We're not supposed to cry," Patrick said. "We're supposed

to celebrate. Susie, his soul was in torment and you set him free. You gave him peace."

Susie smiled, happy that Alfie could finally rest.

They brought Susie back to Krewe headquarters, where she collected Benjamin and said goodbye to everyone, thanking them all profusely.

She left with representatives from the Marshals Service. Then Angela shooed the six of them out of the office. They went to dinner together at a great little Chinese restaurant with outside seating for the dogs. And again, Jordan felt content.

She was comfortable. She had never felt such a sense of belonging.

Dinner was delicious.

And going home was equally wonderful.

Patrick closed the door, locked it, and leaned against it before looking quizzically at Jordan.

"What?" she demanded, smiling, as she had been all evening.

"I start the academy soon."

"Yep."

"And you are going to torment me."

"Oh, you bet!"

"Okay, so, then tonight..."

"What?"

"I get to torment you!"

He pushed off from the door. She let out a laughing shriek. He caught up with her at the bedroom door, swept her up into his arms, and smiled and turned just briefly to command Bry-bo to sleep and guard the front door.

Jordan wrapped her arms around him.

"I don't want you feeling too bad about me being your superior. So, please, feel free to torment away."

He grinned.

"Just the right kind of torment, of course," he assured her.

"All threat, all bark, no bite!" she said. "Get to the torment!"

"Oh, I will," he promised. "And I might never let go."

★ ★ ★ ★ ★

Keep reading for a special preview of

Danger in Numbers

the exciting thriller from New York Times *bestselling author*
Heather Graham!

Available now from MIRA Books.

PROLOGUE

Sam

Fall 1993

Sam Gallagher stood in the forest, deep within the trees, holding his wife and son to him as closely as he could, barely daring to breathe.

They would know by now. He and Jessie would be missed. He could imagine the scene: Jessie wouldn't have appeared bright and early to help prepare the day's meal with the other women. He wouldn't be there to consume the porridge and water that was considered the ultimate meal for the workday—the porridge because it was a hearty meal, the water because it was ordained as the gift of life.

Their absence would be reported to Brother William, sitting in his office—his throne room, Sam thought—where he would be guarded by his closest associates, the deacons of his church.

The family had only been in the woods for a few minutes, but it seemed like an eternity. Jessie was so still Sam couldn't hear her breathing, just feel the tremor of her heart.

Cameron was just six. And yet he knew the severity and danger of his situation. He stood as still and silent as any man could hope a child might be.

Panic seized Sam briefly.

What if Special Agent Dawson didn't come? What if there had been a mix-up and he hadn't been able to arrange for the Marshals Service to help?

What if they were found?

Stupid question. He knew the *what if.*

He gritted his teeth and fought against the fear that had washed over him like a tidal wave. Dawson was a good man; Sam knew he would keep his word. He'd arrived at the commune undercover, having the intuition to realize Sam's feelings, his doubt, and his fear for his wife and his son. Together, Dawson had told him, they would bring down the Keepers of the Earth. His actions would free others. No, *their* actions would free others.

Today was the day. Just in time. Sam had known the danger of remaining, felt the way he was being watched by the Divine Leader's henchmen.

They had to leave. Leave? No, there was no leaving the compound. There was only escaping.

Alana Fisk had wanted to leave, and they knew what had happened to her.

It had been Cameron who had found his beloved "aunt" Alana's body at the bottom of the gorge, broken, lying beneath just inches of dry dust and rock, decomposing in her shallow grave. It had been Cameron, so young, who had become wary and suspicious first. He'd seen a few of the older boys in the area when he'd last seen Alana there, and he didn't trust them. They were scary, Cameron said.

Sam tightened his hold on Cameron. Seconds ticked by like an eternity.

Sam closed his eyes and wondered how they had come to this, but he knew.

He and his wife had wanted something different. A life where riches didn't make a man cruel.

Jessie hadn't hated her father; she had hated what he stood for. And Sam knew the day when her mind had been made up. Downtown Los Angeles. They had seen a veteran of the Vietnam War, homeless, slunk against a wall. Only one of his legs remained; he had been struggling with his prosthetic, his cup for donations at his side. The homeless veteran had looked at Jessie's father and said, "Please, sir, help if you can."

Peter Wilson had walked right by. When Jessie had caught her father's arm, he had turned on her angrily. "I didn't get where I am by giving away my hard-earned money. He's probably lying about being a vet. He can get himself a damned job doing something!"

Sam had been walking behind them. Embarrassed, he tried to offer Jessie a weak smile. He hadn't come from money, and he had lost his folks right after his twentieth birthday, but he was working in a coffee shop, dreaming he'd get to where he could work, go to college, and have time left over to be with the woman he loved.

He had given the man a dollar and wished him well.

Jessie had turned away from her father.

It was the last time Jessie saw her father. Despite the man's efforts to break her and Sam up—or because of them—Jessie and Sam had eloped. The plan was to both get jobs and finish college through night school. Her father had suspected her pregnancy; he'd wanted her to get over Sam and terminate the baby.

Jessie quickly made friends at a park near their cheap apartment. They were old flower children, she had told Sam. Old hippies, he'd liked to tease in return. But those friends had been happy, and they'd talked to Jessie about the beauty of their commune, far from the crazy greed and speed of the city.

In the beginning, Brother William's commune did seem to offer it all: happiness, unity, love, and light.

But now they knew the truth.

Brother William—with his "deacons," his demands on his "flock," and the cache of arms he kept stowed away as he created his empire, demanding absolute power for himself, complete obedience among his followers. And it became clear Brother William's will was enforced; he had those deacons— Brothers Colin, Anthony, and Darryl, and the squad beneath them. They received special treatment.

Sam clutched his family as he strained to hear any unfamiliar sound in the woods. Was that footsteps? Was the rustling of branches just the breeze?

He had to stop dwelling on fear.

He had to stay strong. Maybe not ruminate on what they'd been through.

But there was nothing else to do while they waited, barely breathing.

Think back, remember it all.

CHAPTER ONE

Now
Late summer

The woman had been strung up on a cross, her wrists and ankles tied in that position.

And a spear had been run through her, right in the region of the heart. The weapon appeared to look something like a medieval javelin.

Blood dripped from the body and the stake, only half congealed in the damp heat of the day.

Her head hung low in death and a wealth of dark brown hair fell around her face, tangled and matted with blood. Slashes had been cut through her cheeks, and an eerie mask had been painted on the woman's face, creating a jester's oversize smile and giant, red-rimmed eyes.

A cloud of insects made a strange, buzzing halo around her head.

Special Agent Amy Larson absently swatted at one of the

flies that had deserted the corpse and was humming near her ear. She was aware somewhere in the back of her mind that she was going to be bitten to pieces by the time she left the crime scene. Amy had been called to several murders during her time with the Florida Department of Law Enforcement, but none so grisly, such a gruesome display.

They were almost in the Everglades but not quite. This stretch of old road had once been the main connection between the extreme south of the state of Florida, Central Florida, and all the way on up to the north and connecting with east-west highways stretching out to either coast.

People enjoying the beaches on those coasts probably had little knowledge—nor would they care to have any—regarding the whole of the state. Here in this no-man's-land that was at the edge of the Everglades, dotted with sugarcane fields, churches, and cows.

She drew out the small sketchpad she kept in her pocket; she also kept notes, but Amy liked to sketch out what she saw, always wondering if there was something that would particularly catch her mind's eye.

"Hey, Picasso, you know there will be—"

"Photographs, yes," she told her partner, Special Agent John Schultz of the Florida Department of Law Enforcement.

They'd been partnered for two years and worked well together. He was fifty and had been with FDLE for most of his adult life.

She'd been with the FDLE two and a half years, after a stint with Metro-Miami-Dade. She was twenty-nine, and John had been admittedly annoyed and amused when they'd first been paired on major state crimes, but he was quick to tell others now that they were an odd couple who worked.

Amy sketched every crime scene.

John mentioned it—every crime scene. Even though her sketches had proved valuable in the past, and she knew he liked that she did them.

He gave her an odd, grim smile. He was a tall, rugged man with a sweep of snow-white hair that gave him no end of happiness since most of his male friends and coworkers his age were already bald. But it was hot out here, and he had to swipe back a wavy lock from his forehead; the sweat was causing it to plaster to his face. His smile faded as he took in the scene again.

While no one entered law enforcement without knowing they'd have to face brutality and death, what they saw here was especially grotesque. Despite what he had seen in life— or maybe because of it—John Schultz was a kind man, a good man, and knew the scene was causing an effect on her, as it was on him.

Amy arched a brow to him, and John nodded. They walked over to Dr. Richard Carver. The ME was from this county, which stretched from the beaches to this no-man's-land. They knew him well and had worked together before, though he looked like he should still be boning up for final exams. His looks were deceiving; Carver was in his late thirties.

Carver was just moving up his portable stepladder, asking one of his assistants to check that he didn't pitch forward to the road and bracken, dry in some places, wet in others.

Amy noted the area offered a fine cropping of sharp saw-grass as well.

"Anything to tell us yet?" Amy asked.

"She's been in rigor and out of rigor... I'm going to say she's been here about a day. The insects are doing a number on her."

"Method and cause of death?" John asked hopefully.

"Well, the method could have been this sharp pole sticking into her. With the amount of blood, I'm thinking the cause of death just might have been exsanguination. They were pretty damned accurate in slamming that thing right through her chest and into the wooden pole here. Don't think they got this wood from around here, but I do bodies, not trees. So, sorry—right now, I'm thinking she's been here somewhere between twenty to thirty hours, and she was killed here."

He hesitated; even the doctor seemed bothered by this one. His voice was hard when he spoke again. "She struggled," he said. "I think they cut her face while she was alive. Her wrists are ragged, which shows she tried to escape these ties. And when they came at her with this spear, she knew they were coming."

John turned to Detective Victor Mulberry, from the county's sheriff's office, who had been standing, silent and greenish, behind them. He'd been routed by the hysterical call from a tourist about the body and had been first on the scene. "Do we know of any active cults in this area?" John asked him.

Mulberry shook his head. "Small communities out here, minuscule next to the coast. But we got Lutherans, Catholics, Baptists...and two Temples. I know two of the rabbis and several of the pastors and priests. The people are churchgoing, but in truth, we're a little haven of diversity—all kinds of backgrounds, religions, colors. All the leaders of the local houses of worship get together once a month to make sure there's friendship between everyone. Heck, they put on charity sales and the like together. We have no fanatics, no Satanists, no...no cultists. I guess those church guys made it so it's just...cool. Good, I mean. Good. Folks get along. They like each other. They help each other."

Amy smiled grimly at him and nodded. "Nice," she told him.

But someone, somewhere, wasn't so nice.

She realized Dr. Carver and his assistants had started their work while she and John had silently stared at the scene.

Well, that was work, too, trying to take in every small detail of the scene; it was impossible to know what might become important in the end.

She'd barely been through this area before—and only because both the turnpike and I-95 had been plagued with accidents, and the old road had been just about the only chance of getting up to the middle of the state.

She glanced John's way, shaking her head. "There are a lot of churches, but as far as I know, they're pretty traditional. The population in this area is sparse. Most of the land was owned by the big sugar companies for years, and we're not far from Seminole tribal lands," she said.

She was close enough to one of their best crime scene investigators and forensics team leaders, Aidan Cypress, and she winced when he looked at her with a question that was almost accusation in his eyes.

"This is nothing Seminole, I assure you," he said.

"No, Aidan, I wasn't implying that. This is different than anything...from most anything else in the state," Amy said.

He nodded; he knew her better than that.

"No, nothing traditional, for sure," John said. "Ritual overtones. Both cheeks have been slashed identically. The weapon...half makeshift, as if a poor cosplayer was trying to re-create a medieval halberd. She's naked, but that could be the work of a run-of-the-mill sicko."

"The cross she's on—I *think* it looks like Dade County pine," Amy said. That wood was almost impossible to acquire these days. But the CSI team would know more on that; she was hardly an expert on wood or trees herself.

"I think you're right," John agreed. "And it wasn't recently chopped down—more like crude carpentry. I think the wood might have been taken from various demolition sites, a house or some other building. Though you'd think we'd be preserving our older homes. It was abundant here once, used in most of the Victorian-era houses down in Key West. I'm going to say reclaimed from somewhere."

"We're looking at something planned, yes, with religious overtones," Amy said. "Something extremist…" She looked around at their group. "As we all know well, any extremist is dangerous…"

Dr. Carver twisted on the ladder to look at her. "And you're afraid this is a harbinger of more?"

"Dear God, let's hope not," she breathed.

Aidan Cypress walked over to them. "We're trying to pull tire tracks, but as you see, the ground is mostly muck. And it's rained, so even the paved area is giving us just about nothing. One thing about being on an old road almost no one uses anymore—not a lot of trash. But we're doing our best to get everything, the tiniest scrap. And some of this is sawgrass— long sawgrass, but we're doing our best."

"Thank you, Aidan. You guys are the best," Amy assured him.

"Sketching again, eh?" Cypress asked.

"You never know."

"Okay, Picasso!" Dr. Carver called out. "I'm going to get my crew busy taking her down so I can get her to the morgue. From what I'm seeing, and what I believe, she was killed just as darkness was falling last night, and she was between twenty and thirty years old."

Amy stood just to the side of the corpse, swallowing hard

as she saw the blood had covered the body in such quantities and had dried so it was almost as if she were dressed.

"Like Fantasy Fest down in Key West," John murmured. She turned to stare at him.

"All the blood…it's almost as if she'd been body-painted."

Somewhere inside, Amy trembled at the horror of what they saw. Death had taken the woman in such a way she was almost surreal, like a Halloween prop set out for a wickedly scary party.

"That's what happens," Carver said, "when you pierce the heart and rip up veins and arteries. Anyway, we're good to go, team. We're going to need to get her off the cross—carefully, carefully, my friends," he said to his assistants.

"And we need to get the cross to the crime lab, as much as is possible," Cypress said.

Detective Mulberry had been watching and listening. He spoke up. "Yes, please, get everything. This had to have been wackos from somewhere else in the state—or the country. This sure as hell didn't come from anyone local! And my citizens are going to be terrified. And there aren't a lot of homes with fancy alarm systems out here."

Amy hoped he was right: that the murderer—or murderers—had come from somewhere else, and that they would not strike again. She looked down at her sketch of the scene; it was one that would probably give her nightmares.

She swatted another mosquito buzzing around her face. It was going to be a long morning.

The body was removed from the stake with painstaking care.

Dr. Carver wanted the murder weapon left in the body until he reached the lab; his assistants argued over fitting the stake into their vehicle, but it was done. Then Aidan Cypress's crew began working on the crude cross to which she had been tied.

Amy was watching them work, sketching their efforts, when she thought she saw something tiny fall off the top of the cross as they lowered it.

No one else had seen anything, it seemed, and she wondered if it was a trick of the light, or maybe a small leaf blowing in the something that resembled a breeze that had come up as the day had worn on.

Rain was coming.

Floridians liked to joke among themselves about their seasons: they came in hot, hotter, blazing hot, and then hotter than hell. The atmosphere didn't always acknowledge the changing of the seasons, and while winter caused an ease in the rain that tended to come daily in summer, early fall was still part of their hurricane season.

They'd been lucky so far that day. It had rained the night before, a weak rain, ruining much of the crime scene, but not enough to wash away the pints of blood that had half congealed on the body. Some of the blood had run again; some had stayed hard and crusted.

The forensics crew finally had the cross down.

She walked over to the great hole that had been dug to set the cross. Now it was an area of mucky darkness against the rich sawgrass and foliage that grew around. Her heart sank.

Whatever it had been—*if* it had been anything—had sunk deep.

Amy went down on her knees, wishing her hands were covered by something a bit tougher than crime scene nitrile gloves.

"What are you doing?" John asked her.

"I think I saw something...something falling off the cross," she said.

Dr. Carver shouted out to them, "I'm heading out. She'll be set for autopsy tomorrow. My crew will get her cleaned up and prepped by about nine."

"Thanks!" John called to him. He turned to her. "Amy, come on. We have a fantastic forensics team—"

"They were busy finagling that cross, John. I saw something."

"You're going to cut yourself on all that sawgrass."

She kept her eyes on the ground, scanning. "It will drive me insane if I don't look, John."

He sighed. "All right, I guess I'll get down in the dirt, too. When I'm itching like crazy from all the brush scratches tonight, just know I'm going to be cursing you out in my sleep."

Amy continued diligently pawing through the sawgrass when she vaguely heard the arrival of another car.

Cypress called out in greeting to someone, and Amy finally looked up.

Another man had arrived at the scene. He was tall, dark-haired, midthirties. Wearing a suit, he must have been sweltering in the heat. Then again, both she and John were clad in their daily business suits—blue, light cotton blends, but the kind of outfit that meant work clothing.

The man seemed impatient, pushing back the hair from his forehead, looking around at the scene with keen eyes that were light against the bronze of his face.

She watched him, and John rose, frowning, then smiling in recognition.

"Hey, Hunter! What the hell are you doing down here?" John greeted the newcomer.

"Who is that?" Amy asked.

John hadn't heard her; he'd gone to meet the man.

Apparently, Aidan Cypress knew him, too. After calling out his own greeting, Aidan left his work for a minute to go over and shake hands with the man. "Sent out already, eh?" she overheard.

She shook her head; she'd know soon enough. If she was going to find something, she had to keep looking.

She carefully delved her way through the cutting grass.

But then she had the sense that John had come to stand near her, on the pavement off the mucky embankment.

"Amy, look up for a minute?"

She raised her eyes.

He'd brought the man with him. She waited, watching the stranger. He had the perfect face for law enforcement— which she figured he must be of some kind. His expression gave away nothing. His eyes, she saw then, were a rich, piercing blue that could certainly quell many a suspect. Hard jaw, lean face, high cheeks—the old classic-sculpted bone structure. He stood a few inches over John, which made him at least six foot three.

But she didn't get up; if she did, she'd lose the grid she'd created in her mind.

"Amy, Hunter. Hunter, Amy," John said.

"Mr. Hunter," Amy acknowledged.

His mouth moved in something that might have been a dry smile. A severe one.

"Hunter is my first name," he said.

"Oh, I'm sorry—"

"No, I'm sorry," John said. "I know you both so well that I forget myself. I'll start over. Special Agent Amy Larson, meet Special Agent Hunter Forrest."

"Hunter... Forrest?" she murmured, immediately regretting the words that had slipped out. She quickly added, "You're FDLE? I'm surprised we haven't met."

"No, no, Hunter is a G-man, a fed," John said. "He thinks he had something like this—not as elaborate, but when the info went out…"

"I might have had a practice run for this event," Hunter said.

"Oh?" John asked.

"A practice?" Amy heard the surprise in her own voice.

"North in the state, little town near Micanopy. I'll be joining you at the autopsy tomorrow. Joining the investigation," he said.

She tried to be as expressionless as he was; she wasn't sure what this meant. The FBI had to be invited in, and she wasn't sure how and when he could have been invited, since they'd just started with the crime scene.

And what had he been doing north in a small town near Micanopy?

Maybe he was so confident that he thought he could just make decisions on his own.

"He'd like to see us tonight, go through the cases. You didn't have plans, did you?"

"Not after this," she said.

"Drove here as fast as I could," Hunter Forrest said.

Special Agent Hunter Forrest.

"And I'm sorry I missed the scene in situ," he continued. He looked at John. "But I'm assuming—and I know your guys are good—that we'll have plenty of photographs."

"And sketches," John offered. "Want to see them now?"

"Sketches? You had a photographer and a forensic artist working?" Hunter asked.

"Nope, my partner," John said. "Amy, can he see your book?"

"Really, I'm not trained in forensic art in any way—they're just something I do for myself," Amy protested.

"Amy, come on," John said.

She reached into her pocket, digging out her little pad, and handed it over.

Hunter leaned down and accepted it with a quick "Thank you."

He fell silent, studying her work. Amy went back to her search.

She was startled when he spoke, hunching down beside her, the book still in his hand.

"These are really good."

"Uh, thank you."

"Mind if I ask what you're doing now?"

He was studying her carefully, and she had to wonder if he wasn't thinking she was probably in way over her head, incompetent to handle such a crime and crawling around in the sawgrass just to prove she could do something.

There was nothing to do but explain—evenly and articulately.

"I thought I saw something. A tiny object, but something flew from the body or the cross. I saw it when they were taking the cross down."

"You *thought* you saw something?" he asked.

She smiled through gritted teeth before speaking with assurance. "No, I did see something. I don't know what. We may never find it, but my eyes are good, and I know I saw something."

"Leaf. I think we're looking through grass and leaves—for a leaf," John said, grinning. Of course he was joking with her. He never minded when she had an idea, or when she was convinced she needed to explore in a certain direction.

But his joke didn't sit well there and then—when she was certain she was being looked on as too young and possibly too fragile or maybe even too *female* to handle this kind of job.

"And that's sawgrass," John said. "Careful, it can cut you badly."

Hunter Forrest grimaced. "Only if you let it," he said lightly. "Special Agent Amy Larson has said she saw something. I believe her. We'll search. Let's do it."

Grudgingly, she liked him a little better than her first impression of him.

Special Agent Forrest pulled gloves from a pocket and knelt in a cleared area by the hole in the ground, careful not to press any tiny little thing deeper into the grass or ground.

He didn't seem to give a damn about his suit, or his own physical welfare.

John sighed and got back down.

Aidan walked over. The vans had been packed up.

"What's up?" Aidan asked.

"Amy thought she saw something," John explained.

"Some tiny thing that fell off the cross or the body," she explained.

"Okay, then. I should get down there with you. Amy, can you tell me, what exactly did you see?" Aidan asked, concerned. He took his work seriously. He was never afraid to admit he might have missed something, but if he had, he wanted to get on it.

"Something tiny that, yes, that flew…no, fell, I guess, sorry…when you all moved the cross."

"A piece of flesh? Hair…? Can you help any with a description?" Aidan asked.

"Something like this?" Hunter asked before Amy could reply.

She looked at what he was holding.

It was a small plastic figure.

A horse.

It might have gone with a child's farm or ranch set. It wasn't quite two inches high and the same width. The little creature had a flowing mane and tail.

It was white.

But it looked as if the eyes had been given a touch of paint. Red paint.

Blood, she thought sickly at first.

But it wasn't blood. The paint was too precise. The tiny eyes had been specifically painted a crimson shade of red.

"Maybe it's just some kid's toy, dropped out a car window," John said.

Hunter Forrest was staring at the object, shaking his head. "No, it's not. It was part of the ritual." He looked at Amy.

Aidan grimaced. "It must have been on the body, or attached to the cross, and... I don't know how the hell we missed it. Amy, you're sure it fell off when we moved the cross?"

"There's nothing else I've been able to find," Amy said. "Maybe it got caught in the ties binding her up there or was even behind the body in one way or another."

"Maybe... Let's not jump to any conclusions," John suggested. "We don't know where that came from for sure, or if it has anything to do with our crime scene."

Hunter Forrest was still staring at the small toy.

He looked up at them, shaking his head. "No," he said firmly.

"What is it?" Amy asked him.

"Death rides a pale horse," Hunter said quietly. "And I'm afraid this is just the beginning."

CHAPTER TWO

Hunter heard Amy Larson speaking in hushed, indiscernible tones as he headed down the hallway of the Central Florida offices of the FDLE toward the conference room that had been assigned for their joint investigation. FDLE was still the lead on this case, and since the murder had taken place just about an hour and a half south of Orlando, they'd all decided to come here and make use of what the central office had to offer with support staff and facilities.

Tomorrow morning they'd head back south—the autopsy would take place in the county where the murder had occurred.

While Detective Mulberry would join them at the autopsy, he had been only too happy to hand over the investigation; he didn't see many murders, much less one that had been gruesome in the extreme, possibly the work of cultists, and might relate to other crimes in the state or elsewhere.

At this moment, the investigation had yet to be taken over by the FBI.

It would be.

But Hunter didn't really give a damn who had the lead on the investigation; he knew that something deep and dark was behind this murder, just as it had been in Maclamara. A place, he thought, where there were still lots of old houses that had been built with Dade County pine.

Others would die. How many depended on how quickly they could root out what was happening.

He'd reported in to his superior, Assistant Special Director Charles Garza, and Garza had told him that, hell yes, he was to follow through.

"You feel we need to be concerned and involved, right?" Garza had asked him.

"Beyond a doubt."

"You'll get all the help you need on this. Just call, ask," Garza had told him. "FDLE has been in touch. Stay right on top."

"John Schultz is on it for FDLE. We're good—I've worked with him before."

"Fine. Keep me in the loop."

Mulberry had been absolutely convinced the murder had not been committed by anyone local. Such a thing could only have been done by a crazy person from a large city, probably a northern city, someone who had come down to use the complexity of his county, from the areas of massive population to the boondocks, to commit the atrocity. Therefore, the state or the federal government should take over. He'd be there ready to assist in any way. He was distancing himself from the horror.

Eventually, the FBI would take the lead. For now, Hunter had to hope his old friend John Schultz would make it a dual investigation. He could only assume John would have the final say, since he had so much more experience than his young partner. And John knew Hunter, too.

They'd work together easily.

As he neared their assigned conference room, Hunter could hear John's new partner more clearly.

And he could hear quite clearly that she was talking about him.

"I'm so lost. He was here—I mean, in the state—because of a murder near Micanopy that had shades of a ritual, but why is he *here*? Micanopy is a long drive. And exactly why was he in Micanopy? He's federal. Shouldn't it have been the local police or the county or us, as it proved to be? We don't know the two murders are related. They took place far enough apart."

"He's a specialist in ritualistic killings and extremists and the occult," Hunter could hear John explain. "Hunter came down here because the governor asked him to. Our governor called the FBI's main offices. You remember our governor, right? The guy who is at the top of our food chain?"

"Ha ha, yes, I remember our governor," Amy replied. "I just… Look, we are competent here. Our department is good."

"Good enough to know when to accept help."

"John, we've barely had a chance to begin," Amy protested.

"You just don't like him."

"That's ridiculous. I'm just… Come on. Our state has problems, but we're good at what we do, John. How does one just assume these murders are part of a major plot of some kind?"

"But if they are?"

"Okay, but—"

"You don't like him."

"I can't dislike him. I don't know him."

He heard John's booming laugh.

"That doesn't mean a thing. You didn't like me, remember?"

"No, I had nothing against you. You felt you were saddled with me."

"Guilty as charged, but don't go thinking everyone is an old chauvinist like me."

"I'm just lost as to why the feds are in. He made it from the Micanopy area almost as fast as we did from Orlando."

"Not much difference. And you know Florida. It can be thirty minutes, or two and a half hours, from place to place in certain areas—"

"Depending on traffic. Yes, I know."

Hunter knew he was standing in the hallway eavesdropping.

He pushed open the door to the conference room.

He'd known John a long time—almost a decade, since he'd come into the Bureau. They'd met under similar circumstances when the head of a land-grabbing company had created their own form of a twisted Voodoo-Santeria cult, terrifying the downtrodden into murdering their neighbors.

John was a good investigator.

About this new young partner of his...

Hunter forced a grim smile. She'd just have to live with the chain of power that was going to come down. Live with it—or leave.

Standing, she was about five-ten. He'd thought at first she might have been wearing heels; but no, sensible shoes for wherever one might find themselves walking for the day—or crawling around in the muck on the edge of the Everglades.

Her hair was a deep glossy brown, held back in a sleek low ponytail.

She couldn't have been more than twenty-eight or so, but he thought at least that, because agents with the state department had to have four years of other police work beneath their belts. But she had the look of a college kid—not that looks meant anything, which he damned well knew.

She also seemed severe. Hair so tightly tied back, strait-laced suit—of course, they almost all wore them. She had fine features, but bold, striking green eyes with just a touch of gold at the center.

And she was looking at him as if he might be the anti-Christ himself.

She and John had already set up a board to work with. Crime scene photos were displayed, along with what initial observations Dr. Carver had been able to give them.

Questions were written in marker on the erasable surface.

IDENTITY?
FROM WHERE?
NEXT OF KIN?
GROUPS/CULTS WITH WHICH SHE MIGHT HAVE BEEN INVOLVED?
PREVIOUS MURDER—ASSOCIATED? SAME KILLER/KILLING DUO OR GROUP?

"Hunter, hey, thanks for getting here so quickly," John said, rising to shake his hand again. "We've gotten called out on some weird-ass stuff. Hell, you know, this is Florida. When we don't breed our own wild ones, they find us the same way the tourists do."

Hunter walked to the board, setting the folder he carried with facts and figures from what he considered to be the initial case in the investigation on the table.

He studied the photographs on the board, and then turned to Amy Larson, who had yet to speak and hadn't risen when he'd entered.

He smiled inwardly, thinking he could make up a few labels for a board regarding her.

Young. Suspicious. Ambitious? Resentful of the FBI coming in on what she might see as a Florida case?

She was silent, but watching him—waiting?

He was trying to play well with others. Her turn to lower her guard.

"May I see your sketchbook again?" he asked Amy.

She pointed. It lay on the table by a folder.

"Thank you," he said.

She spoke at last. "What were you talking about, regarding the little horse? 'Death rides a pale horse'? I do realize you're talking biblical, and about the Apocalypse, but I'm not sure how you're so convinced so quickly."

"The slashes on the face of the victim."

She arched a brow, waiting.

"About fourteen years ago, there was a cult leader named Thorne Logan. He started up in the northwest, then brought his family down to farm country on the border between Florida and Alabama."

"You think he did this?" John asked.

Hunter shook his head. "Logan is dead. He fired on one of our agents, who fired back. It was one of my first field experiences. Logan was down on any of his 'harem' straying in the least. To be fitting sacrifices, their faces were slashed. Physical beauty needed to be blotted out because the soul needed to shine in death. And in his teaching, only death cleaned a dirty soul. His principles were...long and involved."

"I remember the case. The media had him billed as Father Killer," John said.

"I do remember something in the papers," Amy said.

"You would have been about ten," John said.

"Seventeen," Amy said, "and I was horrified, but...sounded like they got him. And at the time, it brought up stories of so many other bad cult situations, so it became one for the books."

"Right. It was a big case, but there were others," Hunter

agreed. "Many more that didn't end with so much death and weren't as well-known."

Amy's brows were knit. "But if this man is dead," she said, "it can't be him. You think it was someone who was part of his family or congregation, or whatever you call followers like that?"

Hunter nodded. "You know there are many people—and many religions—that believe in the Apocalypse, right?"

"Of course," Amy said. "There's all kinds of speculation about the Apocalypse, the End of Days, all that. Different religions, sects, ethnic groups. Some people thought the world was supposed to end in 2012, according to the Mayan calendar. I've heard it could have meant the end of one era, the beginning of another. And you get groups who believe comets are omens, or that a certain politician in power means the end is coming. People who have dosed themselves with poison to die ahead of the bloodshed and violence. That's the kind of thing you're talking about?"

"More or less." He indicated the folder that lay on the table. "I was called down to Maclamara to work a murder. It's a little township outside of Micanopy. They're so small up there that any murder is handled by FDLE. I've worked with the detective there before, and when he saw his victim, he called me immediately. And then the FDLE called the FBI and asked for me specifically because I have had some experience with this type of thing. We don't believe the victim was local—no missing person reports from anywhere near the area match up with what we know."

"We?" she asked pleasantly. "As in you and the local authorities?"

"Yes—we—as in me and other authorities on the case."

Amy looked at John, clearly oblivious to the fact Hunter

had heard her speaking just moments ago. There was a query in her eyes. He could almost hear her question to her partner.

One murder—and a fed is called in?

He waited for her to speak.

"You said that murder was similar...or a practice for this?" Amy asked. Her fingers were moving around the paper coffee cup in front of her. She seemed to remember she had the coffee, and she took a long sip of it while she awaited his answer.

He opened the folder, pushing it toward her.

The first photo was of the Maclamara crime scene.

The victim had been stripped and her face had been slashed. But nothing protruded from her chest, though it was a bloody mess.

Amy Larson was appropriately grim and ashen, he thought, even after the day they'd endured.

There was a fine line to tread when working with violent crime. You couldn't let it get under your skin too deeply. You'd be worthless at work from the nightmares that plagued your sleep and kept you up.

But to forget humanity was just as bad. You forgot why you were doing what you did, trying to stop the worst monsters before they did more damage. And every life was sacred, from that of a top scientist or scholar to that of a homeless person on the street.

Danger in Numbers
by Heather Graham
Available now from MIRA Books!